CW01618875

A KILLER GUEST LIST

SARAH BONNER

Boldwood

First published in Great Britain in 2026 by Boldwood Books Ltd.

Copyright © Sarah Bonner, 2026

Cover Design by Head Design Ltd

Cover Images: iStock, Shutterstock and Bella Howard

The moral right of Sarah Bonner to be identified as the author of this work has been asserted in accordance with the Copyright, Designs and Patents Act 1988.

All rights reserved. No part of this book may be reproduced in any form or by any electronic or mechanical means, including information storage and retrieval systems, without written permission from the author, except for the use of brief quotations in a book review. This book is a work of fiction and, except in the case of historical fact, any resemblance to actual persons, living or dead, is purely coincidental.

Every effort has been made to obtain the necessary permissions with reference to copyright material, both illustrative and quoted. We apologise for any omissions in this respect and will be pleased to make the appropriate acknowledgements in any future edition.

A CIP catalogue record for this book is available from the British Library.

Paperback ISBN 978-1-83633-562-7

Large Print ISBN 978-1-83633-563-4

Hardback ISBN 978-1-83633-561-0

Trade Paperback ISBN 978-1-80656-233-6

Ebook ISBN 978-1-83633-564-1

Kindle ISBN 978-1-83633-565-8

Audio CD ISBN 978-1-83633-556-6

MP3 CD ISBN 978-1-83633-557-3

Digital audio download ISBN 978-1-83633-560-3

This book is printed on certified sustainable paper. Boldwood Books is dedicated to putting sustainability at the heart of our business. For more information please visit https://www.boldwoodbooks.com/about-us/sustainability/

Boldwood Books Ltd, 23 Bowerdean Street, London, SW6 3TN

www.boldwoodbooks.com

To Rachel and Alice

PROLOGUE

CASSIE

A fourteen-hour shift in the middle of a forty-degree heatwave has left me in the foulest of moods. So when my front door jams as I push it open, I let out an almighty scream. I've had enough. A commis-chef who thinks he's God's gift to womankind and can 'turn me'. An HR manager who thinks no one has a home life and we can change our schedules at a moment's notice. Three new waitresses with fuck-all experience, who can't even carry a plate each without spilling sauce all over the place.

I shove on the door and eventually it opens, leaving a folded envelope on the mat. I pick it up. Rani and I rarely get post – I mean, everything is online now – and we definitely don't get posh post with the address written in swirling calligraphic script. Inside I find an invitation, an embossed outline of a fancy manor house on the front. On the back, written in that same handwriting, are the words:

Dear Ms Kohl,

You and a guest are cordially invited to the 50th Anniversary of Murder on the Moors.

September 12th-14th at the Holne House Hotel, Dartmoor, Devon.

Return to the golden age of crime fiction at this luxurious 1920s-themed weekend of murder, mayhem and madness.

This is an exclusive event: guests are strictly by invitation only and tickets cannot be exchanged or sold.

Contact our concierge for prices and booking information.

Who the hell is inviting me to a fancy murder mystery weekend? Unless it's meant for Rani? She works for a travel company, but it's mainly booking boring business flights and other such mundanity for CEOs who have no appreciation for how hard she works. She has colleagues who get sent on fancy trips to test exclusive resorts, but Rani doesn't get invited on those. Instead, she gets sent to cut deals with airport hotels and lounges, flying all over Europe but never actually seeing beyond the walls of the airport. Besides, she uses her maiden name at work. We both became Kohl when we married. It's a mashup of both our surnames, Kumar and Ohlson. It also means 'cabbage' in German, which kind of tickled me.

For a moment a frisson runs up my spine. Perhaps it's a job interview? No. That's stupid. I'm a middle-manager at the Raven, a swanky hotel in central London. I'm not considered 'talent'. No one is trying to poach me. Ridiculous.

I do a quick google of the hotel. It looks vaguely familiar. Holne House: where do I know that name from? Of course. Karen! Karen used to work for me at the Raven. She was good, really good, destined-for-great-things kind of good. I wrote her a glowing recommendation and she got herself an assistant manager job at a posh Devon hotel.

Getting us on the guest list must be a thank you. But I bet tickets would still cost a fortune, even if Karen's wrangled us a mate's rate deal. Shame. I think it could be exactly the kind of thing Rani would enjoy, and we could have a weekend away, just the two of us. Leave the puppies with my parents and spend some quality time together. When was the last time we went away? We were meant to go to Greece in June but then Rani had to work and so we cancelled. She said all the right things about how sorry she was, that she was gutted we'd have to miss it, that she'd make it up to me. But I knew deep down she was pleased. Rani is incapable of relaxing and can barely even fathom the idea of sitting on a beach for a few days; she only agreed to Greece in the first place because I nagged her repeatedly about our honeymoon that still hadn't materialised two years after our wedding.

But a murder mystery weekend would be perfect, it would give her enough to sink her teeth into and leave enough free time for some spa action. Plus, I do rather love anything involving puzzles and problem solving. I leave the invitation on the shelf by the front door and head upstairs for a shower. Rani'll be home from walking the fur babies soon and I stink like a badger.

* * *

The invitation has vanished when I come downstairs, hair dripping rivulets down my back. Rani is making coffee and the puppies run to greet me, tails wagging so fast I think they might take off. We rescued these two huge fluffy loons six months ago and they have turned our lives upside down in the very best way. I call them puppies, but Freya is three and Storm is five. They ended up at the shelter when their owner's husky puppy farm was raided. I try not to think about what they went through before, but Rani and I are giving them their best lives.

'I've sent a pitch,' Rani says, after I've petted the puppies. She draws me into an embrace and kisses my lips. We don't ever say hello or goodbye to each other, just continue as if we've been together the whole day. It's a silly superstition. The idea that if you didn't say goodbye then you never really left. But it's something Rani takes seriously.

'Pitch?' I ask.

'For the murder mystery weekend. Sounds like fun. And I think it would do us good to get away. Do you think they'll go for it?'

I'm struggling to understand what she's talking about. 'Pitch? They?'

'You weren't listening, were you?' She sounds almost heartbroken, but it's laced with irritation. Was she talking to me while I made a fuss of the dogs and I didn't pay attention? Again. She says I do this a lot and then she gets annoyed with me. I try to smooth things over with a white lie. 'Of course I wa—'

'It wasn't a question,' she interrupts. 'You obviously weren't listening, because, if you were, then you'd know what I was talking about.'

So much for smoothing things over. But I guess she has a point. 'Sorry.'

She nods, the tiniest movement of her head to show she accepts my apology, this time at least. It's just enough to let me relax, to walk back from the edge knowing I haven't completely messed things up. 'I want to get back into journalism,' she tells me. 'So I sent a pitch to that travel magazine I subscribe to. Perhaps they'll fund the murder mystery weekend for us and then I can write about it.' There's a tinge of hopefulness in her voice, like she's imagining a better life, one where she doesn't have to put up with her bitch of a boss every day and spend half her life in grotty airports.

'I think that sounds like a brilliant idea.'

She gives me a withering look. Because obviously it's a brilliant idea, she thought of it. Her phone dings to say she's had an email. I watch her as she scans the text, her beautiful face cracking into a smile. 'They love the idea. Apparently, they've been wanting someone to cover that weekend for literally years. But it's invitation only and so they've never been able to send anyone.' She looks up at me, her eyes shining with the possibilities.

'I think it was Karen who sent the invite,' I say tentatively, bracing for her reaction. Karen and Rani never got on.

To my surprise all she does is shrug, as if it really doesn't matter. 'Who cares? This is it. The chance I've been hoping for.' She jumps up and down on the balls of her feet, the thing she does when she's super excited. And something she's barely done recently. I love how happy she looks, the stress of her job erased from her features for a few moments. 'We're going to have so much fun.'

PART I

ARRIVAL AND ORIENTATION

1

SADIE

I've attended every single Murder on the Moors event since they started in 1975. It's socially acceptable to be an Agatha Christie fan with a penchant for a murder mystery weekend. And it provides the perfect cover for the real reason I'm so interested in poisons and policing methods and just how easy – or otherwise – it might be to get away with killing.

Fifty years of murder mystery weekends, fifty years of solving problems for my friends. Issues like ghastly husbands and disreputable bosses and even absolute strangers who think the world owes them compliant women who don't fight back. It's amazing how many truly abhorrent people there are in the world, and amazing just how easy it has been to rebalance the scales. It feels somewhat fitting that this year I'm taking Alyssa as my plus one. She's my goddaughter – the granddaughter of my best friend and the first woman I killed for – and a twenty-five-year-old ball of energy who wouldn't exist if it wasn't for that fateful night five decades ago.

Just like her grandmother always did, she arrives in a whirlwind of chaos.

'Aunt Sadie!' she calls across the arrivals area of Gatwick Airport, chestnut-coloured hair flying behind her as she wheels her suitcase at breakneck speed towards me.

I pull her into an embrace. It's been months since we last saw each other and I've missed her.

'What perfume are you wearing?' I ask as we pull apart. There's a jasmine and orange top note, but a more subtle cedarwood base.

She grimaces. 'You wouldn't approve.'

'Try me.' I'm not *that* much of a snob when it comes to fragrance.

'Kylie Jenner,' she says almost apologetically.

I keep my face impassive. It's not the most salubrious but it could have been a lot worse. 'I like it. It suits you. Now then, how was the flight?'

She rolls her eyes theatrically. 'Eughh. You know I hate flying. But they did serve Prosecco, so...' She shrugs her shoulders. I can smell the sweetness of the wine on her breath. I told her I'd pay for a first-class ticket, but she refused. 'I have a job now,' she'd told me, voice tinged with pride.

I've organised a car to take us to Devon; it's a four-hour drive and I'd far rather spend the time chatting with Alyssa than navigating the A303 myself. Plus there's always something so exhilarating about arriving in a sleek black Mercedes complete with driver in one of those peaked caps. I've always had a love for the theatrical.

'Shall we get car snacks?' she asks, looping her free hand through my arm. 'There's an M&S and I've been watching a million "new product" videos on TikTok. Did you know they have a strawberry sandwich? Literally pieces of strawberry and lashings of cream in between slices of brioche bread. God, I've missed England.'

She spends at least ten minutes in the fairly small shop, oohing and ahhing over food I think nothing about ordering every day. But I suppose I don't have to live in New York and consume a diet that is fifty percent corn syrup and fifty percent trans fats.

'Look, they have the sandwich,' she exclaims, dragging me towards the 'Meal Deal' section. 'I've been dying to try this.'

'It looks a little...' I don't really know the right words. It looks like the kind of thing you find in a mid-price hotel that's trying to be 'groundbreaking' and failing miserably.

'You haven't heard about this?' she asks. 'It's literally all over social media.'

'You know I don't understand all that,' I flick my wrist. It's not strictly true. I'm not a total Luddite, I understand the mechanics behind social media and that people are getting absolutely obsessed with all kinds of niche things because they saw them on TikTok. Some of it's even working to my advantage; I've started following a few crime authors who share their research processes and that has been extremely enlightening. I just don't understand why people allow it to suck *all* their time.

Alyssa – or Aly, as she now calls herself – has been living in New York for the last nine years, since her mum passed away and her bounder of a father insisted she went to live with him instead of coming to stay with me and continue her education at St Paul's. I was livid. At him. At the world. But I've tried to make the best of it, visiting Aly in the States every few months and hosting her during the long summer holidays in London. I'd hoped she'd move back to the UK once she graduated, but then she got a job offer she couldn't turn down. Not that I approve of what she does, but, then again, I suppose she probably wouldn't approve of my life choices if she had any idea of the things I get up to.

On the journey down to Devon, Aly tells me more about the job.

'It's just a consultancy,' she says, but I can see from the sparkle in her eyes that it's far more than that.

'What kind of consultancy?'

'We support legal firms to build cases for their clients. There's two main strands: building courtroom narratives to ensure the jury can fully engage with the evidence being presented—'

'Which means?' I interrupt, but not out of rudeness, I just want to make sure I'm understanding what she's saying in the midst of all the buzzwords.

She takes a breath. 'That's the boring stuff really. It means we break down complex stuff like securities fraud into little soundbites so the jury knows what we're talking about.'

'Oh…' I trail off. I don't want to say it but it sounds extremely dull.

'The other strand to the consultancy is much more interesting,' she says with a grin. 'We help advise on the jury selection itself. So I'll research the potential jurors and then we suggest who may react more or less favourably.'

'That feels…' I search for the right word. The most obvious one is 'unethical' but I know Aly is very proud of her job and I don't want to offend her.

'It's fascinating.' She lights up as she talks. 'I mainly work online, seeing what they search for, who they interact with, digging into their prejudices and understanding who they are when they think no one is watching. Last week I discovered a man who we thought was sweetness personified – a kindergarten teacher with two rescue kittens who looked after his sick mother – was actually selling meth over the dark web. More than enough evidence to get him kicked off the jury and a replacement brought in.'

'A replacement who would be more favourable.'

'Exactly. Our client was found not guilty and I'm in line for a promotion.'

I open my mouth to speak but I'm not sure how I feel about this job. It sounds like she helps the wealthy get away with their crimes. You might think – given my own extracurricular activities – that this is the kind of job I could get behind. But here's the thing. I do not condone the uber-rich using their resources to buy their innocence. Yes, what I do is technically a crime, but I prefer to think of it as karma coming back to bite, as protecting women whom society allows to bear the brunt of oafish men who never learned to share.

The first man I killed was Aly's grandfather. Not that she knows that, mind. He was a horrid man, a big brute with no discernible charms beyond an estate in Surrey and a pile of money from a long-dead uncle. My best friend Olivia was only twenty-two, and fifteen years his junior, when she married him at the behest of her own father. She was pregnant within six months and that's when he really let his true colours shine. I knew that he would kill her one day. I can't explain *how* I knew, it was just a feeling deep in my waters. He would kill her and the daughter she bore.

So I killed him first.

I was a silly, spoiled little child and it was the first good thing I ever did.

And, so, I carried on.

Well, if you have a talent, aren't you duty bound to use it?

And I definitely have a talent for murder.

2

CASSIE

Freya and Storm start to whine the moment Rani closes the door. I've promised to be the one who takes them to my parents for the weekend while she finally gets an hour to herself to prepare for our trip.

'We're going to see Granny,' I call toward the boot of the Prius in as cheery a voice as I can muster.

A wanker in a taxi cuts me up as I approach the junction for the motorway and I swallow down the stream of expletives that threatens to erupt from my throat. Rani says I need to swear a bit less and so I'm trying to keep myself in check. I've been doing very well. Instead, I allow my mind to wander to the serious bodily harm I would do to the driver if I had the opportunity.

Dad is waiting at the gate to their property, wearing the same shirt he's worn every day – except Christmas, weddings and trips to his masonic lodge – for the last decade. He bought a dozen in a sale and will wear them until they literally fall apart. They appear to have some kind of magic property and like cockroaches will probably outlast us all. He kisses my cheeks as I get out to greet him. 'You OK, love?' he asks softly, his hands finding my shoulders and discovering the sheer volume of tension I'm carrying in them.

'I'm fine, Dad.' We both know it's a lie. A few months ago, I had a few too many glasses of wine and confessed that sometimes I wonder what my life would have looked like if I hadn't married Rani, hadn't signed myself up to spending large tracts of time on my own when she worked away, hadn't allowed my own world to shrink for her. But we both know that I didn't really mean those things, that I love Rani and the life we've built together, that we shouldn't talk about these things out loud in the cold light of day.

'Is that my grandbabies?' calls a high-pitched voice from the front door. My mum practically runs out, cardigan flying behind her like a cape in her rush to get to the dogs. 'Oh, look at you two,' she coos as she flings open the boot. Some women are born to be parents, some are born to be grandmothers and some are born to look after puppies. Mum is in the third camp, her whole life suddenly falling into place the second she laid eyes on Freya and Storm.

I open the passenger door and begin to hand bags to Dad. 'Rani packed so everything will be there. If you can't find something, make sure you look in all the little inside pockets of the bags, I promise it'll be there somewhere.'

'We used to drop you at your grandmother's with nothing more than a carrier bag,' Dad says as I loop a fourth bag around his shoulder and he staggers slightly under the weight.

I pull the final two bags out of the car and follow Dad into the house. It's where I grew up, a place full of memories and photos and... stuff. So much stuff. I've been leaving hints about this thing called Swedish Death Cleaning, where retirees declutter their lives while they are still fit and healthy to release themselves of the burden of all their unneeded possessions. My parents have not got the message yet.

'Are you sure you're going to be OK with them?' I ask as Dad dumps the pile of bags on the kitchen table.

'We'll be grand. Your mother has been telling the entire world she's getting her furry grandkids for a long weekend. They are guests of honour at the Cancer Research coffee morning in about...' he checks his watch, 'forty-five minutes. And then their presence is expected at Gin and Book Group later, before tomorrow when they will be presented to the other golf widows at the club.' He grins. 'Your mother will tell everyone about their horrible start in life but how they have now been rescued to live in the lap of luxury.' He pulls me into a hug and kisses my forehead. 'Now you go and have a nice weekend at a swanky hotel.' He steps back.

'It's kind of a work trip,' I remind him.

'Work trip, my arse. Just remember it's the first time you can spoil your wife since you two got married.' He raises an eyebrow at me. 'I promise you that the whole "happy wife, happy life" idiom is absolutely true.' He glances at Mum to make sure she isn't listening, but he still drops his voice as he adds, 'Marriage isn't easy, but it's worth it. Just make sure you look after each other, OK?' He ends with his stern 'father' voice, the one he only uses very rarely, and only so I know this is advice I actually need to listen to. The things he tells me like this are the things most people take for granted, but I need to be told. I file the advice away in a folder marked 'important: do not forget'. *Pamper wife who deserves a break.* It jostles against other gems like *make eye contact when talking to people* and *fake it until you make it* and *sometimes a white lie is better than the truth.*

'Love you, Dad,' I say before reaching out to hug him one last time.

I say goodbye to the puppies and then get back in the car. My mum has still not actually said a word to me as she lavishes her attention on Freya and Storm but I'm choosing to let it go. 'Drive safe, love you,' Dad says as he closes my car door. He'll now do his usual thing of directing me out of the driveway. He doesn't realise I have a reversing camera and it'll beep like a maniac for the next few minutes as he stands far too close to the back of the car, the very obstruction the Prius is warning me about. But he means well.

As I pull onto the M23, I instruct Siri to play Chase and Status and crank up the volume. Rani will want to listen to Blackpink all the way to Devon – or possibly the soundtrack to that *K-Pop Demon Hunters* film – and so I need to get my drum and base fix in now. There's something about the heavy beat that quietens my brain in a way that makes zero sense but is a hundred percent effective.

I only contemplate killing two people on the drive back to Clapham – one for switching lanes without indicating and the other for throwing their McDonalds bag out of the window on the motorway – and I feel pretty good as I pull up outside the house. My mood improves further when I set eyes on my wife in a gorgeous black maxi dress, her long dark hair in a braid down her back.

'You look incredible,' I tell her and drop a kiss on her lips.

'I thought I'd try to look like I fit in at the Holne House Hotel,' she replies, affecting a posh accent for the hotel name.

'Let's do this then.' I pick up our little suitcases, staggering slightly with the weight of hers. 'Did you pack bricks?'

'Wine.' She winks.

'You're a woman after my own heart.'

'I am going to lie in the bath and drink red wine and pretend that the outside world doesn't exist.'

'I will rub your feet while you do,' I promise.

'You'd better.'

'Trust me, this weekend is going to be the most perfect opportunity for us to chill out.'

3

SADIE

The Holne House Hotel has hosted Murder on the Moors every year – except 2020 when the event was held over Zoom, but the less said about that debacle the better – and this year is a special celebration of the fiftieth anniversary. I'm expecting this to be the best one yet in terms of how much they pull out all the stops. Of course, the murder mystery element will be dull as all hell. It always is. Nothing compares to the real thing, but at least the Champagne will be good.

Holne House was built in the early nineteenth century, but in the Jacobean style and using local granite from Dartmoor. It's an imposing beast, almost stark in its beauty with its mismatched spires, crenellated ramparts and leaded windows. The Devon sky is uncharacteristically blue, but I can see clouds rolling in over the moors.

I'm expecting to see a few familiar faces as the Mercedes snakes up the winding driveway to the front door. Only forty tickets were available, twenty teams of two, all by invitation only.

I don't even recognise the concierge. She must be new, I have a photographic memory for faces that comes in very handy, so I know I've never seen her before in person. She's wearing a three-piece dark wool suit, with a white starched-collar shirt and plain black tie. It's somehow both incredibly modern – and beautifully tailored – but also in excellent keeping for the 1920s theme of the weekend.

Aly excuses herself – I'm assuming to ring some boy back in NYC – and I head further into the main entrance hall to check us in. The grand staircase rises before me, hewn from a deep cherry-coloured wood, it has a central set of stairs, before splitting into two at the mezzanine level to wrap around the entire hall. It still takes my breath away even after all these years, but before long I feel a deep sense of calm in my bones, as if I've come home.

'Good afternoon, Ms Rose,' the concierge says, leaving her position behind the desk to meet me. 'Such a pleasure to have you staying with us again.'

I'm slightly taken aback. She's acting like she knows me. 'Have we met?' I ask, slightly trepidatious that my perfect face memory is finally failing me in my dotage.

'Oh no, but I have it on good authority that you are our longest-playing sleuth.' She flashes me a smile. Something shines in her eyes, something almost like admiration. She's good, I'll give her that. Obviously a graduate of some fancy Swiss hospitality school, they teach obsequious customer service over there. I'm not a fan, it makes me feel a little itchy, like I'm missing something. But I know plenty of people rave about this kind of thing.

'This is my fiftieth Murder on the Moors,' I tell her, keeping my voice neutral. I don't want it to sound like a brag.

'And to celebrate, we've given you the very best suite in the hotel.' She motions towards the check-in desk.

'The Christie suite?' I ask.

'Of course. Only the best.'

You cannot book the Christie suite and I've never been deemed important enough to even set foot in it before. My senses are on high alert. Something feels off here. But I can't quite put my finger on it.

'Sadie Rose?' A loud voice barks from behind me.

Oh, *merde*. I thought he'd died. Or at least had the kind of heart attack that precluded weekends on the Devonshire moors. I turn and paint a smile on my face. 'Jasper!' I trill, the way it's expected when you meet a man who thinks of himself as an old friend. 'I so hoped you'd be here this weekend.'

He kisses both my cheeks, invading my space and assaulting my nose with the stench of cigars and his liberal application of Frédéric Malle Portrait of a Lady. 'I wouldn't have missed this weekend for the world.' He guffaws a few times like the cliché he is. I've spent my whole life with men like this; I was bored of them fifty years ago and now that has coalesced into an enduring ennui. 'I've heard a new game is afoot.' He waggles an eyebrow at me. He thinks he's being clever with the Holmes reference but, in reality, he is one of the dullest-witted men I've ever had the displeasure to meet.

'I'm sure it'll be just as fun as every year.'

'Another body. More intrigue. More clues.' He taps the side of his nose. 'Not that I'll say any more. You are the competition, after all.'

'Is Mrs Price-Evans your teammate this year?' I ask innocently. Mrs Price-Evans hasn't been to Holne House in over a decade, preferring to stay as far from the philandering old goat she married as possible and allowing him free rein to parade whatever new girlfriend he's spending time with.

'I have a new filly this year.'

I try not to visibly react to his use of 'filly'.

'She's a very clever young thing,' he tells me. I highly doubt it.

'Well, good luck to you both.' I try to catch the eye of the bellhop to help with our bags and get me the hell away from Jasper.

'Sadie?' A woman stops me just as we're getting in the lift.

I turn to face her. 'Yes?' She's young and beautiful and self-assured in the way I always dreamt of being, where the edges are still soft and people's immediate thought is that you must be nice. My edges are hard and people always assume I must be a complete bitch. They aren't necessarily wrong, but maybe that's just because I've always played the role I thought was expected of me. How different my life might have been if I looked like I'd hug you instead of killing you.

'I'm El and I'm with Murderous Intentions.' She points at the cap covering her hair and the logo of the company emblazoned on it. 'We're running the murder mystery element of the weekend.'

'You did last year too, I think?' I ask. I recognise the company name but I've definitely not met this 'El' before.

'The company, yes. But I'm new to the staff. I can't wait to get this story started, though.' She grins.

'Well, it's a pleasure to meet you,' I say, extending a hand to shake hers. Her nails are lacquered in a gorgeous deep red.

'You're a tiny bit early, so we're still running around getting everything ready. There's a folder of information in your room, but this is a special addition.' She flashes me a smile as she hands over an envelope.

'And this is...?' I ask as I take it.

'This,' she says and touches the envelope with a perfectly manicured finger, 'is for your eyes only.'

There's something in the way she says it that sends a frisson up my spine.

As the lift doors close and I begin the ascent, I slowly open the envelope, the paper inside thick and creamy beneath my fingers. No expense spared. I appreciate the theatricality of it, the attention to detail.

Aly catches me up just as I get to the door of the Christie suite, so we get to experience the unveiling together. It truly is magnificent. There are two bedrooms, one on either side of a central sitting area with teal and taupe sofas. The design for this suite at Holne House was loosely based on the vessel that inspired Christie to write *Death on the Nile*.

'Holy shit,' Aly says under her breath. 'This must have cost you a fortune.'

I flap my hand as if to say it was nothing, even though, if I'm honest, this weekend *has* cost an arm and a leg. I didn't expressly book the suite, it appears I was awarded it as the longest-running player. Which is nice. I mean, the suite is gorgeous. But hell, if it doesn't make me feel completely ancient.

Aly picks up a sheaf of paper from the desk area and begins to read aloud. 'Welcome to Holne House and the fiftieth anniversary of our ever-popular Murder on the Moors weekend.' Her eyes flick up to mine as if to check I'm still listening. 'This year we are heading back to the golden age of crime fiction and the heyday of the indomitable Agatha Christie.'

Aly rolls her eyes a little.

'You have read some Christie?' I ask.

She laughs. 'Of course not. Should I have done?'

I motion around the suite named after her.

Aly shrugs. 'Ooh, there's an itinerary.' She hands me a card with the programme for the next few days printed on it. It looks kind of busy. Almost every hour accounted for. There had better be enough time for some actual fun this weekend.

Day One: Friday

2 p.m. – 4 p.m.: Arrival and Orientation

4 p.m.– 6 p.m.: Afternoon Tea on the Lawn

7 p.m. – Late: Dinner, Drinks, and the Day the Sun Went Dark (Lecture from the Astronomer Royal)

Day Two: Saturday

7 a.m. – 10 a.m.: Breakfast (Cooked items from 8 a.m.)

12 p.m. – 2 p.m.: Dartmoor Scavenger Hunt with Picnic Lunch

4 p.m. – 6 p.m.: Afternoon Tea and Games on the Lawn

8 p.m. – Late: Gala Dinner (dress to impress!)

Day Three: Sunday

7 a.m. – 10 a.m.: Breakfast (Cooked items from 8 a.m.)

11 a.m. – 12 p.m.: Denouement and Prizegiving

12 p.m. Guests depart

Happy sleuthing!

The Management Team

Aly takes it from me and reads it herself. She looks up from the page. 'Did they seriously sign this off, "Happy sleuthing"?' She rolls her eyes in a way only her generation can, imbuing the action with a million subtle clues as to what she really thinks about the thing she just read. I've always been fascinated by watching young people and the way they evolve a set of mannerisms and a language that is so uniquely identifiable to their cohort. It's amazing what you can figure out by watching a specific individual. But there are also shortcuts, markers of class and age and lived experience that are so easy to see when you know where to look. I really should have been a police detective; if only I'd lived on the 'right' side of the law all these years.

'It gets worse.' Her tone is bored. 'They signed it off as "The Management Team". Ugh. Like that's a single entity. My boss loves to do that. Sign stuff off from the whole team as if we're all one big happy family and not a load of poor students working for pittance so he can buy another yacht.'

That's another thing about her generation. Money is dirty, and coming from money is something to be ashamed of. Although, it does make her a lot more aware of her privilege and for that I'm grateful.

She picks up a folder and waves it at me. 'Homework?'

'Oh, apparently I have some extra information.' I pull the pages out of the envelope. 'For a Hugo Durbridge and a Jerome Fulker?'

Aly flicks through the folder in her hands. 'No, I have those here. Hugo Durbridge, age 74, from Notting Hill.'

'Yes.'

'And Jerome Fulker, age 52, who splits his time between Reigate in Surrey and New York.'

'Oh well.' I put the pages down. 'Probably just a mix-up.'

I just hope the oversight isn't a sign of shambolic planning. I could do without this weekend degenerating into an utter disaster. Like the time the compere got completely sozzled and blurted out the identity of the killer on the first night.

4

CASSIE

At Rani's behest, I take the motorway rather than the A303. It's longer in terms of mileage but we're less likely to get stuck in traffic and the Prius eats up the miles, the cruise control set to exactly seventy. Rani is a calming influence and I don't threaten to kill anyone, not even under my breath. After an hour, I know all the English parts to the new Blackpink single. Rani speaks four languages and so she also sings along to the Korean parts. Another two hours and I also know every word to the *K-Pop Demon Hunters* soundtrack. It's surprisingly catchy.

'Do you think it's super fancy?' she asks me as we cross into Devon. 'The hotel, I mean.' It's a slightly rhetorical question as we've both pored over the website for the past week, looked at every picture tagged on Instagram, read every review across multiple platforms. It is unequivocally super fancy.

'It's so fancy, you are going to feel like absolute riffraff,' I assure her.

We arrive at the hotel just after three.

'Holy fuckin' shitballs,' Rani says as we travel up the long and twisted driveway, the moors falling away on both sides. 'This place is incredible.' Her voice is so full of childish wonder I can't help but smile. 'One day...' she starts but trails off. This is a game we always play. The 'one day' game. A game of dreams and what ifs and definitely some days. 'One day,' she starts again and I feel her warm hand on my thigh, 'you'll have a place like this.'

'How?' I ask. I know it's against the rules of the game, in the game you're meant to accept that anything can happen. The game is about the outcome not the practicalities of getting there. But I'm tired from the drive and I don't have the energy to play make believe on the life we both know will never materialise, not unless I have some super rich uncle I don't know about who will leave me his vast inheritance.

'Don't we always find a way?' she asks in return, but it's an empty platitude. Guilt tickles my brain, I've ruined the moment and I wish I could rewind a few seconds and simply smile instead.

The hotel is insane. It was once the home of some minor aristocrat with far too much money and that sense of opulence has been carried through all the décor. The entrance hall is panelled in dark wood with huge canvasses that showcase Dartmoor, and the parquet flooring has been waxed to a glorious shine. There's a grand staircase in the entrance hall and I get a glimpse of huge baroque chandeliers. Dotted around the space are large vases filled with hydrangeas in muted tones of green and rusty pink. I'm not really a flowers kind of girl, but sourcing floral arrangements recently became part of my remit at the Raven so I've had to learn the basics.

At the check-in desk we find the first of our fellow mystery participants.

'No. I don't think *you* understand,' a man in a pair of mustard-yellow trousers and a navy-blue knitted vest layered over a salmon-pink shirt says to the woman behind the desk. She is so perfectly beautiful it takes my breath away.

'Sir. The booking was made for a deluxe moor-view room.' She's matter of fact, face neutral, voice still soft even though it is obviously not the first time she's said that sentence to him.

'I need a suite.'

'The hotel is fully booked this weekend, sir.'

Rani leans closer to me, her breath on my neck. 'How long until he asks her if she knows who he is?' she whispers.

'Thirty seconds,' I reply.

'Twenty.'

She's closest, as it is literally the next sentence out of his mouth. 'Do you know who I am?' He leans across the desk a little, taking up the concierge's space.

'Mr Durbridge, sir.'

'And so, you don't think I should have a suite?'

'You booked a deluxe moor-view room, sir.'

The concierge has the patience of a saint and this interaction goes back and forth for another five minutes as Rani and I stand and wait. Eventually Mr Durbridge gets bored and demands to speak to the manager.

'I will gladly get him for you,' the concierge replies with something approaching relief. At least then she can pass him off to someone else. She picks up the phone. 'I'm sorry to interrupt you, but I have Mr Durbridge at the front desk.' She pauses to listen to her boss on the other end of the phone. 'Yes, he's insisting he needs a suite, but we're fully booked.' She nods a few times. 'Yes, his booking is for a deluxe moor view.' She twists a strand of brown hair around her finger. 'I've explained that. He would like to speak with you directly.' She glances up and catches my eye. I give her what I hope is an encouraging half smile.

She puts the phone down and directs her attention back to Mr Durbridge. 'The manager will be down in a few minutes. If I could ask you to move to the side so I can check in the next guests?'

He doesn't even turn to look at us. 'They can wait.'

Fuck that. 'Actually. We've already been waiting. For over five minutes now,' I step forward to tell him. I normally avoid conflict like the plague, but I allow a little of my work persona to take over, the Cassie who takes no prisoners.

'You'd think they'd have more than one member of staff working,' he says. Oh bless, I think he's assumed we're on his side. Ha. Work Cassie knows that the customer is definitely *not* always right.

'I believe you're waiting for the manager? So, you could just step to the side.'

'I'm not moving until my issue is resolved.' He doesn't quite stamp his foot like a petty child having a tantrum, but he isn't far from it. 'I'm sure you and your friend can wait.'

'This is my wife.'

He makes a pinched look, like he's smelt something malignant. 'Oh.'

'So,' the concierge says to me and Rani. 'Mrs and Mrs Kohl?'

I nod and then offer up a smile. She was obviously given a list with descriptions of all the guests arriving so she could greet us by name. It's a nice touch but I don't envy her having to try to distinguish between all the crusty rich white guys I can see milling about.

'I have you in one of our gorgeous suites on the third floor with glorious views,' she says with a grin. I glance at Mr Durbridge and watch him visibly bristle that we have the very room he wanted.

'I didn't know we were in a suite,' Rani says very loudly and not so subtly.

'Oh yes. The Tey suite.'

Mr Durbridge huffs, the set of his shoulders saying he's seriously pissed off. Good. Homophobic wanker. Go stew in your little shithole of a room. Even though we all know that even standard rooms in a place like this are like palaces. It's hardly going to be like booking a room at the local Travelodge, is it?

The Tey suite – apparently named after the crime writer Josephine Tey – doesn't disappoint. It's like something from a movie. There's a huge four-poster bed and a seating area with a velvet sofa and chair. Everything is in deep jewel shades, greens and burgundies and deep blues. It should feel dark and almost claustrophobic, but the designer had such a keen eye that instead it feels warm and cosy and decidedly opulent. If I ever did own a hotel like this, I would decorate it the same way. I take a peek in the bathroom and find a clawfoot bath. Oh yes, this weekend is going to be very good indeed.

Rani does a tour of the room, opening every drawer and every cupboard, commenting as she goes. 'Ooh, there's a hairdryer in the bathroom. And a charger for the toothbrush. Ooh, and a minibar. Fully stocked.'

'Don't touch it,' I bark as she reaches for a miniature bottle of Champagne. Everyone knows minibars are basically extortion.

She pulls her hand back as if I've slapped it. 'I guess I can't expense the minibar back to the magazine,' she says dolefully.

'Actually…' It's a good question. We haven't handed over a credit card or anything for additional charges and we signed a chit to be able to bill stuff directly to the room account. I guess the magazine who paid for this has left a card. Would it be taking the piss to have a little drink in the room? 'How much did this weekend cost?' I ask, realising I never even thought to before.

'Fifteen,' she says.

'Fuck. That's insane, even relative to the Raven's prices.'

'Well, I guess a suite for the weekend, plus two gala dinners, entertainment, unlimited drinks downstairs and wine with dinner... Then there'll be the cost of running the murder mystery part. Extra staff and actors and props...'

'Fifteen grand for a two-night stay,' I mutter under my breath as I cross the room to her. I wrap one arm round her waist as I lean to pluck a miniature Champagne from the fridge. 'But fuck it. A couple of drinks is hardly going to make a difference.'

She whoops and takes the bottle from me. I grab one for myself. We don't bother with glasses, just smash the bottles together. 'Cheers,' she says, making eye contact.

I hold her gaze. 'Cheers. To us.'

She continues her exploration of the room. 'Ooh, what's this?' She flips open the leather cover of the folder on the desk. 'I think this is about the murder mystery thing.'

We move the folder to the bed and make ourselves comfy with our drinks before flicking through.

It's a handbook for the weekend, complete with descriptions of all the players.

'I guess I'd better unpack my new notebook.' I try to sound nonchalant. Like I didn't spend almost an hour traipsing around various stationery stores to find the perfect one. She is black with a foiled art deco pattern, gilded edges and has a matching pen.

I'm so looking forward to this.

5

SADIE

The phone on the side table trills loudly.

'Is that a landline?' Aly asks as she edges towards it, peering slightly as if it's an alien object.

The phone itself is made from cream-coloured Bakelite, the same model my grandmother had. I sometimes forget just how young Aly really is. Or is it how much older I am? The world has changed an unfathomable amount since I was her age.

I pick up the receiver. 'This is the Christie suite.' Ooh, I do like saying that.

'We request the pleasure of your company in the Red Library, Ms Rose.'

'The Red Library?' I confirm, putting the emphasis on the 'red'. There are actually four libraries at Holne House: the original owners were extremely well read, or at least they wanted the world to think that.

'Yes. There is a map of the property in your folder, but someone can come to assist you if required.'

I chuckle. 'I've been coming here for fifty years. I know exactly where to go.'

'As you will. Please bring Ms Williamson with you. Your teammates will meet you there.'

The line clicks off. 'Teammates?' I say out loud.

'Huh?' Aly wasn't paying much attention, flicking through the folder of information instead.

'We've been summoned to the Red Library. Apparently our teammates will meet us there.'

'I thought *we* were a team. Like, the two of us?'

'So did I.' This is highly unusual and for a moment I wonder if perhaps they've decided to break the usual format and try something a little more interesting. Who knows, this weekend might be fun after all. But I won't get my hopes up just yet.

The Red Library is on the top floor of the hotel, tucked into one of the turrets. Personally, I would have called it the Octagon or at least made some reference to the unique shape of the room. But whoever designed the hotel decided to concentrate on the burgundy brocade wallpaper and scarlet heavy curtains and crimson velvet upholstery on the chairs. Even the large table in the centre of the room is inlaid with garnet leather.

The result is really rather fantastic, although it does look a little like the room has been dipped in blood. Perhaps that's part of the appeal? Not that there is any blood when I do my thing: I'm strictly a poisons kind of lady. Far less mess and far easier to walk away from. Why anyone would choose to kill another way, I have no idea.

We find two gentlemen already sitting at the table. The one facing us is handsome, if a little severe in features – his cheekbones are sharp enough to cut glass – and with almost feline eyes. Both men stand as we enter and the other turns towards me. He's the spitting image of the other. Identical twins.

'I'm Sebastian Radley,' one of them says, reaching out a hand.

'And I'm Samuel,' the other says. 'Err, also Radley,' he adds somewhat unnecessarily.

We make introductions and I try to remember which is which. They aren't dressed exactly the same – they're fully grown men, not toddlers – but differentiating by outfit is not going to help when they get changed for dinner later. Formal attire for men is hardly a statement in individuality. Samuel has a tiny tattoo on the inside of his right wrist. Sebastian's hair is longer, curling slightly over his collar. Although comparative differences will only help if they're together, of course.

'Is this your first time at Murder on the Moors?' Samuel asks.

I laugh. 'Hardly. This is my fiftieth year.'

'Fiftieth? No way. You were coming as a small child.'

Normally I hate it when people – but mainly men – try to be cute about how old I am and imply I'm much younger. I don't feel seventy-two, but I know that I look like it. I'm not 'delulu', as Gen Z says. But for some reason, Samuel makes it sound genuine and almost sweet. He has definitely got 'rizz'. That's charisma to you and me.

'How about you guys?' Aly asks.

'First time. We got an invitation and it seemed right up our street.' This time it's Sebastian who answers and I notice he's a little more lacking in the charm department. Fascinating. I'm assuming they grew up together and have been an active part of each other's lives, yet the differences are starting to show already. Given they are effectively the same person – in terms of genetics at least – how can they be so different?

We're interrupted by the door opening. It's the woman I met earlier, by the lift. She's still wearing that awful cap, although I can see her hair escaping in tendrils of pastel pink. Interesting. And apparently very difficult to achieve as a hair colour unless you're so blonde you're almost white to start with.

'You're getting to know each other, I hope,' she says in a singsong tone as she closes the library door behind her. Then she drops her voice. 'After all, you guys have a very special mission to accomplish together.' She sounds genuinely excited about the prospect and her joie de vivre is more than a little grating, if we're being honest. I think I need a drink. Maybe that will help me relax and get into the spirit of the weekend.

She motions to the chairs around the large leather inlaid table and we dutifully sit down in a rough circle. 'So, I don't know if you all got a chance to do some of the pre-reading I gave you?'

It has been almost sixty years – well, fifty-five at least – since I last sat in a school classroom and felt my stomach drop when I realised I hadn't done my homework, but I get the exact same sensation. That feeling I've somehow messed up, got it wrong, failed to reach my potential. Of course, things were different back then, less pressurised, less importance attached to exams and essays and all the academic things. But, even so, standards were exacting at St Paul's and with the amount my father was paying for my fees there was a certain level of expectation in my progress.

'I read the dossier,' Sebastian – I think – says.

'Umm...' Samuel – probably – looks at his twin. 'I didn't even look at it.' He does this almost theatrical cringe and then mimes slapping his own hand.

Sebastian shakes his head and mutters something under his breath. It sounds like 'typical'.

'I read it,' Aly says.

I throw her a look. *No, you didn't.*

'When you were unpacking.' She shrugs. As if it's normal to read a multi-page document in mere minutes. She was always the cleverest.

'Anyway,' El says. 'It was more to give you a head start. You have the most difficult job of all the teams.' A broad grin spreads across her face and she makes eye contact with each of us in turn.

Then she claps her hands. 'But first, let's go through the roles you'll be playing within the game. I know you've been to a Murderous Intentions weekend before, Ms Rose—'

'Please call me Sadie,' I interrupt to tell her. There is a time and place for formality but this isn't it.

She gives me a brief nod. 'I know you've been to one of these before, Sadie, but we've decided to change things a little bit this time round. We're doing away with the cutesy pun names, for starters.'

'Thank heavens,' I mutter under my breath.

'You approve?' El asks with a smile.

'Last year I was the wife of a frozen food magnate called Liz Anya,' I say drily. 'And one year I was a barmaid called Paula Nother.'

El makes a face. 'Well, you'll be pleased to know that this year we've grouped everyone into teams of four, with each of the ten teams being named after one of the tors of Dartmoor. You four are Team Bowerman. And you will each have a role as part of your team.'

'What, like a job within the mystery?' Aly asks.

'Oh no. I mean just like a part to play. It's all based on your relationship to one of the other characters.'

'The Marchioness?' Aly asks, pronouncing the title 'March-ion-ness'.

'Maa-shuh-nuhs,' I correct her. She makes a 'whatever' face at me.

'All will become clear when the games start,' El says. 'But yes. Sadie, you are the Dowager Bowerman, your late husband being a distant relative of the Marchioness. And Aly is your niece.'

'What about us?' Sebastian asks.

'You two are Sadie's nephews and Aly's cousins. You're obviously twins. I couldn't see a way round that. Anyway, in addition to being the Bowermans, the four of you, as a team, are playing a special role this weekend.' This time she waggles her eyebrows. I wish she'd get on with it, get to the point she's so clearly desperate to make but trying to make feel more exciting than it really is.

'Please, please, please,' Sebastian says quietly, eyes closed and the fingers on both of his hands crossed.

'You are going to be the murderers,' El says, spreading her arms wide.

'Yes!' Samuel says. He looks at Sebastian and they beam at each other. 'Get in.'

'Trust me,' El says with authority that breaks into a grin. 'This weekend is going to be a blast.' She turns to me and Aly. 'Is this OK with both of you?'

'Sure,' Aly replies.

I merely nod. Of course it won't be anything like the real thing, but at least it's all adding to the lie I've lived for so many years. Why are you so keen to research grisly deaths and murder? Oh, I do this murder mystery weekend every year. This year I was even the murderer. Imagine that. Ha ha.

'Great. Well, there's a whole lot more to the weekend, and obviously there's a whole story underpinning everything. But Lloyd will take you through that during afternoon tea on the lawn in...' she checks her watch. 'Ooh, we'd better get a move on, the party's about to start.' Again with the beaming smile. Surely it isn't possible to be this relentlessly positive? It's making my teeth hurt. I bet she's the kind of woman who takes Christmas far too seriously, with homemade gift baskets of cookies and too many decorations.

6

CASSIE

We get a call to the room and the man on the other end of the line asks us to join our team in the West Orangery, which appears to be a small conservatory on the side of the main hotel building with views over the formal box maze.

Rani is still giggling like a teenager, hopped up on Champagne and some kind of 'swanky-hotel delirium', when we get there. It's honestly like she's never been in a nice hotel before, although I guess that an all-expenses paid trip to Murder on the Moors is a pretty far cry from the YotelAir at Schiphol Airport.

'Wow, this room is...' she starts but falls silent when she takes it all in. There are huge fronds of fern stretching towards the ceiling and it's warm in that very specifically moist way of a tropical greenhouse. Teal and purple upholstered sofas and small armchairs are dotted around the greenery, giving the feeling of some kind of lush oasis. It's completely beautiful.

There are a cluster of chairs around a central low table and we inch towards them, taking in the rest of the orangery around us.

'Ladies,' a booming American voice from behind me interrupts our investigations.

I whip round to find an older man – probably in his late sixties, but I am normally shit with ages so I try to avoid guessing as much as possible –

standing in the doorway. He smiles and it lights up his whole face. He's surprisingly handsome, like George Clooney, and there's something in his demeanour that makes me realises he both knows he's attractive but also is an absolute sweetheart at the same time. I'm normally suspicious of new people, but he puts me at ease immediately. The effect is almost disconcerting.

The woman next to him steps forwards and closes the distance between us. 'I'm Beatrice. Bea,' she says extending a hand. 'And this is my brother Theodore.'

'Um. Cassie,' I reply, shaking her hand. Her skin is cool to the touch. 'And my wife, Rani.'

There's a tiny pause and my stomach drops. Is she about to say something? She turns to her brother. 'Look Theodore. Lesbians.' But there's a hint of delight there. She turns back to us and grins. 'I am too.' She winks. 'But normally I'm the only one.' She puts her hand on my shoulder. 'This weekend is shaping up to be the best one of these yet.' She sounds so warm, so genuinely pleased to have found common ground. It's kind of endearing.

The door opens and a man enters. 'Good afternoon,' he says. 'I'm Finn and I'm from Murderous Intentions.' He points at the lanyard around his neck, emblazoned with the company logo, as he says it. 'I'll be helping you to navigate the story this weekend.'

'So you know who the killer is?' Theodore asks.

'There's a member of Murderous Intentions allocated to each team and trust me when I tell you that none of us has a briefing into the guilty persons. I have my suspicions, of course, but I'll be working with you to solve the murders in real time.'

He's lying. I can tell instantly.

We make our introductions. Finn's nice if a little standoffish, like he wants to keep us at arm's length. I probably wouldn't even have noticed, to be honest, except that it's in such a direct contrast to the warm openness of Theodore and Bea.

'The four of you are to be a team for the weekend. The game will be explained over afternoon tea in twenty minutes. But this is an opportunity to get to know each other. You'll need to work together if you want to solve the murder and win the prize.'

'Is there a prize?' I ask. I love a prize, even if it's only a token one.

'There's a little something for the winning team, yes.' He smiles.

Well, well, well, things just got interesting. I touch my hand to my bag and the art deco notebook inside. Very interesting indeed.

'Before we head out to the lawn,' Finn says, 'I'd better explain the teams and the roles you will all be playing.'

'Please tell me I have some suitably silly name,' Theodore says, leaning in almost conspiratorially. 'One year I was Felix Fumblefingers, the clumsy yet lovable rogue.' He laughs. 'And once, many years ago now when things were a little less PC, I was Ivor Biggun—'

'Theodore,' his sister smacks his shoulder. 'At least get to know people first before you start making inappropriate jokes.'

'Trust me when I say that we are not easily offended. Cassie's worked in hospitality for years,' my wife says.

'Right then,' Finn tries to bring us back on track. 'Your team name is based on the tors of Dartmoor, so you are Team Cox.'

'You're kidding?' Bea asks.

'No.' Finn looks puzzled. 'Is that a problem?' He frowns.

Bea catches my eye and then Rani's. The three of us giggle. Of all the teams they could have given that name to.

'Right then,' Finn says. 'We're running out of time. Let's go and get things started and then I'll finish explaining things.'

A fun team and a prize to be won. What could be better?

PART II

AFTERNOON TEA ON THE LAWN

7

SADIE

We head through the main ballroom with its gilt details and walls covered in huge paintings of Dartmoor and the Holne family. The furniture has been moved to the edges in preparation of the games later. It's the same every year. I step out onto the stone terrace and walk towards the huge set of stairs that leads down to the lush green lawn below.

The cloud cover from earlier has dissipated, leaving behind a hazy late summer sun, bathing the gardens in golden light. If you didn't look too closely you could almost imagine it was 1927 and we were in the private house of some wealthy aristocrat. You'd obviously have to ignore the corporate branding the hotel has emblazoned over every tiny detail and the Covid-era relics still littering after six plus years: polite notices to keep our distances and all that kind of thing.

I spot Sebastian looking at the same things.

'You'd think they'd remove them,' he says.

I nod in agreement. I might have to watch out for this one, he seems rather more observant than the average person.

Oh *merde.* Theodore Frillish is standing on the edge of the patio area, surveying the lawn in front of him like he owns the place. What is he doing here?

As if sensing me, he turns slowly, a lazy smile across his features. 'Well,

well, well,' he says in that despicable drawl of his. He's from Tiverton in Devon, but pretends he's from Texas. 'If it isn't Sadie Rose.' He bounds over, the ease of his movement belying his age. The bastard has lived the kind of charmed life where nothing bad ever touches him and apparently that includes ageing.

'Theodore,' I say, desperate to avoid him but unable to snub him in quite such a public location.

'It's so great to see you. It's been far too long.'

We both come every year. And every year I try not to talk to him. But he's like a boomerang and, the harder I try to push him away, the faster he comes back to me. 'It's good to see you too,' I reply, my voice stilted.

'Are you going to introduce me to your friend?' There's an almost imperceptible raise of the eyebrow.

'My goddaughter, Aly,' I say, motioning to her. I hope she can feel my discomfort, that she knows I don't want to talk to the man in front of us, no matter how suave he is, or the lustre of his salt-and-pepper hair, the slightly crooked smile that only adds to the handsome proportions of his face.

'Lovely to meet you,' she says as she steps forward to take his hand.

'Ooh, a fellow Yank,' he says and then pulls her into a hug as if they were old friends.

'Weren't you born not far from here?' I remind him.

'You know as well as I do, Sadie, that where we are born doesn't always define us.' Then he has the audacity to wink at me.

'Well, it's been a pleasure.' My tone makes it very clear that I'm trying to extricate myself from his company. 'But we must go and join the rest of our teammates. I feel the games are about to begin.'

'I don't believe the games ever stopped,' he replies. And therein lies the entire problem with Theodore Frillish. He thinks my animosity towards him is a game, a code he can crack to thaw me out. In reality, I'm merely trying to save him from getting pulled into my orbit and crashing down to Earth.

'Oh my God,' Aly leans in to almost squeal in my ear as we walk away to find the others. 'Who was that?' She sounds impressed by him.

I need to nip this in the bud quickly. 'He's nobody.'

'Oh my God.' This time she stops and turns to face me. 'Is he like an ex or something?' She nudges me gently. 'I mean, I get it. He's a total zaddy.'

'I have no idea what a zaddy is.' Although I do. As I said before – I do follow a few authors on TikTok and so I've heard the term before. A zaddy is just an attractive older man whom women of all ages flock to. Apparently, Pedro Pascal is the king of the zaddies.

'A zaddy—' she starts but I interrupt.

'Theodore Frillish is no one. Just someone I met a few times.' I leave it at that.

'But—'

'No buts. Stay away from him.'

Luckily at that moment I spot the twins. 'There they are.' I point to a table on the lawn, the white linen tablecloth flapping gently in the slight wind coming off the moors. 'We should join them.' I hurry over, the fingers on my right hand crossed that Aly will drop the talk about Theodore.

An army of waiters in starched shirts and burgundy waistcoats pour Champagne into crystal flutes and deposit tiers of plates festooned with tiny sandwiches and delicate cakes on the tables. One thing you can never fault Holne House for is the food and drink. It's always excellent, no expense spared.

I raise my glass of Bollinger towards the centre of the table. 'Well, here's to us and our little team,' I say.

The others raise their glasses and echo the sentiment.

The Bollinger is perfectly chilled and, as the apple and peach notes hit my tongue, I'm transported back three decades to a villa in the south of France, the sound of the sea slapping onto the rocks below.

But my reminiscence is interrupted by the arrival of a man in his forties in a rather formal-looking suit. He doesn't look like the other guests, he looks like he's wearing a costume and he's vastly uncomfortable about it. Three-piece suit, white shirt, a bowtie that's been tied incorrectly so it's oddly lopsided. He's carrying a Derby hat under his arm. In short, he looks ridiculous.

He claps his hands a few times to get everyone's attention but most of the other guests ignore him and continue their own conversations. El, our team representative, now dressed in a similar suit – although hers has a fabulous pair of palazzo trousers that vindicate the ensemble somewhat – stands next to him. There's something wrong about her hair, the hairline looks too far forward. Is it a wig? It must be, there isn't a single trace of the pink I saw underneath that stupid cap before. She hands Derby hat guy a microphone.

The screech of feedback as he raises it to his lips stops the babble of conversation around me. 'Umm... Welcome to Holne Hall. And welcome to the fiftieth anniversary of Murder on the Moors.'

There's a murmur through the crowd, some of the guests are glad to be here, people who enjoy this kind of thing and will bore the hind legs off a donkey about these weekends through the whole rest of the year. But there are also a fair proportion of people dragged here by overexcited spouses, people who would otherwise prefer to pluck their own eyes out than go to a murder mystery weekend. Isn't it amazing what we'll do for love? For love, or just a quieter life.

The man clears his throat and plucks at the collar of his jacket. Now that I can see him face on, I recognise him as the same chap who was compere last year. He was... well, not good... but at least somewhat acceptable in his portrayal of the role. Now he looks so uncomfortable he might spontaneously combust. Or as if he has something else on his mind and can barely concentrate on the here and now. I've become rather an expert in reading people over the years.

But at least our El looks like she's got things under control. He gives her a plaintive look. *Please help me*, his eyes say. A moment passes between them. Then she takes the microphone from his slightly limp hand and flashes her smile to the collected ensemble of guests.

Her smile lights up the crowd. This is a woman who *really* loves her job. I'm not going to lie, but it makes me dislike her a little. No one should be that happy; it isn't natural.

8

CASSIE

The woman looks around the tables of guests, her gaze snagging on ours for a moment. I can only assume it's because of how beautiful my wife looks, most people can't help their gaze from drifting to her.

She clears her throat. 'Welcome to Murder on the Moors. The Marchioness of Devonshire is dying and she has no direct heir. For five years, since the tragic death of her husband, the late Most Honourable Marquess, she has been searching for a worthy recipient of her estate.' She pauses for a moment to ensure we're all paying attention. There's something almost magnetic about her and every eye in the audience stares transfixed.

'The Marchioness has whittled down the list of potential inheritors and invited them, along with their families, to spend the first weekend of September at Holne Hall.' The woman drops her voice. 'On Sunday, she plans to announce who she will leave her considerable fortune to.'

'I think the Marchioness may be our victim,' Theodore says with glee. 'I always love these little backstories. The more clichéd the better.' He rubs his hands together and then motions for the waiter to come and top up our Champagne glasses. I have a suspicion my liver is going to take a kicking this weekend if I try to keep up with his drinking.

'You are all gathered here on this lawn as the guests of the Marchioness. So, without further ado, let me introduce you to your host.' The woman sweeps her arm towards the house and, as if by magic, a figure appears at the top of the stone stairs from the ballroom.

Theodore starts to applaud and soon everyone joins in. I'd expected the Marchioness to be old, but the woman walking down to greet us is in her late twenties at most.

'Isn't that...' Rani says, squinting a little to get a better look in the afternoon sun. 'It is!' she exclaims. 'That's Tori Cooper. She's a model. She does the campaigns for that PALETTES makeup kit you bought me for Christmas.'

I should probably know what Rani is talking about, but the truth is, she gives me a list with a specific set of instructions that I follow to the absolute letter and then immediately forget.

Tori – sorry, the Marchioness – is wearing a dusky-pink gown with a dropped waist and chiffon batwing sleeves. She looks like a movie star.

'Ladies and gentlemen,' she says in the pinched nasally voice of the aristocrat. 'Thank you all for coming this weekend.' She pulls a handkerchief from her beaded clutch and coughs delicately into it. 'As you are aware, my darling husband and I were not blessed with children before his tragic passing, and so there are no natural heirs to the title and estate. Each of you has a potential claim.' She coughs again. 'And I am sick. A decision must be made.'

Another cough.

But this time she doesn't stop coughing. Her face turns red and she looks around frantically as if she's seeking someone. 'I... I...' she splutters, the words sticking in her throat as she continues to cough.

It happens in slow motion, almost gracefully. The Marchioness crumples to the floor, the hand holding the handkerchief outstretched. The blood on the fabric is clearly visible from the angle we're all sitting and there's a collective gasp from the guests.

The woman who gave the introduction hurries forward and presses her fingers against the Marchioness' neck. 'She's dead,' she proclaims.

'Uh... we... umm,' the man with the hat from earlier stutters as he steps forward.

'We must call the police.' Luckily, once again the woman takes charge of the situation. I sneak a look at Finn, who is rolling his eyes. No doubt this isn't the first time his boss has fucked up the opening scenes. I'm suddenly kind of glad it wasn't my fifteen grand funding this weekend. 'There's been a murder.'

Theodore gasps loudly. 'Oh, what fun,' he says in a plummy voice, finishing the rest of his Champagne.

'What happened to your accent?' Rani asks him.

'My brother likes to pretend he's American but we're as British as they come. Can you please just stick to your real accent this weekend?' Bea implores him. 'I don't think I can cope with that repellent Texan drawl.'

'Fine,' he agrees. 'Now then, you lot be quiet, someone has been murdered.'

Two of the waiters in their burgundy waistcoats run forward and carefully drape a sheet – or possibly a tablecloth – over the prone body of the Marchioness. I notice the twitch of her hand as one of them gets a little too close, but otherwise her acting isn't too bad. I guess she wants to break away from modelling, but this does feel like kind of a small gig.

There are two men at the next table and they each light a huge fat cigar, wafting the smoke directly towards us. Bea bristles next to me. 'I hate the smell,' she whispers.

'Shall I ask them to put it out?' Rani asks. She's always so quick to rush to someone's aid.

'Oh no, no, I don't want to make a fuss,' Bea replies.

I take a longer look at the men. They are both leaning back in their chairs, a study in casual conduct. But underneath I can see tension between them, as if they are sizing each other up. I wonder if they are really strangers, thrown together for the weekend like we have been with Theodore and Bea. I'm so glad we haven't teamed up with guys like that, I don't think I could stand a weekend of machismo and dick-swinging. They are completely ignoring their extraordinarily pretty – and obviously younger – wives or girlfriends. I stifle a chuckle. Men are so fucking predictable.

The other day, my neighbour's daughter – who I've been babysitting regularly since she was tiny – asked me when I knew I liked girls.

'Since forever,' I replied. It was never a question in my mind.

'I see.' She'd nodded solemnly. Or at least as solemnly as an eight-year-old can. 'So I'd know by now?'

'You sound disappointed.'

She narrowed her eyes and curled her lip. 'Boys are hideous. It would just be so much better to like girls.'

I couldn't tell her she was wrong. Especially as I was so lucky to find Rani.

9

SADIE

Oh yippee.

An estate with no heir.

A dead Marchioness.

A long list of potential suspects.

So far, so boring. It's like this every single year, some stupid backstory that I don't actually care about. I don't come for the story, or the murder, or even the company. I come because then, if the police or whoever decide to look at my search history or the books on the shelves of my Mayfair apartment, they'll find a good reason for my interest in poison and body disposal and how long before you can claim someone is dead after they've disappeared.

El stands in front of the sheet-covered woman. 'The Marchioness has been murdered,' she says. 'But what is this?' She holds up an envelope and waggles it.

'Ooh,' I hear from another table. Well, someone is obviously enjoying this whole charade. I look over. Surprise, surprise, it's Theodore. He always did enjoy this whole weekend a little too much. He's like an overgrown golden retriever with an unhealthy joie de vivre, only exacerbated by a lack of boundaries and an unwavering belief that everyone loves him even if they've done nothing but push him away for years.

El opens the envelope and slips out a letter.

'Dear Guests,' she reads. 'If you are reading this, then I am dead.' El pauses for effect, but I just roll my eyes. Let's get this over with so I can go and find a whisky. All this Champagne is making me feel giddy.

'But I have not died by natural causes. The malady affecting me has not claimed my life. For the last year I have been gathering evidence about you all. Building a dossier of information about who you really are. And I did not like what I found.'

Boring. Secrets and lies. Let's be honest, most people are utter disasters walking around in plain sight.

'I have been murdered, that much is clear. But here's the twist. I have expected this. And I have planned for it. None of you deserve a penny, but perhaps there is one way to redeem yourselves. My will has been rewritten and signed by the eminent Lord Tracey KC himself.' El motions to the man who so far has turned out to be a blithering idiot in these proceedings. 'My colleague will now read the terms of the new will.'

The man steps forward. I can see him visibly sweating under the gaze of forty people who have paid a small fortune for him to entertain them. He is certainly not up to the task this year.

'Here is the last will and testament of the late Marchioness.' He stumbles over the title and I suppress a groan. He clears his throat and looks up nervously. 'I, the Marchioness of Devonshire, do hereby leave my title and estate to the person or persons who solve my murder.'

I thought they were going to pull out all the stops this year? This is probably the worst story we've ever had, not that I remember them all, of course.

Aly excuses herself to go to the bathroom and I take an opportunity to observe the rest of the guests.

As expected, many have returned from previous years, but there are also a surprising number of new faces. When El rejoins us, I ask her about the range of guests.

'Well, my job is just with the story company,' she says. 'But I did hear that there was a bit of a "hoo-ha" in terms of invitations.' She drops her voice conspiratorially and moves her chair in a bit. We all follow suit, huddling into the table to avoid being overheard. I rather enjoy gossip like this. Positively thrive on it. 'So. Apparently there was a guest list drawn up and invitations sent and it was half full of new players, people who had never even been to Holne House before.'

Now that she's mentioning it, I do remember something. A murmur around some of the better restaurants in Mayfair. Some people had been snubbed from an event, one that was being touted as the party of the season. Something everyone would want to attend. I don't really care about that kind of thing. I've lived towards the edge of society my whole life, I stopped seeking out the 'invite of the season' a long time ago.

'But, anyway, the guest list was shrouded in secrecy.'

'Interesting,' Sebastian says.

Aly returns from the bathroom but she's paler than usual, a concerned frown creasing her forehead. I knew a man once who would poke his wife whenever she frowned, his bony finger hard against her skin. 'Frowners get wrinkles,' he'd say with the kind of authority that only complete bastards use. It was just one of the many little ways he would find to belittle her at every available opportunity. I laced his soup with cyanide and left his body in the woods to rot. His wife claimed he was away with work whenever anyone asked where he was. His remains were eventually discovered by some dogwalkers who didn't understand the meaning of 'private property' but by then there wasn't enough of him left to prove his death had been anything other than what God intended.

Aly knocks the table as she sits down and it jolts me back to reality. 'Everything OK?' I ask her as I place a few little sandwiches and a fondant fancy on her plate.

She scowls at the food.

'You need to eat,' I remind her. Too many young girls don't eat properly, picking at their food like little birds so they can fit into some stupidly small size. Well, not my goddaughter. Not on my watch, anyway.

She huffs, but pops the entire cake in her mouth. A look of beatific pleasure colours her features for a moment. 'Fuck that's good,' she says. 'Sorry,' she adds quickly and blushes. 'Pardon my French.'

For a moment I think she's taking the Michael out of me, but then I spot the lick of a grin at the corner of her mouth and realise she's joking. I was brought up by a strict father who didn't believe in cursing and I still find myself unable to let forth a litany of swearwords. However, there's always a loophole and the French have really mastered the art of the profanity. Much to her father's consternation I taught Aly a few choice phrases as a teenager, nothing too bad – *va te faire foutre* and *bordel de merde.* If you do it in French, you can swear like a navvy but still sound like a lady. 'Anyway, talk to me.' I inject an air of authority into my tone. I learned a long time ago that, if you demand answers rather than ask questions, you get a lot more from people. Deep down they all just want to follow someone.

She turns serious. 'I bumped into someone. Just outside the bathrooms.'

'Who?'

'His name is Jerome Fulker. I recognised his signet ring. The symbol on it.' She sounds worried, or frightened. 'It reminded me of something I read a few months ago. About this gang in NYC.'

'And...?' She obviously has more to add.

'So, I went back to the room and grabbed my phone.' She pats her pocket. 'I know I'm not meant to have it... but this is important. I went digging. And there are rumours, certain people saying things in various forums about him. I went on the dark web.'

My eyes flare with concern.

'Chill,' she says. 'I know what I'm doing. This is kind of my job, remember? Anyway, I found something. This gang is involved in a whole load of different activities, but they mainly specialise in moving things.'

'What kind of things?'

'Drugs. Guns. Exotic animals. Anything that requires a permit and you don't have one.'

'Exotic animals?' My memory snags on something I read earlier as I flicked through a few pages of the folder El gave me. 'That's what it said... in the dossier...' I whisper.

Aly looks at me like I've gone senile. 'The dossier just says he's on Team Shilstone and gives some skeleton details like his age and where he lives.'

'There was an additional notes section.'

'There totally wasn't.'

How bizarre.

'I'm going to have another look,' Aly says, before she drops a kiss on my cheek and turns to leave.

I resist the urge to shout 'be careful' as she walks away.

10

CASSIE

Theodore offers to take us on a tour of the hotel. 'I've been here about twenty times over the years, so I know it like the back of my hand.'

'I think that's probably meant to be my job,' Finn says, 'but I'm more than happy to let you lead the way. Although we do still need to talk through your team and the characters you're playing this weekend since we ran out of time before.'

The communal guest areas on the ground floor of the hotel are truly beautiful in a slightly stark and quintessentially masculine way, with lots of dark wood and muted tones of green and blue and burgundy. It isn't how I would have decorated this part of the building, I would have chosen a brighter colour palette, something that would contrast with the view of the moors from the huge windows. I think the designer who last renovated was trying to keep it historically accurate. I can imagine a rather sombre lord rattling round here in the dim and distant past, but in reality it was probably just the fashion of the time. Perhaps he also found it rather austere and was desperate for some laughter and joy?

In the main entrance hall, I stop to marvel at the ornate staircase.

'Fabulous, isn't it?' Finn says. 'Imagine making an entrance back in the day, coming down the stairs to greet your guests.' He sounds genuinely enthusiastic and it's kind of sweet. 'Oh, and look at this.' He points to what looks like a low mahogany sideboard with three dials on the front. 'This is an original Zenith electric radio from 1927. It would have been absolutely cutting edge at the time.'

I wait until he's moved away to pull out the notebook and jot down a few notes and then hurry to catch up with the others.

Rani slips her hand into mine as we walk through an impressive library with a mezzanine and double-height bookcases filled with leatherbound books. In the middle is a huge globe, above which a massive crystal chandelier glitters. 'This place is fucking mental,' she whispers in my ear. 'I feel like royalty. But like the poor cousin who somehow inherits everything because by some weird twist of fate everyone else has died, and then they come to live here and it's like a whole other planet.'

'A manor house would suit you,' I tell her and she squeezes my hand in return.

'Please remember you are meant to be looking for clues,' Finn reminds us.

'What kind of clues?' I ask.

He shrugs enigmatically. 'Things that seem interesting, or out of place, or deliberately left in plain sight.' He drops his voice to almost a whisper. 'We're not trying to catch people out this weekend, it's meant to be fun. The answers are in front of you.'

I don't think subtlety is his strong point. I drop Rani's hand as I look around the library, searching for the clue he's literally just told me is here. Finn coughs and nods his head towards the table in the centre of the room. There's a newspaper lying on it that looks almost antique.

Theodore picks it up and unfolds it to reveal the front page. 'The *Devon Times*. Dated 27 June 1927.'

'I'll write that down,' I tell him.

We continue the tour, waiting for Finn to point us towards the things that may be clues. I keep my own eyes peeled – I don't like to rely on other people – and eventually we find ourselves in a small parlour room. Everything is a vibrant teal, from the walls to the upholstery to the rugs. It should look tacky and gaudy but it doesn't. I might even take a little inspiration for our guest room that still hasn't been decorated. Rani said she'd do it months ago but nothing's been done and so I guess I'm going to have to take over.

There's a fireplace on the left wall and on the mantelpiece is a photo of a woman I recognise. 'Isn't this the Marchioness?' I ask.

Rani steps closer to look more carefully. 'Yes, you're right.'

Theodore looks too. 'That's the Criterion,' he says, pointing to the sign behind her. 'It's a restaurant in Piccadilly. They do a fabulous osso bucco.'

'Shall I write it down?' I ask, directing the question at Finn.

He shrugs but I can tell from his little smirk that yes, yes I should. 'Now then,' he says. 'We probably need to pick up the pace a little.' We follow him out of the parlour room.

'I imagine there are hidden passages all over the hotel,' Rani says as we follow a corridor lined with huge oil paintings of the Dartmoor countryside and moody pictures of the sea in the middle of a storm.

Theodore falls into step next to us. 'There are rumours of those secret passages,' he says conspiratorially. 'Perhaps we should have a look later. It might give us a bit of an advantage in the game.'

'That sounds like an excellent idea,' I say under my breath. I know it's only a game, a story for the weekend, but I am nothing if not competitive and if there's something to be won, if only for kudos, then I will do everything in my power to win it.

I wonder how competitive my fellow team members are. Bea is like the fun aunt I always wanted. Not that my aunt isn't fun, but she is slightly staid and with a penchant for crochet and bridge. Bea, on the other hand, looks like the kind of aunt who would have taken you to a nightclub back in the day and let you smoke her Sobranies. I wonder if she does actually smoke Sobranies? I gave up during the pandemic but I could devour a cigarette right about now.

The final stop on our tour is what Finn describes as the evidence room. 'This is where you'll find more information, pieces of evidence, newspaper clippings, all that kind of thing,' he says, motioning inside. 'The portfolio will be added to over the weekend so make sure you come back here regularly. And there are notepads and pens on the side.' There are too many people already inside for us to see much so we decide to return later to go through the detail. I do spot a small leatherbound book right at the entrance and have a quick flick through before I join the others. It's the Marchioness's diary and the last entry is 27 June 1927. Hmm, interesting.

That's the same date as the newspaper. But I'm sure it's meant to be the first weekend of September in the game. Weird.

We head back to the lawn and find our table. The plates have been cleared, but a red-waistcoated waiter brings a new place setting for each of us. It feels decadent to the point of being wasteful.

'Right then,' Finn says. 'Teams. So you're Team Cox—'

Bea laughs and spits Champagne towards him. 'Sorry, sorry,' she says quickly, covering her mouth with her hand.

'Anyway. The four of you represent an animal welfare charity called Stop Animal Cruelty, or SAC for short.'

'I feel like a little more effort could have gone into selecting the name, but OK,' Theodore says, but I can tell he's joking.

'Anyway, Theodore, you are the Director of Communications. Bea, you're the Executive Director.'

'Does that make me his boss?' she asks, pointing at her brother.

'One hundred percent,' Rani confirms. Bea pumps her fist in the air and Theodore pulls a face.

'Rani, you are the Head of Fundraising, the kind of job that involves lots of schmoozing, which I'm sure you're very good at.' There's a tiny undercurrent of something in his tone but I dismiss it. 'And you, Cassie, are the CFO. Chief Finance Officer.'

Rani looks at me and bursts out laughing.

'I think there's been a mistake,' I say. 'I'm not really a numbers gal. Patterns and problem solving, yes, but numbers aren't really—'

'Chill,' Bea says, touching my arm. 'I don't think they're going to expect you to actually do the bookkeeping, it's just a role for the game.'

'Right,' I say quickly, my cheeks starting to blaze. Of course it's just a title for the game. What was I thinking?

I stew in my embarrassment. Why can't I just be normal and not say the first thing that comes into my head? I try to cover my shame by eavesdropping on the table next to us.

'The skirt who did the intro?' I hear one of the cigar smokers say. 'She must be one of the more senior people, right?'

There are nods of assent from his cronies. 'Bit too perky for my liking,' one of them grumbles. 'Pretty though.'

'She's been assigned to one of the groups.' He says it with a sly tone, like he's figured it all out. 'So they must be important...' He dangles it there, a juicy titbit for his friend to latch on to.

'You think one of them is the killer?' one of the girlfriends asks.

'Nah,' the other guy says as he lights the end of his cigar again and takes a few puffs. 'She's been assigned to them because of Sadie.' His tone is clear. He does not like this Sadie. I assume she's the older of the two women and I wonder what she ever did to elicit his dislike.

'She thinks she's a VIP,' scoffs the first man. 'Thinks she's more important than everyone else.'

'But couldn't she be the killer?' the girlfriend asks.

'Hardly! She's what? Seventy?' He says it likes she's fucking ancient, even though she looks like she would run rings around him without even breaking a sweat. He must be sixty himself, if he's a day. But then I guess men are allowed to age and women are meant to fade into the background as their years advance.

11

SADIE

I'm waiting for the actual game to begin. This is all feeling very slow. So, we have a murder and a task to find the killer. Now, obviously it's my team, but I'm assuming that doesn't let me off the hook entirely for the weekend. I'm going to have to at least pretend to be innocent.

'What's next?' I ask El.

'Patience, Ms Rose,' she says enigmatically.

'This is feeling kind of…' I wave my hand around and raise an eyebrow. I think my meaning is pretty clear.

'I promise it's going to get a lot more interesting.'

A minute later, she excuses herself from the table and then Sebastian follows suit less than thirty seconds after that. Hmm. I guess he's being briefed on whatever this 'more interesting' thing is going to be.

'I assume Sebastian is preparing to get away with murder,' I lean over to whisper at Samuel, careful that none of the other tables could overhear me.

'What?' he says, jumping back a little like he's been given a small electrical shock. So melodramatic.

'I said that I assume Sebastian is pre—'

'Yes, I heard you. Umm…'

I take a deep breath. 'You remember that we are the murderers, don't you?' Perhaps he's just a tad slow.

'Of course.' He seems to have composed himself. 'I just don't think we should discuss it in public, that's all. You never know who might be listening.'

I tap my finger against my nose. 'Right you are. Secret squirrel time.'

He shoots me a look that says he thinks I'm a batty old woman. It isn't the first time someone has looked at me like this. Ageing has been really rather useful in my line of work. Partly because no one imagines a grandmother killing people. And partly because any discrepancies can be explained by my 'declining mental faculties'.

Aly returns from her research mission, looking even more pale than before.

'You're right,' she says, eyes darting from me to Samuel, who has pulled his own phone out of his pocket and is looking rather engrossed in a game of Candy Crush. Aly gives him a look that manages to combine jealousy that he's flouting the 'no-phone' rule so casually, and irritation that he's flouting it in the first place. There's even a tinge of judgement that he's doing something so banal. Her mother must have taught her that one, she was something of an academic snob.

'What do you mean, I'm right?' I ask her.

'That other dossier. The one El gave you? It's different to the one that was already in the room, the one I read.'

'Perhaps a misprint. A mistake?' I used to spend my life doing mental gymnastics and trying to come up with elaborate plans and reasons for things. Then I read about Occam's razor and the idea that the simplest explanation is the most likely. It's been revolutionary.

Like the time I was questioned following the death of a prominent Mayfair business owner. 'Why were you in the home of the deceased?' the officer had asked me.

'His wife and I are friends,' I replied. In the past I might have said 'I forgot my bag and went back to get it.' Or 'I heard a noise and it sounded like a cat had been shut inside.' The simpler the better. Always. The police never found his killer.

'I don't think it's a mistake.' Aly lowers her voice even further, her lips so close to my ear I can feel the heat of her breath. 'Something weird is happening. The other guy in that envelope? Hugo Durbridge? I think it's real.'

'What do you mean, it's real?'

'Your additional pages say that he was responsible for a big Pharma cover-up in Bolivia a few years ago. He was the Chairman of the company at the time. It looks legit, like he actually did that. In the real world.'

'You really think so?'

'I think those pages might just be pointing a big fat finger at two of our fellow guests.'

'But why?' I ask.

'I don't know. Not yet. I need to do more research. This whole not having our phones thing is bullshit.' She raises her voice on that last sentence and Samuel has the grace to raise his eyes from his screen to meet hers. He merely shrugs and goes back to his game.

She steps back, eyes roaming the people on the lawn. I follow her gaze.

'You know, normally I know everyone here at these weekends,' I say. 'They are normally repeat players, or friends of friends, or at least passing acquaintances. But this year... there are all these strangers.'

'They said half the guests were new invites,' Aly says.

'Yes. But you'd think I'd know some of them. I've been running around Mayfair for decades, I know pretty much everyone. And I do have a photographic memory for faces.'

'Do you know anyone who hasn't been to Holne House before?' she asks.

I take a long look around the guests. At each table there is one couple I recognise from previous years and then two strangers I've never seen. Except... 'Monty Braithwaite,' I say, pointing towards a man on the opposite side of the lawn. 'We've met at a few charity things over the years but he's never been to Murder on the Moors before.'

'Any idea if he's a secret criminal?'

'Epstein.' I say the name quietly, as if I'm trying it on for size. 'There have always been rumours...'

'Interesting.' Aly taps her forefinger against her lips as she thinks. It's the same action her grandmother used to make. 'So, we have all these newbies, people who have never been to this weekend before, even though it's been running for fifty years. And three of them are potentially terrible people. Hmm... I guess I'd better do some more research.' She stands still for a moment and then leans back down to whisper in my ear once again. 'But why would someone give you an envelope with some of their crimes in it?' She kisses my cheek and walks away, leaving me to contemplate the question.

Why would someone want me to know about these men and their real crimes?

Occam's razor comes into play.

Because someone thinks that information would be of interest to me.

But why would they think that?

Because I'm a serial killer with a penchant for taking out the rubbish.

But that means someone knows exactly who I am.

A cold hand creeps up the back of my neck and I take a slow look around the clusters of guests scattered across the lawn of the hotel.

Who knows?

And how did they find me?

My hand shakes as I reach for my glass of Champagne. The most important question of them all hangs in the ether. What will they do about it?

12

CASSIE

Some of the guests take up a game of croquet and are soon fully into it, whooping and shouting at each other.

'Honestly, this is all so much of a cliché I could die,' Rani tells me, her eyes shining.

'You're glad we came?' I ask her.

'Are you kidding? This is amazing.' She grins and then squeezes my waist. I want to believe that she's having a good time but something tells me she's playing a role. It isn't anything specific, just a prickly sensation in the back of my brain that she's faking it.

A waiter brings fresh sandwiches and miniature cakes, eliciting another squeak of excitement from Rani. This reaction, however, I *can* trust. The quality of the food is exquisite, every tiny attention to detail perfectly crafted: finger sandwiches filled with cream cheese and cucumber; mini pretzel rolls with salt beef and sauerkraut; blinis with smoked salmon, watercress and caviar; individual carrot and walnut cakes with cinnamon-infused frosting; tiny choux buns filled with lemon curd; the most incredible blood orange macarons I've ever tasted.

'Look, these have HH embossed on them,' I say, showing Rani one of the shortbread rounds.

'Trust you to notice,' Rani says.

'The details are important,' I reply.

'Oh, believe me, I know.' She says it like the long-suffering wife, but I can hear the edge of the joke in her voice. She's told me a hundred times that one of the things she loves about me is how excited I get over small things. My little nerd-out moments. Maybe that's why I think she's faking her own excitement, because it feels like she's mirroring and we both know I'm the weird one in our relationship. 'Besides,' she adds, reaching over me to snag a pretzel roll. 'When you run a place like this, you'll need to remember these kinds of details.'

'If,' I correct her.

She leans in to whisper, 'Allow yourself to dream... just a little.'

'So, does anyone have any ideas about the Marchioness?' Theodore asks, bringing our attention back to the murder mystery at hand.

'Do we really have to do this?' Bea asks in reply. She sounds like a petulant kid who's been told they need to visit their least favourite grandmother.

'Do what?'

'This.' She motions around.

'I thought you wanted to come this weekend.' Theodore sounds a little hurt.

'For the spa and the food and the wine and the opportunity to meet some other lovely people. And to gossip. Of course.' She raises her glass of Champagne towards us and I can't help but raise mine back in response.

'But the murder mystery?' I can tell Theodore is trying not to splutter.

Bea sits back in her seat and crosses her legs, smoothing her skirt down with the hand not holding her glass. 'Oh, brother dear. Are you sure that's a good idea?'

'I like murder mysteries.' But I can tell they're not talking about murder mysteries any more.

'You're trying to impress her and I don't think it's a good idea.'

'Am not.'

'Are too.'

They sound like children arguing. Isn't it amazing how any time with our siblings causes us to revert to being teenagers, no matter how grown up the rest of the world thinks we are? The same thing happens whenever I see my two brothers: we fall straight back into old habits, with them wrestling and me trying to keep them quiet so we don't get into trouble with our parents. It's always been my job to maintain the peace.

'It isn't like that,' Theodore says, somewhat petulantly. 'I like murder mysteries and I want to figure out who killed the Marchioness.'

'Sadie Rose is trouble and we both know it.'

'Umm...' Rani interrupts. 'Who is Sadie Rose?'

The tips of Theodore's ears turn pink. 'No one.'

'Ha!' Bea directs her gaze to one of the guests a few tables over, the same woman the cigar-smoking idiots were saying was too old to be the killer. 'That is Sadie Rose.'

'Are you two... Or were...?' Rani fishes for more information.

'She's an old friend,' Theodore says. 'That's all there is to say.' But there is clearly far more to this story than he's letting on. Perhaps later on we can needle more information from him. Or at least get a few gin and tonics into Bea and get her to spill all the tea on her brother.

I spend a few moments watching Sadie Rose and her teammates. A pretty, young woman slides onto the seat next to her and nibbles the edges of a sandwich. The man is on his phone, flagrantly flouting the rules. He's one of the identical twins I saw earlier. The two men were so alike and watching them was almost mesmerising. They were so similar in the way they carried themselves, sitting in the same positions and mimicking each other's hand movements like they were performing an intricately choreographed ballet. I remember reading something once about how Benedict Cumberbatch had spent days watching ballet dancers to perfect the hand movements for his role as Dr Strange and I saw something similar reflected in the twins. A quiet grace.

'Earth to Cassie,' Rani says, breaking my reverie.

'Sorry, just...' but I don't really have an answer. I kind of zoned out for a few moments. It's something I've always done. Sometimes it works in my favour, I have a knack of looking like I'm intently listening in meetings or in lectures. But sometimes I find my mind drifting and my gaze blurring... but then I realise I've been effectively staring at a stranger, slack-jawed to boot – for far longer than would ever be considered appropriate. I've had a few comments about it, if we're honest. But I don't know I'm doing it until it's too late. 'Sorry,' I repeat instead and try to bring my focus back to the people immediately in front of me.

'So, now that we've established my brother wants to impress his paramour with his superior sleuthing skills...' Bea manages to sound both horribly condescending and endearing at the same time; a rare feat only reserved for siblings. 'Are you two "Team Winning" or "Team Having Fun"?'

'Cassie is "Team Winning",' Rani replies without missing a beat.

'I... I...' But she's right. 'Yeah, I guess. I can be a little competitive.'

Rani snorts. 'A little. Ha.'

'You're competitive too,' I remind her.

She pauses for a moment. 'Maybe.'

'You should get some rest this weekend, though, when you're not concentrating on the article, of course,' I say. 'Rani is trying to break into journalism and get away from her corporate job. This weekend is actually kind of a commission for her,' I tell the others.

'Congratulations!' Bea exclaims and garners looks from a few of the other tables with her exuberance. 'That calls for more Champagne!' She waves the now empty bottle at one of the waiters.

But just as the red-waistcoated man is crossing the lawn towards us, a fresh bottle on a tray in front of him, there's an almighty crash from another table and a shrill scream pierces the air.

The scream dissolves into a laugh. 'Oh my God, Hugo. You nearly gave me a heart attack,' says a high-pitched voice.

A man comes into view, clutching his tie as if trying to remove a noose, his face turning redder and redder by the second as he stumbles about.

Everyone begins to ask questions at once.

'What the—'

'Is he—'

'Ladies and gentlemen.' A disembodied voice comes over the speakers dotted around the lawn. The man takes a final gasp as he falls to the ground. 'It would appear there has been a second murder.'

There's a synchronised 'Oooh' from the crowd.

'Hugo Durbridge, AKA the late Marquess' uncle and evident patriarch of Team Brent, has been killed. It's well documented that the uncle was allergic to shellfish.'

We all turn to look at the man lying in the middle of the lawn. There's a raucous round of applause.

'That was very convincing,' Rani says, nudging me with her shoulder as she joins in the clapping.

'It really was.'

13

THE HIT LIST

Dossier One: Hugo Durbridge

I open the file and scan down the questions we've already written to help us build up the character set. Every person at Holne House needs to have a sheet that details who they are playing within the game, their relationship to the Marchioness and a few key facts about them. And then there are the additional notes that will only be provided to some specific guests.

'All right. Let's start with the easiest. Victim one.'

'Hugo Durbridge?' he asks.

'The one and only,' I reply, as I start to fill in the details.

Name: Hugo Durbridge
Team: Brent

'What's his role?' I ask, fingers hovering over the keyboard. I've painted my nails a gorgeous festive red and there's a certain satisfaction to watching them clack away at the keys like I'm some kind of businesswoman. I've never had a job like this before and it's kind of fun.

'Relative?' he suggests.

I screw my face up. 'We've already used that on someone else, remember?'

'I'm fairly sure there can be more than one relative.'

Hmm. It's actually a fair point. 'Fine.'

'How about the uncle of the Marquess?'

'Perfect.'

Role: Relative

Relationship to the Marchioness: Uncle of the Marquess

'Wouldn't that give him the greatest claim for the fortune and therefore make him the most obvious culprit for the Marchioness's murder?' I ask, sitting back a little and picking up a pencil to nibble.

'That is why he's the first,' he says.

'Ooh, good. I like that. You're quite clever, you know.'

'Borderline genius, actually.'

'Ha.' I blow him a kiss and he pretends to catch it with both hands.

I fill in some of the other details quickly, copying them from the surprisingly neat handwriting on Mr Durbridge's booking form. I can only imagine he has an assistant who completed this on his behalf.

Age: 74 years

Residence: Notting Hill, London

Occupation: Banker (Retired)

'Do you know what the collective noun for bankers is?' I ask, looking up from the page.

'The what?'

'Like, the fancy name for a group of them.'

He shakes his head, looking at me like I'm an alien, but one he's rather fond of at least.

'They are a wunch. A wunch of bankers.'

He smirks and then breaks into a full-blown chuckle. I knew that would tickle him.

We have requested photos of all the players to make some of the evidence boards and things. Hugo Durbridge is an utter cliché of the wealthy gentleman entering his twilight years, even down to the tweed jacket – yes, with elbow patches – and the ruddy complexion of a man who rather likes a glass of port.

Personal Life: Married, but attending with a 'lady friend'

I make a face as I type that out, from what I can see he doesn't even try to hide his philandering ways. But, anyway, onto the more interesting stuff. 'Can you pass me the iPad?' I ask.

He catches my eye as he hands it over.

'Do you think this is going to work?' I ask.

'Of course. Have faith, *Rakkaani*.'

I smile at the term of endearment.

On the iPad is the result of months and months of meticulous research. Hours spent trawling the deepest recesses of the internet, cross-checking facts and dissecting rumour from reality.

Additional Notes:

In 2019, Hugo Durbridge held the position of Chairman for a large pharmaceutical conglomerate.

After more than a dozen deaths in La Paz, Bolivia, concerns were raised over contaminated painkillers making it onto the local market from a small manufacturing facility in the city. The conglomerate made a bland press statement and nothing further was done. A few months later, the same thing happened again. But, by this time, the facility had been expanded and was now supplying a larger area and the death toll increased to the hundreds. The conglomerate promised an investigation. But this was cut short when the facility burned down, killing fifty-three workers in the process. There was speculation of a cover-up, but nothing further was done.

Is it fair to blame the Chairman for an accidental fire in a manufacturing plant ten thousand kilometres away?

Who do you think ordered that the problem be "dealt with" without delay and without raising suspicion on the world stage?

One down, many more to go.

14

SADIE

Aly turns to me. 'That's Hugo Durbridge.' She motions towards the man lying still on the ground. 'Chairman of that Pharma company I mentioned. The one who ordered a problem to be covered up and didn't care about all the people who died in the process.'

'Did the dossier say he was from London?'

'Yes,' she confirms. 'Why?'

'And the factory was in Bolivia?'

She nods.

'I heard a story once. About a man on a flight from La Paz to Heathrow via Bogota. A rich Englishman with no class. A rich man with no class and a fairly significant seafood allergy that he insisted on making everyone's problem. He hadn't informed the airline in advance and so they served crab filled pasta in a spicy sauce. They had to divert the plane and it was all a bit of a thing.'

'I did find something in my searches about him having an allergy.' Aly tells me. 'So it was pretty clever to have him fake die from that.'

I guess...

If he is acting.

All I'm going to say is that was very realistic.

And I have seen a lot of men die over the years.

* * *

Two people dressed in white paper overalls appear with a stretcher. They carefully move Hugo so he's lying flat on his back and then roll him onto it before covering him with a sheet. He doesn't help them at all, just stays limp like a sack of potatoes. The overalls struggle to lift the stretcher with their uncooperative cargo and they make a slow march towards the back of the house.

I do not know Hugo Durbridge, or at least not beyond the words written in that dossier Aly has helped verify. Does he strike me as the kind of man who wouldn't try to help make someone's life easier by breaking the fourth wall just a little to help get him away from the scene of the crime? Yes. I'll admit, he is exactly that kind of man. But playing dead is actually surprisingly difficult.

When I was in my early thirties, I had to pretend to have taken a large dose of wolfsbane to make the police think I was one of the intended victims rather than the killer. Lolling your head like your neck has no bones, keeping your facial muscles relaxed and not opening your eyes even if they jolt you are all extremely hard to do, especially if you're put on the spot with little notice.

So, is our Mr Durbridge just a good actor? Or is there far more going on here?

El interrupts my thoughts as she strides back to the patio area to address us all.

'Poor Hugo, the Uncle Brent. Cut down in his prime.' She levels her gaze across the assembled group. 'Someone has been very naughty.' She grins then motions to where Hugo Durbridge just keeled over. 'Why would anyone murder one of our most esteemed guests?'

Silence descends on the lawn. El coughs quietly, then again more loudly. 'Lloyd!' She hisses eventually to get his attention.

He jumps and almost drops the cue cards in his hand. 'Err... Err...' He frantically shuffles the cards, obviously looking for the correct one. He glances up at her and then back at the cards as if expecting her to rescue him. 'Oh. Umm...'

One of the Murderous Intentions staff from another table – Theodore

Frillish's table – jumps up. 'Is this murder connected to the Marchioness?' he asks. I appreciate his correct pronunciation of her title.

'What an excellent question.' El shoots daggers at Lloyd before smiling at the other man. 'Well, I think it would be a little unusual for there to be two murders that were entirely unconnected.'

'So do we need to solve this murder too?'

'Your task remains the same. Solve the Marchioness's murder. The untimely demise of Mr Hugo Durbridge – God rest his soul – may indeed be a clue. Or it may be little more than a distraction.'

A silence settles over the lawn as the guests try to mull over what she means by that rather cryptic remark. Surely it must be a clue, you don't plant a new dead body as a red herring. Even if you've never been to a murder mystery weekend before, you'd know that isn't how this works. Not that I really have to concern myself, I suppose. After all, I know who the killers are.

Sebastian puts his hand up and Samuel shoots him a look. 'We're not in fucking school,' he hisses.

'Will there be more?' Sebastian asks.

For a moment I'm confused. We're the killers so why does he— Oooh. Clever. A trick. Pretend to be like all the other guests.

'More?' El asks.

'Bodies? Murders?'

El's whole face breaks into a smile. 'Only time will tell.'

'That means yes,' someone calls from the other side of the lawn.

A cacophony of questions are shouted towards the patio area.

'How many?'

'When?'

'What happens if you get murdered?'

'Now then,' El says to bring the focus back to her. 'I'm not going to give the whole weekend away.' She chuckles softly. 'But whoever asked about what happens if you are "murdered",' she makes air quotes and adds a wink for good measure, 'raises a good point. Well, you are obviously out of the game.'

There's a ripple of laughter from the lawn. I'm going to be honest and say I didn't think it was that funny, but perhaps I just missed something?

'If you are killed... well you must stay away from the rest of the teams. The eastern wing has been set aside for you. There you will find a truly luxurious VIP experience laid out. Some of the best rooms in the hotel. Your own library and bar area, fully stocked with all the very best the Holne House cellar has to offer, of course. A team of staff to ensure your every need is met. There are even staff on hand to offer a range of spa treatments, including a signature massage.'

'I think getting bumped off sounds like a great idea,' comes a loud voice from the table to my left. He's a large man with a ruddy face and a waistcoat stretched over his rather ample middle. Obviously the kind of man who likes the finer things in life.

'I think that can be arranged,' a young female guest at another table says, before her companion gives her a nudge.

Theodore Frillish raises his hand. 'So, we need to figure out who the killer is. But how do we actually play?'

El shoots him a look. 'You will find a range of clues around the hotel, and by talking to each other, trying to figure out who is lying about their whereabouts as the weekend unfolds. You will need all your detective skills. There will also be periodic games and acted scenes to help you. In addition to tomorrow's scavenger hunt across Dartmoor.'

A murmur flows across the lawn.

'And how do we determine the winner?' This is Theodore again.

'The winner is the team who solves the Marchioness's murder. But, just in case you all figure it out, we'll be asking for guesses at intervals over the weekend. The first team to guess correctly will be crowned on Sunday.'

PART III

DINNER, DRINKS AND THE DAY THE SUN WENT DARK

(LECTURE FROM THE ASTRONOMER ROYAL)

15

CASSIE

Rani and I head back to the room to change for dinner. I'm buzzing. I'm not going to lie.

'This is fun,' I tell her as we get into the lift.

She grins at me. 'It shouldn't be. But I feel the same. I was thinking the whole 'murder mystery' element might feel a little tired, but this is... it feels kind of fresh.'

'I wonder what all the people who've been coming here for years think about it? I don't think this is standard.'

'You'd think they'd be pleased to get something a bit different. Anyway, who do you think the killer is?' Rani asks.

'I think we need to have another read through all the potential suspects before we speculate.' I say the words in the exact same way Theodore did on the lawn a few minutes ago. He's a sweet guy, but he really is taking this very seriously. Obviously, I want to win, but apparently there are rules, ways of doing things, procedures to follow. He's demanded we meet him in the bar in half an hour so we can start working on whittling down a list of suspects.

'Come prepared,' he told us. Like he thinks there is time in half an hour to get ready for dinner and read an entire dossier of information.

'It's going to be someone we wouldn't expect,' I say, thinking out loud as

I try to decide between the two potential outfits I bought for this evening. I'm not a girly girl, I much prefer jeans and a t-shirt to getting dressed up. And I almost never wear makeup, I just hate the feeling of all that gunk on my skin.

'Wear the black trousers,' Rani says, coming up behind me and wrapping her arms around my waist. 'You know they do funny things to me. Especially if you pair them with that pale grey silk top.' She motions to the one she means. It's cut asymmetrically and it does make my boobs look really rather spectacular, even if I do say so myself.

I take the two items out of the wardrobe and lay them on the bed. The top has just enough beading to demonstrate a token effort at meeting the 1920s dress code, especially with the Gatsby-esque headpiece I found in Oxfam the other week.

'What do you think the deal is between Theodore and that Sadie Rose?' I ask as I take off my trainers.

'Why do you care?'

'You know I love to know about people.' I eye up the heels I'm meant to wear this evening with trepidation. I hate heels. But I don't think this is the kind of place a woman can get away with trainers at dinner, no matter how uncomfortable I'm going to be.

Rani just rolls her eyes at me.

It's true that I'm nosy. Really, really, really, nosy. And if I don't know actual facts about people then I make stuff up, give total strangers complete backstories. Perhaps I should have been an author?

* * *

We make our way to the bar. We didn't explore it as part of the tour earlier and I'm almost speechless when I see it. It's reminiscent of an old-style hunting lodge, with a double-height ceiling arching overhead, from which hang huge chandeliers made from deer antlers. Enormous leaded windows look out over the moors, with stained glass in the upper panes that fill the room with a reddish hued light. There's a huge wooden fireplace at one end, and a curved bar at the other, behind which a hundred bottles of high-end spirits glitter like diamonds.

We're five minutes late to meet Theodore and Bea and he tuts under his breath.

'Sorry,' I say, doing this weird, almost obsequious little bow I instantly regret. Why can't I just be normal?

'So,' Theodore starts. 'Did you get time to go over the dossier?'

I open my mouth to say sorry again, but Rani gets in before I can speak. 'We had a quick skim read. Looking this good takes time, Theodore.' She motions between herself in her gorgeous dusky-pink halter neck dress and me with my headpiece. 'Surely you must appreciate that.' Her voice is smooth as honey and she gives him a slow smile.

'I can never begrudge a lady indulging in a little self-care,' he replies warmly. Rani is so good at this, at knowing exactly how to get people on her side. The cynical part of my brain thinks it's a little manipulative but I try to shut down that voice. Especially when it suggests that she does it to me sometimes. I think sometimes I need to be manipulated, otherwise I get stuck in a spiral of my own inability to get moving. Apparently, it's called executive dysfunction, but fancy names don't make it any less debilitating.

Rani's hand on my knee brings me back to the here and now. 'What are you drinking?' she asks.

'Um... Well, seeing as it's the roaring twenties,' I touch the headpiece. I'm starting to feel a little self-conscious about it as most people don't seem to have opted for something quite so obvious. 'How about a White Lady?'

'A what now?' Rani asks.

'Gin, Cointreau, lemon juice,' says Bea. 'An excellent choice.'

Cocktails acquired, we take a seat at one of the small card tables dotted around the bar area. There are larger armchairs and sofas closer to the fire, upholstered in a muted tartan fabric, but they are already taken. I guess that's why Theodore was so irritated about our late arrival.

'I think it's Jasper Price-Evans,' Bea says. 'But it's more of a hunch. I don't like the way he was looking at some of the wait-staff.' She shrugs.

'You know you can't decide the killer based on who you think is a bad person in real life?' Theodore tells her. 'This isn't some kind of morality contest.'

'Well then, brother dear, do tell us how you are going to solve the murder on the first evening without seeing any more than the most basic of clues?'

'We already have all the facts. It's all about motive.'

'So, enlighten us then.' There's an edge to Bea's smile. I can only imagine that's what happens when you've put up with an insufferable sibling for over sixty years. I don't see my brothers that often, to be honest. One lives in Canada and the other went to Edinburgh for university and never came back again. It didn't used to bother me much; we'd see each other for Christmas and special occasions like family weddings and whatnot and it was fun and games. All the years of fighting left at the door and just enjoying the good parts now we didn't all have to actually live together.

But now... well, now I'm starting to feel like I'm the glue holding the whole family together. The one who organises everything. Who makes sure they remember Mum and Dad's birthdays and wedding anniversary. Who buys the gifts and signs their names on the card in case they forget to send their own. And then, when Mum was sick, who was the one who went to check on Dad? Who took him meals and drove him to the hospital when he broke his glasses and couldn't drive himself? It was just a glimpse of the future. And, I'm going to be honest, it's scary.

A loud gong breaks me from my reverie.

'Jesus, what was that?' Rani asks.

'That, my dear,' Theodore says, 'is the dinner bell.' He chuckles. 'I suppose we should find out what delights Holne House has in store for us.'

The dining room is massive and in a similar style to the rest of the hotel, with wooden panelling, dark upholstery and large chandeliers hanging from the high ceilings. The walls are decorated with a combination of landscapes, portraits and hunting trophies. I really hope we aren't having venison with all the deer eyes staring at me.

We're seated at tables of eight, two teams squashed together at round tables like it's a bad wedding. On each place setting is a small envelope with our names on it. *Please keep me safe for the next round* it says. I slip it inside my fancy notebook.

We do a round of introductions but I'm barely paying any attention. All I can see is the way one of the men, Mitchell, is looking at Rani. I do not like it one bit, and not in a weird jealous way. I know my wife is objectively attractive. I mean that there's something in his stare. Predatory. Wanting. Like he's waiting to pounce.

I'm probably just overreacting.

But my instincts are usually right.

16

SADIE

I know dinner is about to start but there's somewhere I need to visit first and I want to go before it's dark.

The air is still warm as I push open the small door out into what would once have been the kitchen garden. Now the vegetables and herbs are bought in by truck and the garden is purely decorative. Or at least that is the story the gardener tells.

He inherited the job here at Holne Hall after the disappearance of his uncle and guardian back in 1982. Uncle Barry vanished one night after he tried to walk home from the pub in the nearby village of Lustleigh. For a while there were rumours about a Beast of Dartmoor – although it's now considered that the Beast was actually a puma released from a zoo – and it was enough to fan the flame of speculation that Uncle Barry had met a grisly end at the claws of the Beast. In the end, the police never even came to the hotel to look for him, not that they were likely to notice the new herbs in the kitchen garden, the earth underneath freshly tilled. The human body is a magnificent fertiliser, and there's something 'circle of life'-esque about a man killed by the same herbs he went on to nourish.

If I was just a little older – not much: a few decades at most – there would have been some who called me a wise woman or described me as one of the cunning folk. Others would have called me witch. Women would have come to me when they had a problem. A husband who drank too much. A father who refused to let them leave. And I would have offered them a discreet solution from my garden. A little belladonna. A snippet of thornapple.

It isn't magic but it may as well be. How can something so simple, something that grows straight from the ground, solve so many of the world's ills?

I pick a few foxgloves and a sprig of hemlock. I'll take my usual haul later in the weekend when everyone is bored of the games and just wants to chill out. If someone catches me now, I can tell them I'm sneaking clippings for my window boxes at home.

* * *

One thing I will say about Holne House, the food is always fabulous. For dinner this evening they have taken inspiration from the Criterion Restaurant in Piccadilly, somewhere with an exceptional literary pedigree as the place Dr Watson and Sherlock Holmes first met. I believe it also featured in *Downton Abbey*. There are oysters to start, followed by French onion soup, steak for the main and pineapple upside-down cake for dessert. Of course, the actual menu sounds a lot more adventurous, with some items even described in French for extra pomposity: *gâteau renversé à l'ananas*, anyone?

The food would, however, probably taste better if I wasn't sharing a table with one of the most insufferable men I have ever had the displeasure to meet.

I'm not being hyperbolic.

'Jerome,' he says by way of introduction before we've even got all the way to the table. He doesn't stand. Now, I'm not a stickler for manners, even though I was raised in a very specific way by a father who had rules for literally everything. But there are certain things that are considered good etiquette, and they are things I do expect, especially in places like Holne House. And one such thing is to at least vaguely stand – even if it's a half-hearted pathetic effort to rock forwards in such a way that mimics an attempt to stand – when a woman approaches the table.

'I'm Sadie Rose,' I say, clipping my words just enough that he should know I'm a little pissed. 'And this is my goddaughter, Aly.'

He barely looks at us. Well, I suppose we are women. His view on women is made very clear by the fact that he fails to introduce the one next to him, who I can only assume is his long-suffering wife.

Aly nudges me with her shoulder and then I realise. This is Jerome Fulker. One of the men she has been researching, the one who imported rare animals. I take a sip of water to try to wash the bad taste from my mouth at having to sit with him this evening.

The twins are a few minutes late, leaving me to make the smallest of small talk with Jerome. I ask him about his teammates.

'Patrick and Susan. Or is it Sharon? Something beginning with "S" anyway.'

They arrive with the twins and Jerome instantly changes, almost as if a light switch has been flicked. He becomes the soul of the party, insisting on choosing wine for the table.

'I think we should go for a Châteauneuf-du-Pape,' he announces before beckoning over the waiter.

'I'd rather have white wine,' Aly says softly.

Jerome whips his head round to look at her. 'We're having steak.'

'Yeah.' She motions at the menu card on the table. 'I can read.'

He narrows his eyes. 'You cannot drink white wine with steak.'

'Umm, I can drink what I like.' She says it in a way that makes it sound like she thinks he's a moron. I'm extremely proud of her.

'No.' He's forceful. 'You cannot drink white wine with steak. There are rules.'

Aly arches an eyebrow. 'There are also rules about standing up when a lady approaches your table, but you already chose to ignore that one.'

'Well, that's—'

'A glass of sauvignon blanc, please,' she interrupts him to speak to the waiter. 'And can I have an ice cube in it please.' She throws a grin to Jerome. 'I like to make sure it's extra cold.'

'You can't put ice—' he starts but cuts himself off to shake his head instead.

Talk turns to the usual boring topics as dinner progresses. Careers. Sport. Politics. It probably won't surprise you that Jerome leans pretty far to the right. 'Le Pen had it right,' he says at one point. Followed later by, 'I just hope Farage can hold the line.' I keep my fingers crossed that we don't have to sit with them later, or tomorrow.

Jerome quaffs his way through almost an entire bottle of Châteauneuf-du-Pape before dessert is even served and his speech starts to get a little sloppy. I hate sloppy drunks. I have no issue with people drinking – and I am rather partial to a gin and tonic or a good Sancerre myself – but you have to be able to keep control of yourself. Otherwise, who knows what kind of secrets you might blurt out to a group of strangers over a slice of pineapple cake? It's definitely not worth the risk. It has its downsides though: when you're one of the most sober people in the room, you start to realise how badly behaved a lot of people are.

The talk moves to holidays. 'We spent a glorious week in Barbados,' Sara – not Susan, or Sharon – says, placing her hand on her husband Patrick's arm.

'It cost me an arm and a leg,' he says, not entirely happily.

'Silly goose,' she says, tapping him gently. 'It was worth every penny. We had this fabulous suite with its own infinity pool looking out over the ocean. Just incredible.'

I'm so bored, I'm struggling to keep my eyes open.

'Why don't you tell them about your safari?' Jerome's wife is petite and blonde and I still don't know what her first name is.

Jerome takes a deep breath and puffs out his chest. 'Well. It wasn't like your ordinary safari. This was in South Africa.' He chuckles to himself. I wish a lion had eaten him out there in the bush. Then I wouldn't have had to sit through this particular brand of *connerie*. 'They let you hunt the animals,' he says quietly, but with this expectant little smirk on his face, like he knows you'll still pay attention to him.

'What, like you can help track them to find them?' Aly asks, a tinge of suspicion in her tone. She's read the additional information we have about him but she's doing a good effort at pretending he's a stranger to her. However, she's obviously not afraid to let him know that she thinks he is utterly vile.

'Oh no. They let you hunt them. Properly.' Jerome sits back in his seat like he's a king surveying his subjects. He's studying our reactions, waiting to see how we will all react to this nugget of insight into a truly odious man. I keep my expression impassive. I have a really rather excellent poker face.

Aly – on the other hand – does nothing to hide her disgust. 'You hunted endangered animals?'

'They aren't endangered,' he corrects her with a smug tone.

'Semantics,' Aly counters.

'You have no idea of the feeling of power as you wait in the African bush for a lion to come close enough. I was looking directly in his eyes. This apex predator. Just him and me. But he knew who was the master here. When I raised the gun and "pow".'

'You think you were the master because you had a gun?' Aly scoffs.

'I was the master because I killed him.'

Aly puts down her knife and fork carefully. And then she starts to clap. Slowly. All the while she maintains eye contact with Jerome. 'Well done. You managed to shoot an animal at point blank range, one who had been drugged to make him more docile.'

'He could have killed me at any moment. You have no idea of the rush.'

'What did you say this place was called?' Aly asks.

'Riverthorn Lodge.' He sits back in his seat and then he smiles at her. 'But I don't think you'd qualify for a trip. It's very exclusive.'

We finish our food in silence and then Jerome excuses himself to head to the bathroom. Aly's shoulders visibly drop as he leaves, she's obviously been holding a lot of tension just breathing the same air as him.

I also excuse myself and head to the ladies' room. I return to find Jerome weaving his way back to the table.

We both sit at the same time and then I notice how pale he is, his face as white as a sheet. 'I... I... I...' he stammers.

'What's happened?' his wife asks, jumping from her seat to grab his arm and pull him into his own chair before he passes out. His right hand is clutching inside his jacket. He draws it out slowly. It's bright red with blood.

'I...' he tries again but no more words come out.

He slumps forwards, his head thumping onto the table and causing his glass of Châteauneuf-du-Pape to fall, the remnants splashing onto the table and mixing with the blood dripping from his hand.

'Jerome?' his wife screeches, the noise making the rest of the room fall silent. She reaches out for him, touching his face, panic etched into her own features.

'Ladies and gentlemen,' a voice booms out over the speaker system, grabbing everyone's attention. 'We have our third murder. Jerome Fulker of Team Shilstone.'

'It's just the game,' Jerome's wife whispers as she stumbles backwards into her own chair. 'I thought...' but her words trail off as a slightly manic laugh bubbles from her lips. She clamps her hand to her mouth to stop it.

The disembodied voice continues. 'Jerome has been killed by a knife wound to the torso. Now then, if you could all calmly make your way to the ballroom, refreshments will be served while the crime scene is cleared.'

I look up as Sebastian and Samuel both stand. They've been sitting at the table this whole time.

So, if all four of us on the killing team are here, who just took out Jerome?

17

THE HIT LIST

Dossier Two: Jerome Fulker

Jerome was one of the easiest to confirm. He didn't help himself by constantly bragging about his adventures. What a fool. Everyone knows that, if you want to get away with things, you keep your mouth shut. But it will be his downfall.

'I'm going to enjoy this one,' he says when he realises that I'm preparing Jerome Fulker's dossier.

'Me too,' I grin.

'Paring knife?' he asks with a raised eyebrow.

'Of course.' As if there was any other choice here.

I copy the details carefully, the clack clack of my nails on the keyboard becoming a metronome, beating out the time of this man's eventual demise.

Name: Jerome Fulker
Team: Shilstone

'Do you think we should pick a different team name?' I ask, after I mistype 'Shilstone'.

'They're all tors on Dartmoor.'

'I know. But I'm going to say "Shitstone" a hundred times over the weekend.'

He snorts. 'You'll be fine, *Rakkaani*, I have faith that you can keep your shit together.' He chuckles at his own joke, even though it wasn't really that funny.

Role: Almoner
Relationship to the Marchioness: Member of the same masonic lodge attended by the Marquess
Age: 52 years
Residence: splits his time between Reigate, Surrey and New York
Occupation: Importer
Personal Life: Married to Jenny, his partner for the event

It was Jerome who started this whole thing, who inspired us to form the list of diabolical individuals who would eventually form the guest list for the weekend. I take a deep breath before I write out his crimes, a heavy feeling in the base of my stomach over the things this man has done.

Additional Notes:

Jerome Fulker likes to hunt wild animals. Any animal will do, as long as he can shoot at it. But it was on a trip to the Riverthorn Lodge that he discovered his true passion for killing big cats and other exotic species. In the intervening years he has been back to Riverthorn three times.

But the last time wasn't just for pleasure. Last time it was a fact-finding mission regarding a potential expansion to his import business.

Since 1993, Jerome has been trading in the "exotic pet" market, supplying wealthy idiots with wild animals they can use for bragging rights around the dinner table. Since the advent of social media, his business has soared, making him tens of millions of pounds.

In 2024, Jerome brought three male lions from Riverthorn into the UK. They were sold to a Russian oligarch living in London. Three days later, the same oligarch sent pictures of the lions to his son, as a permanent reminder of the fabulous weekend of sport they had enjoyed. All three of the majestic cats had been shot and killed.

Everyone in this story is guilty.

18

CASSIE

'Well, well, well, another murder,' Theodore says with glee as we file past the table where Jerome is still splayed. 'I can't wait to see the new evidence,' he adds and does this funny little skip.

But my mind is elsewhere.

I can smell it. Like pennies.

Blood.

Real blood.

19

SADIE

There's a frisson in the air, a ripple through the crowd as everyone forms small groups to discuss the most recent murder. For a moment I feel myself getting caught in the swell. But then I remember both twins watching Jerome 'die' from the other end of the table.

The only thing I can assume is that we are basically cheating. What if it was El? Staging the murder so that no one could possibly accuse Team Bowerman? It's the only thing that makes sense. Now, I'm not exactly a stickler for the rules. I never have been. Some of the things I could tell you about what I did in the past would make your hair curl.

But it's one thing to cheat at life, to rebalance the terrible cards you were dealt into something better. But why bother to cheat at a stupid murder mystery game? Then I turn round and see the intense look on some of my fellow players' faces. Of course. Some people take these things very seriously. Some people live for these weekends, for unpicking the clues and taking their shot on the identity of the killer. Would some of these people cheat to nudge a simple game in their favour? You bet they would.

It still makes me feel a bit funny though. Underhand. Sneaky. I've always tried to avoid being sneaky. Cunning? Clever? Yes. Strategic? Oh absolutely. There's a brilliant Taylor Swift interview where she says something about how women are only ever allowed to be calculated, whereas men are called strategic. I know it's probably odd to take life advice from a woman half my age, but she's right. The words we use to describe ourselves and each other are important.

I spot El toward the back of the room. She's wearing a smile, one that's slightly coy around the edges. Oh yes, she definitely did this. And she thinks she's being oh so smart. Not on my watch, and I'm not having some clever dick on Sunday pointing fingers at me for cheating.

But, as I try to part the crowds to get to her, I'm accosted by a woman I've never met.

'Felicity Atkinson,' she says, thrusting her hand towards me.

'Sadie. Sadie Rose,' I reply, trying to keep my face neutral as she attempts to break my hand with her vice-like grip. She's typical of a certain breed of woman, the ones who used to tell their peers that the only way to get ahead was to emulate the men. The women who would stab you through the heart with a stiletto heel and then use your dead body as a stepping stone. Whatever happened to the sisterhood? 'Hoes before bros', as I've heard some of the young people say?

'I hear you're the longest standing guest of these weekends? Perhaps I could pick your brains sometime.' It feels more like a demand than a request.

'Of course,' I reply, but she's already turned her focus to the man next to me. For a moment I'm blindsided by the sheer rudeness of her, but then my attention is snagged by the women next to me.

'Darling,' a woman with a shrill voice and so much makeup you can see the cracks around her eyes says as she embraces Jerome's wife. 'Oh, how exciting that it was your better half. Jerome, isn't it? And so realistic too. You must be very proud.'

Jerome's wife nods mutely.

'Was he excited to be selected?' the overly made-up woman – her name is Veronica; we've met a number of times over the years – asks.

'I... well... I didn't know.'

'Oh, what a cad! To keep it a secret, even from you! Ha ha.' The woman takes Jerome's wife's hand. 'Oh look. You've got blood on you. Ha ha. We must go to the bathroom and wash it off. You wouldn't want it to stain.' Veronica grabs my arm. 'You must come too. I want to hear all the details.'

I get swept up with them like flotsam in the surf. I've never been a girl's girl, one of a gaggle. But, for a moment, it feels almost nice to be considered part of the team. However, the camaraderie quickly dissipates in the bathroom as I stand awkwardly to the side as Jerome's wife washes her hands, scrubbing at the red stain.

'Gosh, it looks just like the real thing,' Veronica says. 'How fun. Obviously, no expense has been spared here. Do you think your husband's going to be upset, or is he the kind who will enjoy the VIP area?'

Judging from the man I met over dinner, he will be as happy as a pig in shit as long as he has someone to bore with his hunting anecdotes.

'I think he'll be annoyed that he's not in the centre of things,' Jerome's wife says quietly. Actually, she might have a point.

'Do you get to see him? If only for a quick visit?'

'I don't think so.' To be honest, Mrs Jerome doesn't sound that upset about it. 'But no doubt Jerome will kick up a fuss about getting cut off like that.'

'My husband is gagging to get killed quickly. He hates these things. But I wouldn't miss this event for the world. You're a veteran too, aren't you, Sadie?'

'Fifty years,' I confirm.

'It's our first,' Mrs Jerome says. 'I didn't really know what to expect. Jerome thought it was such an honour to be invited. And now he's...' she tails off.

Do I really think that Jerome is on his way to the VIP area? I'm not sure what I believe, to be honest. Is it possible that two men – two terrible men who have done atrocious things – just happen to be able to act out such convincing deaths? Deaths that make someone like me, who has more than a little experience, question if they might no longer have a pulse?

I think I need to see for myself. The VIP area is officially out of bounds for those of us still in the 'land of the living'. But I've been coming here for five decades. I know exactly where the bodies are buried – figuratively, I've never actually got my hands dirty here at Holne House, it's generally better to avoid defecating where you eat and all that – and where all the secret tunnels lead.

I mumble some excuse about needing to find Aly and leave the two women in the bathroom. I've never really understood this burning desire for women to go to the ladies en masse. It all feels a little unnecessary if I'm honest.

There are access points scattered all through Holne House, hidden behind paintings and tapestries, secret doors in bookcases, fireplaces that rotate, fake panels in walls. The main entrance hall is basically empty so I slip behind a rather desolate painting of Dartmoor in the fog and let myself into the secret passageways.

It's cool inside, with lighting provided by intermittent lightbulbs embedded in the smooth stone walls. Part of the network is used by staff to get around without the guests seeing them, a hidden army keeping the hotel operating seamlessly. But there are branches that even the staff probably don't know, hidden rooms and nooks no one ever sees.

I navigate to the West Wing, where the VIP area has been set up. There's another ballroom – in my opinion better appointed than the main one I've just come from, although it has no windows so can feel a little claustrophobic in the summer – and a selection of parlour rooms, in addition to a number of suites, all of which feature William Morris wallpaper and four-poster beds.

Hmm... that's odd.

I've made my way to the ballroom and I'm behind one of the massive canvasses that grace its walls. It is completely silent.

I let myself inside and have a wander about.

There is no one here. No Hugo Durbridge. No sign of Jerome Fulker having a fit.

But there's also no staff.

No hospitality set up with drinks and nibbles.

And the biggest giveaway of all.

No lights are on.

* * *

In the gloom, I spot a thin strip of blue light under the door to one of the parlour rooms. Hmm... perhaps there is someone here after all. I sneak back through the tunnel to the other side of the area so I can peek into the room.

Inside are two women facing away from me. They both have a laptop and a couple of extra screens. They must have been the source of the blue glow. They are watching CCTV of the guest areas.

The two women have an easy camaraderie, like they've been friends for a while. I recognise the concierge from her dark wool suit. And then the other turns towards me, almost as if she senses I'm there. I hurry away. Something tells me I don't want to get caught skulking around by these women. But it doesn't make sense.

Aly said she was a model. Fair enough that she might take a small part to dress up as a Marchioness, but then why would she be watching CCTV in the semi-dark?

What is going on here?

20

CASSIE

The guests fall silent as the gong is struck and the woman who took over the compering earlier strides out to the small makeshift stage area next to the bar. Her shirtsleeves are rolled up and she has a small smear of red just above her left elbow. She must have been helping with the victim. I just hope they used a non-staining faux blood: I was managing the Raven's laundry the year we did a Halloween party and some of the fake stuff leaves an awful mess.

'That's El,' Theodore says, bumping my shoulder with his. 'She's the actor assigned to my friend's team.'

'Friend,' snorts his sister. 'He means Sadie Rose.'

Theodore shoots her a look. 'Anyway,' he changes the subject. 'This El is very accomplished.' He sounds thoroughly impressed by her. 'Just look at how she takes control of the room.'

'My darling brother has a thing about strong, independent women. You might have noticed,' Bea says drily, but there's an edge of pride there. Given the way some of the other men here have been acting – especially the leering Mitchell we sat with at dinner – I can only imagine the pride is that her brother isn't a disgusting perv.

'Ladies and gentlemen,' El addresses the crowd. 'We have a third murder. Someone has been *very* naughty indeed.' She smirks.

'You know,' Theodore whispers, 'Murderous Intentions are very lucky they have someone to take over the compere role when the initial guy turned out to be such a disaster. It's weird, though, as he was here last year and was fine. A little boring may—'

'Shhhh.' The tall woman on the other side of Theodore hisses. 'I'm trying to listen.'

'Sorry,' Theodore replies. 'I was just say—'

'Shhhh.'

'So, you have now been the witnesses to three murders,' El says from the front. 'The Marchioness. Then Hugo. And now Jerome. Have you solved the case yet?'

There's a mumbling from around the room.

'No? Oh well, that just won't do. I think it's time for some sleuthing. Perhaps an opportunity to learn a little more about who may be a potential killer.' El pauses for a moment. 'Now then, you'll remember that when you sat down for your dinner there was an envelope on each place setting? I trust you all have those with you?'

There's a murmur of assent and some grumbled curses.

'I'll take it from the lack of victorious waving of said envelopes, that not all of you did in fact keep them safe for the next round.'

In slight defence of my fellow competitors, *please keep me safe for the next round* was not an explicit instruction to take it with you when ushered from the dining room after another murder.

'Numpties,' Theodore says as he slips his own from his jacket pocket. He hands one to Bea. 'We all have ours, right?' He checks with me and Rani.

'Of course.'

There's a few minutes' pause in El's instruction giving while some of the others rescue their cards. 'The body's gone,' someone behind me observes. Like Jerome Fulker might have still been lying there playing possum.

'Now then,' El says. 'Are we all ready? Great. Then I want you to open your envelopes and read the cards. Please don't let the people around you, including other members of your own team, see what is written on the cards.'

On the back of the envelope are the words *Where were you on the day the sun went dark?* I glance up and can see that the others also say the same thing.

I slide the card out carefully.

Cassie – CFO of SAC (Team Cox)

You were in the office. You do not need to lie. Your alibi can be corroborated by your secretary.

'The card you just read should contain three pieces of information. Where you were on the day the sun went dark. If you can tell the truth to the other guests. And, lastly, how that information may be confirmed.'

She pauses for a few moments as everyone re-reads their cards.

'But, before we go any further, you may be wondering what on Earth we mean by the "day the sun went dark".' There's a murmur of confirmation from the guests. 'We have a very special treat for you all. If I may present the Astronomer Royal, Sir Frank Watson Dyson.' She motions towards the door and a man appears. He is dressed in a well-cut black three-piece suit and sporting a very thick lustrous moustache. I have no idea who he is meant to be or if it's an accurate portrayal, but Theodore brims with excitement next to me.

'Dyson's observations confirmed Einstein's theory of the effect of gravity on light,' he tells me.

Thankfully though, we're not about to get a lecture on that, but on a solar eclipse that occurred recently. Well, recently in terms of the game anyway.

'On the 27th June 1927,' the actor begins, but I stop listening. Isn't that the same date as the newspaper? And the Marchioness's diary?

What is the relevance of the date? What else happened that day? Were there other clues in the hotel, ones we missed or dismissed as unimportant?

The actor playing the Astronomer Royal talks for about ten minutes, most of which I barely hear as I force myself to concentrate on all the details I saw during the tour. Nothing jumps out at me.

'And so, as you now understand, the solar eclipse on the 27th June was a truly monumental occasion. A day to be remembered. So where were you that day? Where were you on the day the sun went dark?'

The question lingers in the air for a few moments before El steps forward and starts a round of applause. 'May I extend a warm thank you to our special guest this evening, Sir Frank Watson Dyson.'

The applause dies down as he heads through the guests to the door. I'm assuming he is one of the Murderous Intentions staff who got roped into dressing up and putting on a plummy voice and he'll return shortly in the uniform black outfit with the lanyard round his neck.

'Now then, ladies and gentlemen,' El addresses the group. 'The game is simple. You must talk to each other, get to know your fellow guests. Ask them questions. Try to determine where they were on the day of the eclipse.'

She pauses again and waits for the attention to drift back to her.

'We will serve drinks and petits fours to keep things lubricated and there are small notebooks in the evidence room for those who didn't bring their own.'

I touch mine and feel a little smug that I had the foresight to bring it.

'Now, go mingle. At 11 p.m. we will ask you for your first guess. Can you solve the Marchioness's murder by then?'

Theodore turns to me and grins. 'Shall we make a plan?'

'I think I already have one.'

21

SADIE

Hidden deep within the West Wing is a secret room accessible only via the passages. It's tiny, a perfect pentagon that I could maybe lie down in at a push but only if it was empty. There are no windows, but I flick the light switch and cross my fingers the bulb still works. Success.

It was obviously designed so you would never know about its existence, even if you tried to map every inch of the house. Was it originally a priest hole? Or a room for activities that should never see the light of day? Well, it is a pentagon. There's something extremely calming about this room, as though it sits under the veil of a witch's protection. That sounds a bit batty, I know, but I've always thought there was some truth in witches and magic and the female ability to bend the rules just a little.

The only furniture is a small side table flanked by two high-backed leather chairs. I pull a tissue from my bag and use it to flick a fine layer of dust from one of them. The room is so well hidden that no one comes to clean it, but a secret room can't attract that much dust.

I need time to think about what I've just seen.

The VIP wing is empty of VIPs.

So where are Hugo and Jerome? I could understand if Jerome has gone to pack a few bits for his stay in the suite, but that still doesn't explain Hugo. He's been 'dead' for hours.

Then there's the two women watching CCTV of the whole space. Could they be part of the company running the event? Are they just keeping an eye on things? Or is it something more sinister?

And let's not forget the dossier of crimes in my room.

I give myself a little shake. *Pull yourself together, woman.* How many mystery weekends have I been to here? How many crimes have I already solved within these walls? Follow the evidence. Put the pieces together.

So, I have 'dead' VIPs who aren't in the VIP suite.

Two women watching CCTV in a room far away from the action.

People who have committed some heinous crimes in real life.

Hugo 'died' via anaphylaxis. But what if it wasn't fake?

I can feel myself drawing closer to the truth. I trust my intuition and close my eyes as the picture comes more into focus. A dossier of crimes, enough to classify as a hit list? A gaggle of unwitting guests who think it's all just fun and games. A team to make sure it's all going to plan.

The murders are real.

It's the only conclusion that makes sense against the evidence I have.

A thought hits me like a bolt of lightning.

Am I on the hit list? Has someone discovered my penchant for poison and decided it's time I face judgement for my actions? Perhaps someone who is less grey in terms of morals, who thinks there is never an excuse for murder. They're wrong, of course; there are so many excuses for murder, the list is longer than my arm. But no, the person behind all this can't be moralising like that. They wouldn't approve of two wrongs making a right like I do. You don't punish a vigilante by acting the vigilante against them. Hugo and Jerome were objectively terrible people, men whose actions have destroyed the lives of innocent people and animals. They deserved to die.

I do not.

Besides, if I were on some hit list, why would I be on the 'killer' team in the game? You can't take out one of the killers, that would ruin the whole game. And I'm under no illusions that whoever is in charge wants to see this game played out. There will be more deaths, more people who the other guests assume have played a role and then gone to get pissed in the VIP section. So, no... I'm not a potential victim.

But that leaves two questions.

Who is the real killer?

And how are they planning to get away with this?

Because they will want to walk away. Of course they will. No one would put on such an elaborate display of theatrics and then allow themselves to get caught.

Of course. The realisation slaps me in the face.

How do you get away with murder?

You blame someone else.

If they know all about the complex crimes of people like Hugo and Jerome, it isn't a leap to assume they know about – at least some – of mine.

And who better to blame for the murders this weekend than an existing serial killer?

I'm the scapegoat.

22

CASSIE

This weekend is basically a big logic puzzle. And if there is one thing I enjoy, it's a logic puzzle.

'Something happened on the 27th June,' I say to the others. 'We don't know what yet, but it must have something to do with the Marchioness's murder. So we need to figure out where everyone was on that day.'

'But some of them may be lying,' Theodore says.

'Exactly. So let's figure out where they all say they were first. Then we can go through all the clues in the evidence room and see where there are discrepancies.'

'Which will tell us who is telling fibs.'

'Exactly.'

Both Rani and Bea look thoroughly unenthused by the plan. I suppose I'm going to have to pick up the slack for them.

'Are any of you lying on your card?' Theodore asks.

'Hey, that's cheating,' Finn says, joining us at the table.

'Spoilsport,' I reply, before drawing a huge grid in my notebook, taking over a double page spread. For a moment I feel bad at using the notebook and not keeping its leaves blemish free, but then I pull myself together.

Theodore goes to find drinks. 'Proper drinks,' he tells me with a wink.

'Theodore has very specific rules about what he drinks and when,' Bea says with a world-weary tone, like she's put up with his bullshit for far too many years. 'He won't drink wine after dinner.'

If it was anyone else, I'd think they were pretentious and a bit of a douchebag. But Theodore manages to be constantly charming and his idiosyncrasies feel like harmless foibles to be considered endearing rather than serious character flaws.

He returns with a tray of crystal tumblers with a good two fingers of whisky in the bottom. He also has a small bowl of ice cubes and a little pair of tongs.

'Lagavulin for the ladies?' he asks with a grin and a flourish.

'Women shouldn't drink whisky,' a voice booms from behind him. Fuck's sake. It's Mitchell, who we sat with at dinner.

'Women,' says Bea pointedly, 'can drink whatever they bloody well like.'

'You're going to put up with that kind of language from your sister?' Mitchell asks Theodore.

'Trust me when I say I have zero control over what my sister says,' Theodore replies. His tone remains pleasant but I can hear the bite in his words.

'Yes, well. I like my females a little more respectful,' he says, his eyes latching onto Rani.

I feel my hand clench into a fist at my side. I can't help it. If he gets any closer, I will punch him in the face. And I'll probably enjoy it.

'The problem with Western women is they have no class. And they don't understand the natural order of things. They've lost sight of the way things are meant to be. The way God intended. Man as master.'

The rest of us just stare at him as some of the most misogynistic bullshit I've ever heard continues to dribble from his mouth.

Eventually Theodore steps towards him and places a hand on his shoulder. 'All right then, old boy. It's been a pleasure but I need to take my team to do some more sleuthing. There is a murderer to be caught after all.' And then he turns to the rest of us. 'Shall we?' He jerks his head towards the door.

I follow him in relief, flanked by Rani and Bea.

'Jesus Christ, that man is...' Bea trails off as if searching for the right word and not finding any that even come close to describing that disgusting pig.

23

SADIE

Nothing seems to have changed when I get back to the ballroom, except everyone keeps peeking at little cards in their hands as they chat. Are these the ones on our place settings at dinner? They must be. I pull my envelope from my bag so I don't look out of place. I'll need to figure out what the game is quick smart to avoid arousing suspicion.

It all feels wrong. If I'm right about the murders being real then I suspect more people in this room are going to die this weekend. How many I don't know, but it's only the first evening. I've only had two dossiers, but I can feel it deep in my waters that there are many more awful people in this room. And, if I'm right about being the scapegoat, I will be blamed for them all.

There will be evidence to support it too.

Hugo went into anaphylactic shock, I'm assuming after he ate some seafood. Anyone could have switched out one of the sandwiches on his table, it would hardly be difficult. And it would be impossible to prove who it was with everyone milling around at that point in the games.

I was in the bathroom when Jerome was stabbed so there will be witnesses to both of us returning to the table at the same time.

In my room they will find papers suggesting I knew about the real crimes committed by the victims.

Merde. If they look more closely, they'll find the bottom layer of the fragrance box I carry with me. People might think I'm a fragrance aficionado, but in reality it's a cover for carrying small vials of liquid. No one asks to unstopper vintage vials of rare perfume, especially not if they think they'll get a lecture from a boring old lady about what they all are.

How do I stop this?

'Ah, Sadie.' One of the twins appears at my elbow. 'There you are. I've been looking for you.' He smiles at me and motions a waitress over with her tray of wine. 'Shall we have a drink?'

I take a glass of red and study the man in front of me. Which one is he? Sebastian or Samuel? They are wearing the exact same suit this evening, the same shirt, the same cufflinks. 'Do you always dress the same?' I ask.

'Ha. Well. Not always. And, to be honest,' he looks almost embarrassed and for a moment I feel bad for pointing it out. 'It's Sebastian. He loves the whole matchy-matchy thing. But, then again, for guys, it's difficult not to look like clones in formalwear. Men don't exactly get a lot of choices.' He motions around the space. Almost all the men are dressed the same. Black suit, white shirt. Perhaps the odd splash of colour here and there. You can tell them all apart because they're different heights and builds and carry themselves differently. Jasper, for example, has such terrible posture he's already developing a hump and he's barely sixty. But the twins are the same height and build and they both have that easy grace of former sports players, gymnasts if I had to put my own money on it.

'So where is your brother?' I ask.

'Oh, he's around.' Samuel smiles. 'We need to make it look like we're really trying to figure out who the killer is, after all,' he says softly, glancing around to make sure no one can hear him.

'And who—' I stop myself in mid-sentence. I was just about to ask him who he thought the killer was. The real killer, that is, the one who decided this wasn't actually just a game. Perhaps I shouldn't have this wine, if I'm ready to blurt things out like that. Of course, he thinks *we* are the killers and that this is all just a game.

'Shall we mingle?' Samuel asks me.

'I think I might just stay here for a few more minutes. Compose myself.'

'You mean consider the possibility of who the killer is?' he says with a grin.

'Exactly.'

I take the time to actually look at the envelope I'm holding. *Where were you on the day the sun went dark?* Inside is a card.

Sadie – The Dowager (Team Bowerman)

You were in London, meeting others at the Criterion Restaurant. You need to lie. But think carefully about a potential alibi, you want one that is difficult to disprove.

I don't know what it means.

But, then again, in the grand scheme of things I don't suppose it matters. What's important is figuring out what is really going on and how I can protect myself. And Aly.

24

THE HIT LIST

Dossier Three: Mitchell Jameson

Mitchell Jameson was an easy one to add to the list. He is the epitome of the disgusting human being. A foul man with so little in the way of redeeming features that I genuinely think his own mother would approve of what we're going to do to him.

Name: Mitchell Jameson
Team: Pew
Role: CEO of Marquess and Pew Marques
Relationship to the Marchioness: Business partner of the late Marquess
Age: 55 years
Residence: Edinburgh
Occupation: Business Owner
Personal Life: Single

Additional Notes:

If you ask Mitchell what he looks for in a woman, he will tell you that he likes 'the exotic'. In an interview last year, he said, on record (just to be clear how truly vile this man is and how untouchable he sees himself):

'I have travelled extensively for years, sampling the delights of what all the continents have to offer.'

What he did not say in that interview was that many of the 'delights' he 'samples' are subsequently trafficked to work in the strip-clubs and brothels he owns across Scotland. He also offers a sideline in domestic labour and child-care workers.

May he rot in hell forever.

25

CASSIE

I'm chatting to a guy around my dad's age who doesn't seem to actually understand the game. So far he has asked where I was on 25 June three times – despite me correcting the date for him – and shown me his own card to 'make sure I know he isn't lying'. But he's just taken the conversation off at a bizarre angle.

'So, it's the Astronomer?' he asks.

'Sorry?'

'The murderer.'

'You think the Astronomer Royal is the murderer?' I ask in a neutral voice, the one you use with the elderly who you think might be going a little senile.

He leans in a little closer. 'Makes perfect sense, doesn't it?' he whispers and then steps back so I can see him tap the side of his nose like he's party to a secret.

All of a sudden, there's an almighty bang and all the lights go off. In the darkness someone screams.

'Ladies and gentlemen,' El's voice rings out. 'Please stay calm. I'm sure the power will be restored imminently.' By the bar, there's a flicker of light as she lights a candle.

Other candles soon help to throw a warm glow over the ballroom. This must be part of the game given how prepared they were. A murmur fans across the collected guests. I pick out a few sentences. 'What's happening?' And 'Is it another murder?'

We stand around for a few more minutes, no one quite sure what to do. I keep my attention on El, she's the only one who actually seems to be in vague control.

Eventually she nods towards the door behind me. I turn to see one of the twins. Interesting. I file it away under 'potential clues to tell Theodore' and then focus back on El.

'We have another murder,' she says and the rest of the room falls silent. 'Someone has tampered with the electrics and now one of our guests has been cruelly electrocuted. In the main entrance in front of the stairs.'

Chaos erupts as everyone turns and starts to head towards the door to have a look. I am jostled by a woman with an oversized handbag and a resting bitch face. 'Watch yourself,' she growls at me.

In the entrance hall, there is the set of magnificent stairs that dazzled me during our tour earlier. They start as a single flight up to a mezzanine level and then split into two that wind upwards on either side of the hallway. They are carved from a deep dark wood that glistens in the candlelight. We are directed to head slightly up them, so there is space for all of us to take in the view of the body lying at the foot of the stairs.

'It's Mitchell,' Bea says as she comes to stand on my right-hand side. 'Thank goodness! Now we don't have to put up with him for the rest of the weekend.'

The woman on my left adds, 'Thank heavens for small mercies.'

I look over the banister and there he is. Mitchell Jameson, lying on his back, with one hand outstretched. In his fist is a power cord attached to a large mahogany cabinet with three dials on the front – the very old radio Finn showed us during our hotel tour. Ha! I knew it would be important. The scene has been staged so it looks like he was trying to plug it into the socket on the wall close by. The socket emits a small puff of steam.

'Can you smell that?' one of the guests asks.

'It smells like chicken,' says his companion.

But they're both wrong. It smells like slow-roasted pork.

26

SADIE

Once again, two people arrive in white overalls and take the body away. They are both extremely wary of the electrical cord still in his hand, despite the fact that it's no longer connected.

The man, Mitchell Jameson, looked pretty dead to me and so I can only assume this is body number three. I spot movement out of the corner of my eye and turn in time to see Sebastian slip behind one of the large paintings in the hallway. I know that one leads to the secret passages.

But why is Sebastian going in there?

I have the sudden thought of the two women in the room with all the CCTV. Are they watching me now? Watching me to see if I'm acting off. If I look like I know more than I should. If I saw Sebastian slip behind the picture?

I need to follow him. But that will definitely look suspicious. Except…

I walk carefully towards the ladies' bathroom, waving to Veronica as I pass her. 'Must dash. I'll be out in a jiffy,' I mutter. No one is going to stop a woman on a mission to the bathroom.

Inside I head to the cubicle in the far corner and relief flashes through me when I realise it's empty. I lock the door: I might need to make my escape route back this way. I leave my shoes. A cursory look under the gap in the door frame will have someone assuming the cubicle is in use.

Besides, there is no way I can run in those shoes and the blisters on my heels are begging for release.

I dig into my beaded clutch bag and pull out the Swiss Army knife I've carried since my first husband, Tommy, passed away. 'Aww sweet. To remember him?' people ask when they see it.

'The love of my life,' I always reply.

And he was. He really was. But, in reality, I carry the Swiss Army knife because Tommy always told me to be prepared for anything. Including removing the small screws holding a board to a wall to reveal another entrance into the secret tunnels.

I am trying to remember if any of the feeds in that CCTV room showed the tunnels, and I don't think they did. But I cross my fingers as I follow the curve of the passageway just in case. It's superstitious codswallop, I know that, but it still makes me feel better. And there is good science in the efficacy of placebos.

I can hear breathing up ahead and I round the corner to find Sebastian in the open doorway to a room off the passageway. He's kneeling on the ground in front of me tying up his shoelace.

His shoulders tense as he senses me behind him and he slowly rises to standing. On the ground next to him is another pair of shoes, the ones he must have been changing out of. Workman's shoes. The type with a thick rubber sole. A thick rubber sole that would help insulate the wearer from an electric shock.

He must realise I've seen them because he takes a step towards me, hands up in a placatory gesture. 'Sadie, I—'

He's moved just enough for me to be able to see behind him into the room before the door swings shut.

'You can't kill me,' I blurt out.

'What? I—'

'I know you're part of this...' I wave around him. 'Whatever this is. But you can't kill me.' I inject some bravado into my voice. It sounds fake in my own ears, but that's OK, he probably thinks I'm reacting like any normal – ha! – person would do if they came upon a murder suspect. In a dark passage. *A secret dark passage where there are no cameras and no one knows where you are*. I try to quiet the voice in my head.

'What are you talking about? You know we're the murderers in the game?' He says it like I might be a bit dumb. But he glances again towards the shoes.

And then it dawns on me. I could try to bluff this out, pretend I didn't see what I just saw. And then what? I end up taking the blame for these deaths and spend the rest of my life in a dank prison cell. Or I could try to find a way out of the net they are trying to close around me. But how?

'If you staged the murder, why would you need to change your shoes?' I ask. 'And why would you have Hugo and Jerome's bodies in the cold store?'

The shock registers on his face. 'I err… I don't know what you think you just saw but…'

He trails off as he sees the smile on my face. He knows the gig is up. Once upon a time, the room behind him was used to store exotic cheeses and other expensive perishable goods, hidden from the inquisitive eyes of the staff and any other guests staying at Holne Hall. It's the perfect place to hide a few bodies. Bodies who are meant to still be living and breathing and having the time of their lives being pampered in the VIP area.

'You can't touch me,' I say with all the bravado I can muster. 'Aly would come looking for me.'

'Aly? Would she though? What if I told her that it would really throw off the scent about Team Bowerman being the killers if one of them were to be "killed"? Would she believe that? If I made your real death look fake and then told her you were in the West Wing?'

His eyes are hard. Impassive. As if there is no emotion running through his veins. Under normal circumstances I might be impressed, he certainly has all the hallmarks of being a highly successful killer. In another life might we have been friends? Mutually respectful of each other's skills? Perhaps. But none of that matters because we aren't on the same side.

If he lets me walk away, he knows I won't stay silent about what I've seen. Especially not as he's trying to make it look like my fault.

But he can't kill me without causing a tonne of trouble for himself.

I reach into my bag and pull out the Swiss Army knife once more. It's not the most impressive weapon in the world, but if you're going to have to fight for your life, you will take any weapon – no matter how small – you can get your hands on.

27

CASSIE

On the stroke of eleven, the gong is once again sounded and we gather back into the ballroom.

'Well, ladies and gentlemen,' El says from the stage area. 'What an eventful day we've all had. It's hardly believable that in just seven hours we have borne witness to not one, not two, not three, but *four* murders.' She pulls out a handkerchief and wipes her brow. 'I don't know about you, but I'm exhausted.'

There's a ripple of laughter from the crowd.

'So, it's time for you to give your first guess. Now, if you don't have everything figured out, don't worry. There will be plenty more clues to uncover tomorrow and some things may become considerably clearer.'

'I hope that means we can figure out who is lying about their whereabouts,' I whisper to Theodore.

'Me too. I have no idea who is lying or why it matters,' he replies.

We turn our attention back to El. 'A member of staff will bring round some cards and pens imminently. Please confer among your team and then make your guess. If you don't have a solid answer yet, please feel free to jot down your theories, we may award some early points for teams who come close. All will be revealed on Sunday. Good luck.'

The four of us from Team Cox huddle up. 'Does anyone have any suspicions?' Theodore asks. 'I don't feel like there's been many clues.' We all nod our agreement. I have no idea how these things usually work, but it does feel pretty light on that front.

'I still think it's Jasper,' Bea says.

'You can't vote for him because he's boring,' Theodore tells her.

'Which one is he?' I ask.

'The group by the door, the one with the terrible posture.'

'Oh. He's not the killer,' I say with surety. He's the one who didn't understand the rules of the game. Unless being utterly inept was an elaborate act, there's no way he would have been able to avoid just telling me straight he was the murderer.

'What do you think?' Bea asks me.

I pause for a moment to consider the evidence we've gathered and the clues we've seen. Like the newspaper and the diary and then the lecture from the Astronomer Royal. 'It's definitely something to do with the 27th June. And people being where they shouldn't. Note that it's "people" plural and not a singular person.'

'You think there is more than one killer?' Theodore asks.

'Yes.'

'Genius.' He sounds genuinely impressed.

'But I don't know who,' I say.

'How about we put down that there is more than one murderer and it's linked to an event on the 27th June?' Theodore suggests and offers me a beaming smile.

'Shall we pick a team to name?' I ask.

'Good idea,' Theodore replies. 'But which one?'

'Someone who hasn't lost a team member? Belstone?' I make it clear this is a stab in the dark, but it's better than nothing.

'Great, Any objections?' Theodore asks the others.

Bea and Rani shake their heads.

'Well, that settles it then.' He waves over one of the staff with the cards and writes up our guess. 'Righto, shall we have a few more drinkies and a debrief?' he asks. How does he still have the energy of an enthusiastic toddler who's just woken up from a nap?

Although another drink does sound nice. It's been a long time since

I could wind down with a few beverages. I'm either working or on call from work or waiting to drive to the airport to pick Rani up from a trip.

'Rani?' I turn to my wife. 'Another drink?' I add an optimistic spin to the question so she can't be in any doubt which way I'd like to go.

'You go,' she says, leaning in to kiss me lightly on the lips. 'There is a clawfoot tub in our room, complete with some seriously fancy toiletries and I fully intend to get our money's worth.'

'You're sure?' We usually go to bed together, we always have. Or at least, we do unless Rani's away with work, but that doesn't count.

'You go and have fun,' she says, kissing me again before turning to walk away. She doesn't say goodbye. For a moment I want to call out to her retreating back, but I don't want her to go to bed irritated by me not respecting her superstitions.

Theodore and I find a spot at the bar and order some brandies.

'So here's the thing,' he says, swirling his Hennessy around the glass. 'There have been three deaths now, not including the Marchioness of course,' he adds before I can interrupt to correct him.

'One from each of three teams.'

'Exactly. Do we think one person from each team is a target?' He twerks his eyebrows as he waits for me to catch up.

'So, what you're saying is that one of us will be "murdered"?' I do the speech quotes with my fingers.

He nods. 'So, who do you think it will be?'

'Does it matter? Except that I don't really fancy being in the VIP area with Mitchell and Hugo and Jerome.' I wrinkle my nose.

'That's true. They are all insufferable bores with very few redeeming features. Jerome is one of those chaps who likes everyone to think he's important.'

'You know him?'

'Our boys were at Eton together.'

'And I guess you've both been at these weekends before,' I add.

'No. I've never seen him here at one of these. Actually… I've never seen any of them here before.' He pauses for a few moments. 'So, are the "victims" all new to Murder on the Moors?'

I fake a shiver. 'I hope not, because that means it'll either be me or Rani who's killed.' I make another face.

'We'll come and visit you.'

'You won't be allowed.' I grin. 'Gosh, that sounds like prison.' We both laugh.

'Am I interrupting the fun?' a voice says from behind the bar.

'Karen!' I exclaim, jumping up to give her an awkward hug over the bar. 'This is Theodore, my teammate. Theodore, this is Karen, she's an old friend of mine.'

'Pleasure to meet you,' Theodore says. He sounds genuine. He really is one of the good guys. You can always tell a lot about a person from the way they treat the staff in bars and restaurants and at the airport; anyone in customer service. 'I was just saying that, if Cassie gets "killed", I'll visit her in the VIP area.'

'Me too. I'll bring you care packages of decent cocktails and premium snacks.'

'Promise?' I ask them both.

Karen puts out her little finger. 'Pinky promise.'

I intertwine my finger with hers.

'But why do you think you'll end up in the VIP suite?' she asks. She points at our almost empty glasses and we both nod for a top up.

'Well, so far, it's one person from each team. And we noticed a pattern,' I say.

'*I* noticed a pattern,' Theodore says. He might be an absolute sweetheart, but he's as competitive as hell.

I roll my eyes at him. 'Each team is made up of a couple who's been here before, and one who hasn't. It's only the newbies who have been victims,' I explain to Karen.

'So far,' she says. 'Is three enough to see a pattern?'

Theodore and I look at each other.

'Sorry to burst your bubble,' Karen says. 'My brother is a data analyst and he's always banging on about "statistically significant sample sizes".'

'I remember that,' I say, before letting out a groan. 'There was that party we went to and he was trying to chat up some girl and he would not shut up about it.' We both laugh. 'I had to pull him to one side and say that would never ever fly as a chat-up line,' I add for Theodore's benefit.

'Oh, but here's the thing,' Karen says. 'He just got engaged.'

'No way!'

'Yeah. She's also a data scientist. It's kind of sweet.'

'Bless him. Send him my congratulations.'

Theodore drains the contents of his glass. 'Right then, ladies, I think it's time for me to retire. It looks like you two have a lot of catching up to do and I don't want to interrupt. Just make sure you get some sleep,' he tells me with a waggle of his finger. 'I need you nice and sharp for tomorrow's games.'

'Yes sir,' I say, making sure it sounds like the joke I mean it to.

'I have a feeling tomorrow is going to be a particularly exciting day,' he says as he skips out of the bar.

28

SADIE

Sebastian takes a few steps backwards when he sees the glint of silver from the knife.

'You know, knives aren't really my thing,' he says, his gaze snagging on it once more.

'No, they're more mine,' a voice says behind me.

I whirl around to see El standing in the passageway. She's also holding a blade, but hers is more impressive than mine. It looks like a Japanese paring knife, with an ornate hilt and a blade that would slice through flesh like butter. 'El?'

'Hey Sadie.' She adjusts her grip and I can tell it's muscle memory; she has had a lot of practice with this knife.

'I... I...' But I don't actually have any words. I'm vastly outmatched. Two against one. And they have a better weapon. What can I say to walk away from here?

'You know, Sadie,' El says. 'I was really hoping it wouldn't come to this.' She motions around herself. 'It didn't have to be this way.'

'What way was it meant to be?' I ask bitterly. 'You were going to frame me anyway.'

Confusion skitters across her face. 'Frame you?' She cocks her head. 'Whatever are you talking about?'

'I know the murders are real.'

'Yes, well, evidently you saw inside the cold store.'

'And I know you've planted evidence in my room. Evidence that I was researching the men who have died.'

'And why, Sadie, would we want to frame you?'

'Because you know,' I whisper. Perhaps, if nothing else, this can be my confession. My chance to bare my soul and ask the universe for forgiveness for taking all those lives. I don't regret them for one moment, but it's probably not a bad idea to rebalance the weight of my heart before it's measured against the feather of Ma'at.

'What do we know?' She takes a small step towards me, as if by closing the distance I might share my sins more readily.

'About the people I've killed.'

The words hang in the fetid air of the passageway. I have never spoken them out loud before.

Confusion returns to El's face.

'You... you... do know...?' Have I just confessed to murder without needing to? Could I have taken my secrets to the grave after all? Even if my grave is about to become the secret tunnels at Holne Hall. In some ways it's really rather fitting. Almost comical. If it weren't me who was about to die.

El laughs. A long loud laugh that reverberates around the narrow space. 'Oh dear, Sadie. Of course we know.'

'So that's why you're going to frame me.'

'Frame you? Oh Sadie, we didn't want to frame you. We wanted you to join us.'

'Join you?'

'Haven't you always wondered what it would be like to be part of a team? To slay together?' El asks.

'But—'

'It was meant to be perfect. I like sharp objects.' She throws the knife in the air and catches it as a wicked grin flashes across her face. 'Sebastian here likes to stage an accident. And you might have noticed he comes with a built-in alibi in the form of his brother. It's truly brilliant. And then there's you. You have a specific skillset that would have been delightfully complementary. I hear you prefer a more subtle approach. Apparently, you're a true master.'

'So, you want to recruit me?' I can feel a bubble of hysteria building in my chest. Perhaps I will not die tonight.

'Wanted,' El says and the bubble bursts at her sharp tone.

'But I had no idea.'

'Perhaps,' Sebastian pipes up, 'we could give Sadie a second chance? A little time to think about what she wants to do.'

'Fine,' El says. She glances at her watch. 'Besides it's getting pretty late and the party will be winding down for the evening.' She turns to direct her attention back to me. 'Read the proposal. Think on it. We'll rendezvous tomorrow morning.'

'I have one more question,' I say. She nods as if to give me permission to ask it. 'Who are you?'

'El.' She says it like a fait accompli. Like that is all she's going to say on the matter.

I don't say anything, but I settle my weight into one hip and stare her down. It's a look that never fails to get people to crack and one I've perfected over the years.

'Fine.' It takes less than thirty seconds for her to break. 'Eloise Gunner.'

The name rings a bell, albeit a small one. 'Why do I know that name?'

She smiles. 'I didn't have you down as a true-crime fan.' She arches an eyebrow. 'There was a documentary recently. About the man who killed my family.' There is almost no trace of emotion in her voice. But I can tell that isn't her being callous, it's a survival mechanism.

'The Christmas Massacre?'

'Yep.'

'But the documentary said you were missing, presumed dead.'

'Yeah, well, I used a few aliases over the years. And then, as Jessica Williams, I found myself in Ellsbury. It's a little town in Sussex but they have a gorgeous Christmas market every year. And that's where I met Alvi.' Her whole face breaks into a smile. Whoever this Alvi is, she's obviously madly in love with him. 'He encouraged me to reclaim my own name, said I shouldn't have to leave my history behind because of the actions of a dead man.'

'I thought they never found whoever was responsible for killing your family?'

'If by "they" you mean the police, then no. *They* didn't. But *I* did.' Her voice isn't just tinged with pride, it's positively dripping in it.

'And then you what… carried on killing?'

'I'm extremely good at it. And I don't think you should let talent go to waste.'

'I couldn't agree more.' It's the same sentiment I've used myself a number of times.

She beams at me and I smile back. Perhaps we could make a good team.

'Just one thing,' I say before I head back to the party. 'Where do I find this proposal?'

El and Sebastian look at each other.

'It's in your room. I gave it to you when you arrived.'

'No, you didn't. All that was in that envelope was information on Hugo and Jerome.'

'You must have missed it. But we put another envelope under your door.'

'When?'

'Before dinner. It had the information about dear Mitchell Jameson and then a request to join us before his death.'

'*Merde*.'

'What?'

'I left the room half an hour before dinner.' I quietly berate myself for visiting the garden. 'And I haven't been back to the room since. But Aly has.'

'Would she read a letter addressed to you?' El makes it sound like that is something that just wouldn't happen. She's wrong.

'Aly is a nosy twenty-five-year-old who has been digging into Hugo and Jerome and has already figured out that the crimes you shared with me are real.'

'So that's a yes?' I hear El say, but I've already turned away from her and I'm running back down the passageway, skirt hitched in my hands to avoid tripping.

Is there a chance she hasn't got to it first?

29

THE HIT LIST

Dossier for Insurance: Sadie Rose

I turn to look at him. 'Are you sure about this?'

'What do we always say?' he asks with a raise of his eyebrow.

'That it's always better to be safe than sorry,' I reply. He's right. And it's a mantra that's kept me safe for a long time. I open another character sheet and begin to type.

Name: Sadie Rose
Team: Bowerman
Role: The Dowager

'Do you think she'll hate it?' I ask. 'Being called the Dowager?'

'Why would she hate it?'

'It sounds kind of old and fusty.'

'From what I've seen, she's anything but.'

'Exactly. That's what I mean. It just feels like a bit of a cliché.'

He takes off his glasses and rubs the bridge of his nose in an infuriatingly attractive way. I have no idea how he can still make me feel like a giddy teenager. 'This whole thing is a cliché. The 1920s theme. A

Marchioness with a fortune to leave. A gathering of potential benefactors. The murder of said Marchioness. A scavenger hunt.'

He has a point.

Relationship to the Marchioness: Distant Relative

Now, on to the real facts about Ms Sadie Rose. Formerly Mrs Sadie Duggin. And Mrs Sadie MacCarthy. And Mrs Sadie Rochford. Our very own Dowager Bowerman has certainly had her fair share of husbands. Not that she dispatched *all* of them.

Age: 72 years

Residence: Mayfair

Hmmm. Occupation. That's an interesting one. I can't find any evidence that she's ever had a job per se. Or at least not since she was in her early twenties and spent a handful of years with British Airways as an air hostess. But an apartment in Mayfair is certainly not paid for with air hostess money so I can only imagine that trail of former husbands was helpful in the financial department.

Occupation: Unknown

Once again, I pause when I get to the section marked 'personal life'. From the looks of it there were multiple husbands but no children of her own. 'Why do you think she never had kids?' I ask.

He raises an eyebrow. 'Are you really asking that question?'

I feel the flush burn my face. He's right. I should be ashamed to ask. Especially after last night. We went out for dinner, just the two of us, for a romantic meal. It was bliss. Until some idiot at the next table asked us if we were planning on starting a family of our own soon. It was so rude and so invasive I had a mind to... well, obviously not, but you know what I mean.

Personal Life: Multiple marriages. No known children. Godmother to Alyssa Williamson (accompanying Sadie this weekend).

It'll do. I roll my neck to work out the kinks.

Additional Notes:

Sadie Rose has a very specialist skillset, honed over many decades of practice. If you go to the East Wing and head out of the fire exit close to the kitchen you will find a small walled garden. To the untrained eye it looks like nothing. To those in the know, it looks like someone has a love of Agatha Christie and has emulated the garden at Torre Abbey.

But what most people don't realise is that the garden was planted by Sadie and maintained by a trusted groundskeeper. Every year, on the second weekend in September, Sadie comes to Murder on the Moors and, under the cover of a jolly good weekend, picks the plants she will need for the year ahead.

She is also a perfume connoisseur, carrying around a small Louis Vuitton travel case of vials of her favourite scents. I too like the smell of almonds in the morning.

People in Sadie's life have a habit of heart attacks, falling overboard on cruises, or even just disappearing altogether.

I don't think it takes a genius to put these things together.

30

CASSIE

I keep Karen company in the bar for a while longer. It's very slow, just a trickle of guests who don't quite know it's time to call it a night. This is one of my favourite times when I'm working though, there's a sense of peace in pottering about behind the bar, making sure everything is just so for the next day, the handful of punters providing just enough company to stave off the loneliness.

But Karen doesn't seem to be enjoying these quiet hours of her shift. She's acting a little off, like she's worried about something.

'You know, if there's something worrying you, you can always talk to me,' I tell her.

'It's fine.'

'Really?' I sit back and appraise her. 'Just talk to me, OK?'

Eventually she says, 'I don't want to set hares running if I'm just being silly.' Hares running is such a Karen thing to say, she was always the queen of the odd idiom. Cat among the pigeons. Spanner in the works. I decide not to press the issue, she'll tell me when she's ready to share.

The other guests start to head off to bed and pretty soon it's just me on one side of the bar and Karen on the other.

'What time do you finish?' I ask her.

She checks her watch. 'Probably in an hour. It doesn't exactly look lively in here.' She motions around the now empty room.

'I should have said something earlier, but thank you for the invite, it's been good to see Rani getting excited about something, even if it's just some fake murders.'

'Invite?' Karen asks.

'I'm assuming you pulled some strings to get us on the guest list.'

She looks at me blankly. 'I have no idea what you're talking about.'

'It wasn't you who snuck me onto the list?'

'No. Why would I do that?' She sounds genuinely puzzled.

'I just thought…' What did I think? That we were friends and she might want to see a friendly face? But she's obviously settled here, being her usual brilliant self and slaying at her new job. 'Never mind.'

'Well, it doesn't matter why you're here, but I'm really glad to see you.' She smiles. 'I want to hear all the gossip from the Raven.'

We spend ten minutes chatting about the people we used to work with, who is still there and who has moved on to other places.

I regale her with a tale of one of the bartenders who was convinced one of our patrons was Cate Blanchett, even though she blatantly wasn't, both of us giggling like schoolgirls, leaning over the bar from each side with the easy camaraderie of friends who have known each other for years. I've missed this. Missed the person I am with people who just understand me, where I'm not putting on an act, acting like the person I think they want me to be, rather than the person I actually am. Masking is exhausting.

'Any chance of a drink?' a voice calls from the other end of the bar, interrupting my story. 'Or are you too busy?' He sounds pissed off, the kind of man who is used to people doing exactly what he says. The kind of person who can turn a shift from fun to bullshit in an instant.

Karen gives me a look. It's so fast, he won't notice. 'Coming,' she calls to him.

'Well, take your time.'

'Arse,' she whispers under her breath as she leaves me to serve him.

I watch idly as she runs him through every single whisky they stock. It's a high-end hotel so this takes quite a long time. Eventually he picks one. I can't make out his exact words, but I can tell from the way Karen steels her shoulders that he's made some kind of dodgy comment. This is the dark side of hospitality. Although sometimes it leads to comedy gold.

She comes back from serving him and gives me a pointed look. 'He told me I'd better be careful or he'll have to bend me over his knee.'

I mime being sick. 'Gross. But at least it's good fodder for the book.'

'True,' she says and pats the pocket of her apron. For years she's being collecting little snippets of things that customers say, conversations she overhears, stupid things that go wrong. She's always said that one day she'll write a book about it. Like an exposé on the truth of hospitality.

But obviously this anecdote doesn't make the cut because she changes the subject. 'How are things going with Rani?'

It was actually because of Karen that Rani and I got together in the first place. Rani had been into the hotel a few times and of course I'd noticed her. She's stunning, she would sit at the bar in a skimpy dress and sip a cocktail like the literal woman of my dreams.

'You should ask her out,' Karen told me one night when she saw me looking.

'She's a customer.' I had a very strict 'no dating' rule when it came to the clientele.

But Karen kept going on and on about it. She'd just started seeing some guy and she was desperate to matchmake for everyone else too. In the end I capitulated. And the rest – as they say – is history.

'Didn't you guys get puppies?' Karen breaks me from my reverie.

'Yeah.' I pull out my phone and show her the lock screen. An uncomfortable prickle runs up my neck, as if someone is watching us.

'Adorable.'

'They are.' I put my phone back in my bag. I spot movement out of the corner of my eye, but when I turn to look there's no one there.

'You OK?' Karen asks.

'Yeah, sorry. I just thought I felt someone watching us and then there was movement... but I must have imagined it.'

'And is everything all right with you and Rani?'

'It's fine. Great. Perfect, in fact.'

'But that's a problem...'

I told you she knew me too well.

'I just... I keep wondering what I'm going to do to fuck it up,' I say quietly.

'Why would you fuck it up?'

'Because I always do. I'll do something stupid, or say the wrong thing, or... I don't know... But then she'll realise she made a mistake.'

'Ooorr,' she drags out the word. 'Perhaps she loves you and you love her and you'll live happily ever after?'

'Maybe.' I glance at my watch. It's almost one in the morning. 'I'd better go find her.'

'Less than six hours until I need to be on breakfast duty,' she says as she yawns. 'Sometimes I hate this job.'

'You love it really,' I remind her. You can't work in hospitality for a long time without loving it. The haters quit within months and go to find easy jobs, like sitting in an office and playing with spreadsheets.

'I do. And I really think this is the place that's going to make my career.' She beams. 'The senior management are noticing my efforts. I've even been offered a training course. Like a proper one.'

'I'm so proud of you.'

'Thanks.' She blushes.

'Look at you being the employee of the month.'

'Oh no, that's the new concierge.' She rolls her eyes. 'She only started a few weeks ago and they already put her in charge of running the whole VIP area for the "victims".' She raises both eyebrows pointedly. 'But I'm not jealous.' She obviously is. 'Now, bugger off so I can finish closing up and then get a quick run in before I try for at least a few hours' sleep.'

Back at the Tey suite I find Rani fast asleep, the only source of light the bedside lamp on my side. She always makes sure my light is on if I'm coming to bed after her. Such a simple thing, but it saves me from crashing around in the dark. She can be thoughtful like that.

I slide into bed beside her and she scooches over to be little spoon. I bury my face into the base of her neck. She smells like blackcurrant and patchouli, her perfume with the name I can never remember. 'I thought you were having a bath?' I whisper into the dark.

'I did. It was delightful.' In my arms she stretches slightly, as if to demonstrate how relaxed she is.

I try not to stiffen behind her. That was a lie. But why would she bother? If she wanted to go to bed instead, it isn't like I'd care. I just want her to be happy. 'I love you,' I say instead.

'I love you too,' she replies.

31

SADIE

How did I miss a letter? I ask myself as I hurry down the passageway towards the ladies' bathroom. Without shoes, my stockinged feet make no sound on the stone floor. I need to get back to the Christie suite as quickly as possible. Is there a chance that Aly didn't see the new envelope? That she didn't just open it, wanting to see if it contained information about another awful human about to meet his maker in the game. She's too curious for her own good, that girl.

I slip my shoes back on and close the cover to the passageway. I only put back two of the four screws, who knows if I'll want to make a quick exit into the tunnels at some point this weekend. Just in case there's anyone else in the bathroom, I flush the toilet before I leave the stall. Of course I find that brusque woman from earlier standing at the hand basins. What was her name again? Oh yes, Felicity Atkinson.

I make a show of washing my hands. I don't want any rumours going around that Sadie Rose doesn't take care of appropriate hygiene.

'Would now be a good time to pick your brains.' Once again, it's more demand than question. I guess Ms Atkinson is so used to getting her own way that she doesn't feel the need to actually ask for things.

'Sorry, I need to find my goddaughter,' I reply smoothly.

'Oh. I thought she was your granddaughter.' Emphasis on the 'grand'.

People always assume that, the same way they assumed Aly's mother was my daughter.

'No. Goddaughter.' I don't offer up any further information. I really don't want to get into a discussion as to why I've brought my goddaughter and not a blood relative with me. There are only so many times I can tell people I didn't have children of my own before I want to employ some violence. I know I'm nosy and I like to pick into other people's lives, but I don't appreciate them doing the same to me.

'I think I saw her heading up the main stairs,' Felicity says. 'Probably heading back to your room.'

'Lovely, thank you.' *Merde!* She can't go back to the suite before I get there. What if she sees it? Finds the letter and realises all that I am?

'So you do have time now,' Felicity says.

'Sorry. I have to find Aly,' I say as I start to walk away. I'm not lying.

'How rude,' Felicity mutters under her breath.

I manage to avoid bumping into anyone who wants to chat on my way to the lift. I spot Jasper as I'm desperately pushing the call button but thankfully he doesn't approach. The lift feels like it takes a year to arrive and then transport me up to the second floor.

The electronic lock beeps as I tap my room key against it and I push open the door.

Aly is sitting on the edge of her bed, a letter in her hand. The envelope on the duvet next to her says 'Sadie' in flowing script, the same handwriting as on the previous ones.

'You shouldn't open someone else's letters,' I say softly as I take a few tentative steps towards her.

'I knew it.' Aly's eyes flash. 'I knew you were hiding something.'

'You don't seem...' but I trail off. She should be terrified of me, trying to put as much distance between us as possible. Or curling her lip in disgust as her eyes fill with loathing. Fear or loathing are the only two responses to discovering someone is a murderer. Aren't they? But she looks almost like she's in awe.

'What?' she asks.

'What?' I repeat.

'You're looking at me like I'm some kind of alien species,' she clarifies.

'I thought you'd be...' I spread my fingers out. 'I thought...'

'You thought I'd be what? Horrified?'

I nod.

'Aunt Sadie. You are a fucking badass.' She looks at the letter. 'But you should probably decide what you're going to do.'

'Do you think...' but I trail off. I can't ask my twenty-five-year-old goddaughter if she thinks I should join a killing spree.

'If the others on the list are anything like Jerome Fulker, Hugo Durbridge or Mitchell Jameson, then I think the answer is obvious. As long as they have the right fail safes in place, of course. What reassurances have they given you?' She sounds so professional. So astute. My heart swells with pride at this incredible young woman I had at least a small hand in raising.

'Well, err, they—'

'Did you even ask?'

I open my mouth to answer but I'm saved by the phone on the side table ringing.

Aly answers. 'It's for you,' she says, handing me the receiver.

'Sadie speaking,' I say into it.

'It's El.' She sounds businesslike. 'You ran away before we got to finish our conversation.'

'Sorry... I...'

'Does she know?'

'I assume you mean Aly. And yes, she read the letter.'

'Will she be a problem for us?'

'No.'

'Will *you* be a problem for us?'

'No.'

'We need you to prove yourself. A new envelope will be delivered shortly. Make your decision. If you wish to join us, come to the Red Library in the morning.' There's a click and the line goes dead.

'What did she say?' Aly asks.

'Apparently I need to "prove myself".'

I turn to see an envelope coming underneath the door.

Quick as a flash, Aly moves to the door and peers through the peephole. 'One of the twins,' she says.

'Sebastian,' I confirm. 'He's part of this too.'

'Yeah. I could spot the serial killer in him a mile off. He needs to improve his poker face if he doesn't want to get caught.'

'You knew something more was going on here?'

'Err, dossiers, realistic "deaths", identical twins who can be in two places at once and you'd never know which one you were actually talking to...' She says it like it was always so obvious. 'I did some research on Sebastian and Samuel. They seem to have had such tragic lives, so many people in their orbits ending up dying in freak accidents.' She gives me a pointed look.

'Apparently that is Sebastian's preferred method.'

'Anyway.' She waves the envelope toward me. 'Shall I open it?'

'Please.'

'It's another dossier. Diego Perez.'

'What did he do?'

Her eyes scan the page until she gets to the section where his crimes will be listed. Assuming this is the same as the last one, anyway. 'Identity theft. On a rather epic scale.' She looks up from the paper and her eyes meet mine.

'What do we do now?'

'I guess I get to work.' She walks over to the small desk and opens her laptop. 'Give me half an hour to do some research.'

32

THE HIT LIST

Dossier Four: Diego Perez

I'm daydreaming about lunch – we're having bacon, brie and cranberry paninis: festive flavours are my favourite – as I start the next dossier.

'Oops,' I say as I delete the title I just typed.

'Did you head it up as "The Naughty List" again?' he asks.

'Guilty as charged.'

'Who are you doing now?'

'Diego,' I reply.

'Diego, Markus, Lionel, Terry, Paul.'

'All of the above.'

Name: Diego Perez
Team: Cleave
Role: The Cleave Organisation doesn't have roles
Relationship to the Marchioness: The Marquess owed significant sums to the Cleave Organisation at the time of his death.
Age: 55 years
Residence: Oslo, Norway
Occupation: Unknown

Personal Life: Unknown

Additional Notes:

Little is known about Diego Perez. Mainly because that isn't the only name he uses. We have traced dozens of false identities under which he has travelled, racking up huge credit card bills in the names of his victims. And when I say huge, I'm meaning tens of thousands, hundreds of thousands. He even spent a month at the Venetian Hotel in Las Vegas pretending to be Herr Schmitt, heir to some rambling Bavarian estate, while he accumulated a total bill in excess of a million dollars. It was all anyone could talk about on the poker circuit that year.

On the one hand, this seems like a purely financial crime and therefore not necessarily worthy of inclusion, but it is only the tip of the iceberg. In his various guises, Diego has committed more crimes than I can list and his prodigious catalogue has catapulted him to fourth on this list.

PART IV

BREAKFAST

33

CASSIE

I wake up at six forty-five. Over five full hours of sleep. That feels like a record recently; I don't think I've slept like that for months. I feel... almost human, despite the thump of whisky – or possibly brandy – behind my right eyeball. That is nothing a strong coffee and a croissant can't fix.

Rani is still fast asleep, her hair fanning across the pillow. She looks peaceful, her hands thrown up over her head. She's always slept with quiet abandon, and can sleep through the kind of racket that normally heralds the end of the world. It's a rare talent. 'You learn to sleep through anything when you're at boarding school,' she told me once. 'There were eight of us in my dorm when we were younger and it was total chaos. Good training though.'

I decide to leave her to get some more sleep and head down to the breakfast room. I can bring her back a fruit platter and selection of pastries so she can have breakfast in bed. It'll be romantic.

She doesn't stir as I pull on a pair of jeans and a t-shirt, before scraping a comb through my hair. After the dressiness of last night, I actually look like myself in the mirror. No CFO of an animal rights charity right now, just a woman getting her beautiful wife something to eat.

It's quiet inside the breakfast room, I'm obviously one of the first to come down. I guess everyone else is waiting for the hot food to start at eight.

There's a slightly stressed-looking woman laying out the pastries and I'm pleased to see they look freshly baked. I have a great love for croissants and I've even made a list to rate them all so I can avoid disappointment by getting shitty ones. For reference, if I have to go to a chain – I work stupid hours and the smaller local places aren't always serving croissants at midnight – then it has to be Pret. I will sometimes accept Co-Op (I know, it feels like an odd choice but they do a particularly good hazelnut-spread filled one). But a lot of the others can get in the bin with their long shelf-life rubbish that is drier than the Sahara.

'I'll be there in a moment,' the woman calls out when she sees me loitering by the pedestal with the sign telling me to wait to be seated in aggressively large capitals.

I wait for a few minutes, running my eyes down the list of guests and their room numbers. I probably shouldn't look to be honest, but I'm intrigued as to the names of all the suites – all named after famous mystery writers – and then the way a boutique hotel decided to use four number designations for the other rooms. Seriously? Room 4139 in a hotel with like twenty standard rooms? There must be some kind of coding attached. Like 4 is the floor, and 1 is the wing, and 3 is the grade. Utter overkill. I file it away under 'things not to do if I ever get to manage a hotel like this'.

'Sorry,' she says, running over to me. 'We're a little short staffed this morning.' She flashes me a million-watt smile, but I can see the cracks around the edges and how it doesn't go anywhere near her eyes. It's the smile we all learn on day one of working in hospitality. 'Short staffed' is code for 'some arsehole didn't make it to work on time'.

I want to tell her she really doesn't need to pretend around me, that I know exactly how it feels when someone doesn't show up for work and you have to do their job as well as your own. It sucks. But I know it would be weird and inappropriate and make her feel super awkward so instead I just smile. 'No worries. I was wondering if I could make up a tray of breakfast for my wife? She's been working flat out recently and I think this is the first time she's had a lie-in in months.'

'Aww, that's too sweet. Of course you can. Umm...' She looks around her as if to gauge everything else that still needs to be done before the other guests descend on the breakfast room.

'Just coffee, some fruit and a plate of pastries,' I say, injecting my voice with hopefulness. 'I can make up the tray if you just point me in the right direction.'

'Sure. Sorry.' She offers me this funny half grimace. 'I'm a bit off balance this morning.'

'Perhaps Karen could help me?' I ask. 'She's working this morning, isn't she?'

A dark cloud crosses her features and her lips purse. 'She was meant to be.'

'Oh.' So, it was Karen who didn't show up for breakfast duty. Which feels... I don't know. It feels wrong. I worked with her for years and she never missed a shift. Not even when she thought she might have appendicitis and I eventually had to threaten to fire her if she didn't go to the hospital immediately to get checked out. 'Is everything all right with her?'

The woman's professional facade cracks for a moment. 'I'm sure she'll turn up later with a hangover and a lame excuse.'

I plate up the breakfast and head back to the room to wake Rani. It doesn't sit right with me, this whole Karen thing. I know her. I know she wouldn't not turn up for work.

Unless something has happened.

34

SADIE

Aly wakes me up before it's even fully light, which feels like an affront. I never get up before dawn – well, unless I'm travelling or for other really good reasons.

'It's not even seven,' I say as I look at my watch. It's a Jaeger-LeCoultre Reverso One, with a burgundy leather strap and pink gold face. A gift I bought myself a few years ago after I dispatched a particularly loathsome creature.

'And you need to meet El and Sebastian in half an hour.'

'Oh.' She's right. I have half an hour to decide if I am going to join El's murder posse. What was it she said? 'Haven't you always wondered what it would be like to be part of a team? To "slay together"?' Like there needs to be a slogan for murder these days. I know branding is one of the cornerstones of the 'late-stage capitalist hellscape' – Aly's words – that we're apparently living in. But I didn't think that extended to the way we think about serial killing. I'm not sure I like it, to be honest. And I've never been much of a team player.

'Have you decided?' Aly asks.

So, I might not be convinced about the whole team effort thing. But I am rather itching to indulge myself. It's been a fair few months since I last killed a man.

Actually, it isn't only men I kill. I have also dispatched a few women in my lifetime. But only the really, really bad ones.

Like my friend Tilly's hideous mother-in-law. And yes, I know it's a cliché, the whole terrible mother-in-law thing. But with her it was legitimate. Her mother-in-law, Nora, was one of the worst people I have ever met in my entire life. Constantly nit-picking and telling Tilly she wasn't good enough for her darling son. 'He's only marrying you because you're young and pretty and he's thinking with his pecker,' she said to Tilly once with a completely straight face. 'Once you've popped out an heir and a spare, he'll see the truth and then he can move on and find someone better.' She wore a permanent sneer whenever Tilly was around.

Tilly was a sweetheart, the kind of woman everyone falls in love with. The kind of woman who would give you the shirt off her back, literally. I once spilled strawberry jam down my white blouse before a date and she swapped with me in the ladies' room of the Ritz-Carlton. But Nora ground her down.

And then her husband got sick. Really sick. Tilly juggled his care with raising their three daughters (a lack of sons obviously yet another point of contention with the mother-in-law, male-preference primogeniture is still very much alive and well. Not that there was any money left, Nora's husband had gambled away the family fortune and left them on the brink of bankruptcy). Nora would come to visit her son. And then she would sit there, like a goddamn queen, and expect Tilly to take care of her too. 'You really should make tea in a pot when you have guests,' she would say when Tilly slapped a mug of tea in her ungrateful hands. Or, 'What's for dinner?' When Tilly had been so busy she hadn't even had a pee for five hours. Or, 'You're hardly giving him a reason to fight, looking like that.' This was said with a pointed look at Tilly's unwashed hair and sweatpants. It is very hard to look fresh and clean when you can't have a shower in case your husband chokes on his own vomit. But did Nora offer to watch her son so his wife could wash? I think we both know the answer to that.

I'd offered to pay for a nurse to come and help out. But, in my stupidity, I'd suggested it within earshot of Nora, who had muscled in with an adamant refusal. 'No stranger is looking after my boy. That's the duty of a wife.' I went back a few days later, this time armed with casserole and gin and colouring books for the girls to try to keep them out from under Tilly's feet. I'd found a nurse who was going to arrive the following morning at 10 a.m. and there would be no further questions about it.

But I found Tilly squeezed in the corner of her kitchen, the lights off as she cowered like a terrified animal in its burrow.

'What's happened?' I exclaimed, running to her.

'Nora.'

'What's she done this time?'

Tilly waved towards the kitchen table and the stack of letters. I picked the first one up and read it gingerly. Nora had taken out a loan against the family home, the last remaining thing of any value. And then she'd taken out another, this time making her son the guarantor. And then a handful of credit cards in his name, with her as the secondary cardholder. I scanned the bill. Hundreds of pounds in various restaurants around London, hundreds in Selfridges and Fortnum's and all the other places they couldn't afford to shop in.

'How much?' I asked softly.

'More than I can ever repay.'

'But it isn't your debt.'

'It's Marcus's. Stupid fucking woman.' There was so much venom in her voice.

The next morning, Nora went to The Wolseley for breakfast.

She died three hours later.

'Causes Unknown' it says on her death certificate.

Ha! Causes Unknown, my foot.

Cyanide is a wonderful thing.

'Hello?' Aly interrupts my musings. 'So, what are you going to do?'

Just thinking about Nora has made me remember why I started doing this in the first place. Some people do not deserve to live. Does Diego fall into this category? Of course he does.

* * *

El and Sebastian are waiting in the Red Library when I push open the heavy wooden door.

'Have you made a decision?' she asks, without any pleasantry. Not even a 'good morning', or a 'how did you sleep?'

'I'm in.'

'Excellent.' El hands me a piece of paper.

'What's this?'

'Let's call it an audition. You need to make the death look like it's part of the game.'

35

CASSIE

Back in the Tey suite, Rani is sprawled in bed as she leisurely makes her way through the items on the tray I made up. But my brain is racing at a million miles an hour and I'm too hyped up to relax over breakfast. Instead, I tear a croissant into tiny flakes on my plate.

'What are you doing?' Rani asks, putting her hand over mine to stop me shredding baked goods.

'Karen's missing,' I tell her.

'What do you mean, missing?'

'I mean she's literally missing. She didn't turn up for work this morning and no one knows where she is.'

'She probably overslept,' Rani says. She sounds so nonchalant. Like it doesn't even matter.

I stand up and start to pace. I don't know what to do. If no one else seems to care, then how do I even begin to look for her?

'Will you please sit the fuck down,' Rani says, a little more forcefully than seems necessary.

'Sorry,' I say softly.

'Don't be sorry, just stop it.'

'Sorry.'

She rolls her eyes. She always tells me I don't need to apologise so much. 'I'm sure she's fine. She'll just have switched her alarm off by mistake or something.'

'But wh—'

'She isn't your problem, you know?'

'What's that meant to mean?' I can't help but jump into defensive mode.

'I mean, if she gets into trouble with her manager then it's not your problem. She doesn't work for you any more.'

'But what if something's happened to her?'

'Can you please just stop, Cassie?' She sounds close to the end of her tether.

'It's just...'

'Just nothing. For fuck's sake, Cassie, not *everything* is your problem to fix.'

I go to have a shower. My eyes are stinging with tears at the little jibe. I know deep down she doesn't mean it, that she isn't trying to be critical and pick holes and that it isn't her fault that I'm so weirdly sensitive about being told I'm in the wrong. It isn't something I want to fight over and I know from bitter experience that is what will happen.

I feel a lot calmer after my shower. Rani heads into the bathroom to have hers as I try to decide what to wear today. Apparently, we're off for a picnic on Dartmoor. I really should check the weather forecast. It looks sunny right now but who knows what will happen as the day progresses?

But as I bring up the weather forecast site, I remember that I didn't actually try to call Karen. I thought about it but I didn't actually do it. Why am I so shit at remembering stuff like that?

I'm scrolling through my emails when Rani comes and looks over my shoulder.

'What are you doing?' she asks.

'Trying to find Karen's phone number. She changed it last year and I'm sure she sent me an email, but I can't find it.'

'And you didn't save her number at the time?' Rani asks as if that is what any normal person would have done. I mean, it *is* what any normal person would have done, but I did not do it. I'm so bad at keeping in contact with people. It isn't that I don't want to, that I don't want to have loads of friends and messages flying back and forth and a general sense of being part of a group. But I'm so bad at it. I read my messages and then say to myself that I'll remember to reply later. And then I forget. And then, by the time I remember again, a week has passed. It's ridiculous how many of my messages start with the phrase 'I'm so sorry about the delay in replying' or the white lie 'Only just saw your message' or even the blatant untruth 'Oops, must have turned off notifications, only just got this'.

Anyway, it's all coming back to bite me as I can't find the damn email she sent.

'You're sure it was an email? Not a message on Instagram or something?'

Oh. I open Instagram and head to my messages. And, sure enough, there it is. 'You are a fucking genius.' I nestle back against her and she leans over me to drop an upside-down kiss on my lips.

When I try Karen's number, no one answers. I send a message via WhatsApp and watch as the two grey ticks appear to say it's been sent. No blue ticks appear to say she's read it though. I try ringing the number again. How many times can you try without looking like a lunatic?

'We really need to be heading down for the games,' Rani reminds me. 'Theodore will be upset if we're late to join him for coffee in the breakfast room.'

'True,' I agree with her. 'He is seriously competitive. Oh, I didn't tell you. Last night he went through all the deaths and tried to find the pattern for which one of us it'll be.'

'Which one of us what will be?'

'It's pretty obvious that there'll be more murders and it looks like someone from each team. So, one of us is going to die. You, me, Theodore, Bea. But which one?'

'I... I hadn't thought about that.'

'Apparently the first three were newbies to the games, rather than people who had been here before.'

'Which means it's one of us two?' Hmm, that sounded almost hopeful from her part.

'You don't sound bothered.'

'I obviously do not want to get sent to the VIP section without you,' she says, taking a few steps towards me so she can draw me into a hug. 'This was meant to be a chance for us to spend some time together,' she whispers in my ear. My stomach turns somersaults. I wonder if she realises she still has this effect on me?

36

SADIE

A red-waistcoated waiter brings coffee to the Red Library for us. I make a joke about how well camouflaged he is but no one laughs. I'm not sure Sebastian and Samuel actually have a sense of humour. Especially Samuel, he's looking extremely tired this morning. But at least the bags under his eyes are helping me figure out which twin is which.

'It was because of you, you know,' El says as she pours herself a coffee from the French press.

'What was because of me?' I ask.

'Why we're here at Holne Hall.'

'I don't understand.' I look at her expectantly. She really needs to be better at explaining herself, there is far too much ambiguity in the things she says. This isn't a murder mystery, she can talk like a normal human being.

'We knew we needed a team. With the sheer volume of people on the list, this job always needed at least four. But ideally six. And so we went looking. For other people who might have specific skills. And that's when we found you.'

'How did you find me?' I keep my tone casual but my heart is thumping in my chest. If they found me so easily, then that means other people can too.

'Don't worry, I doubt anyone else will.' It's as if she read my mind.

'That doesn't answer the question.' Nor is it particularly comforting.

'You must realise there are rumours, whispers around Mayfair of someone who can fix certain problems for you. You don't do this for fifty years and not pique the interest of a few people, Sadie. So I watched you for a while. You can hide yourself from the police but we can recognise each other, we can see the things no one else would.'

I don't like it one bit. The idea that killers recognise killers sounds utterly ridiculous. Is she lying to me? I will demand answers when this is over and make sure no one else can stumble into my secrets, but for now I'm just going to have to accept her explanation. 'And you saw how often I come to Holne Hall?' I ask.

'We saw Murder on the Moors and realised what a perfect opportunity it would be. A murder mystery weekend where the guests are picked off slowly, like an Agatha Christie novel. But the twist is that the deaths aren't faked.' She pauses for a moment. 'And then I saw your garden.'

Anxiety starts to bubble in my chest. It is one thing for El to have been able to figure out who I am, but it is quite another to have found the garden. All the other evidence is circumstantial at best. But the garden? That is the evidence that ties it all together.

'How?' I ask.

El smiles. 'Oh, come on now. Everyone knows what belladonna looks like.' She grins. 'Or at least anyone with half an interest in gothic literature.' Her smile drops for a brief moment. 'Fine. I have a friend. She's kind of more like a niece really, my best friend's foster-daughter. Anyway, she's eighteen and very much into romantasy novels. You've heard of them?'

I nod. Why does *everyone* assume that I'm so entirely out of touch with popular culture?

'She was reading a book and it was called *Belladonna*. I used to know someone who went by the name Bella Donna and so it piqued my interest. There was an illustration on the cover, purple bell-shaped flowers and black berries, it matched what I saw in the kitchen garden here.' She shrugs. 'It wasn't hard to put two and two together.'

I have to remind myself that the police have a much higher threshold of evidence requirements than this woman. It's one thing to make a leap when no one is in court asking for a jury to consider the facts of a case. *Yes, your honour. I recognised a fairly common plant in a hotel garden and, knowing Sadie Rose had been a guest here, I decided it must be the source of all her poisons.* It would get laughed out before it got anywhere near a trial.

* * *

Diego Perez's file had made him sound like an utter psychopath running around pretending to be anyone but himself. But the man standing in front of me in the queue for a breakfast omelette looks just like any other. He's fairly short and rotund. Maybe five foot seven and around fifteen stone. I calculate the dose I'll need. Luckily, I already have that much prepared. If he'd been over eighteen stone I might have had a problem. A non-fatal amount would be a disaster.

I strike up conversation as we wait for our breakfast to cook. I've come to eat on my own, Aly doesn't eat until at least midday apparently and the twins had breakfast early. I don't mind. It's much easier this way.

'Are you enjoying the weekend?' I ask, deliberately keeping it bland.

'My wife wanted to come.' He sounds rather bored with the whole thing. Not that I can blame him.

'And is she enjoying herself?' I ask. I wonder how much she knows about her husband's crimes.

He shrugs. 'I suppose.' He rotates slightly, just enough to signal the conversation is over, that he has nothing else to say. I pretend not to notice.

'I love this place, Holne House,' I say, edging further into his space.

'Hmm,' he says.

'Breakfast is always such a delight. The pancakes are also excellent.' I point to the pancake station. 'Award winning, in fact. You have to try them, they're perfect after an omelette.'

I watch him from my table by the window as he sits with his wife. She picks at a plate of fruit as he finishes off his omelette. His gaze drifts to the pancake station. I knew it would work to tempt him. He's certainly the kind of man who likes a sweet treat.

And atropine is so easy to disguise in maple syrup.

I make my move just after he does, so I'm directly behind him in the queue for the pancakes. The syrup is in little jugs, the perfect amount for a single serving. It will massively reduce the risk that his wife consumes any. He pays me no attention as I select a jug and carefully slip the atropine inside.

On my way back to my table I nudge him, just as he's reaching for his own little jug. He knocks it and it falls to the floor.

'Fuck's sake,' he says under his breath.

'I'm so sorry,' I say. 'Here, have mine, I'll get another.' I hand him the jug from my own tray.

'Fine,' he huffs. Ungrateful pillock.

I stoop to pick up his original jug and deliberately drop a vial labelled 'Belladonna' under his table. It's obviously not *the* vial, just a prop I made for the game, something I thought might get the guests talking. I head back to the pancake station and select a new serving of syrup, slathering it over my pancakes before I go back to my table. I like to give it time to seep into the batter. There's a tray of fresh bacon on the side and I add a few rashers to my plate. Murder has always given me a hearty appetite and I have a particular soft spot for bacon and maple syrup, even if it is an American import to the breakfast array.

Diego shovels his own pancakes into his mouth.

It'll take ten minutes before he notices something is wrong.

Eleven minutes later and I stand to leave the breakfast room.

As I'm walking towards the door, there's an almighty racket as he falls face first into the plate of pastries he had taken to round off his meal. I scream, just a poor old lady confused by the sight of a man suddenly collapsing not far from me. Then I giggle and point towards him. Oh to be so overt! Normally I slip out of a side door before my victims keel over, it's far better for avoiding capture. But now this kill is part of a wider game. And there's a team of people to help cover it up.

El was right.

Slaying together really is more fun.

37

CASSIE

There's a collective gasp as we realise it's another murder. I hear someone at the next table muttering that it's a tad off-putting to have someone die while they're still eating, but to be honest they've moaned about every single thing since Rani and I sat down fifteen minutes ago. They were especially vehement that they shouldn't have to wait for the chef to cook their omelette 'like this was Butlins'. I'm not sure they've ever actually been to Butlins, I don't think Butlins has a Champagne station with Bollinger for your morning mimosa – or buck's fizz, depending on the ratios you prefer. Even that didn't make this miserable bastard happy, though, apparently the orange juice was too warm for his taste, ungrateful git.

Anyway, the victim appears to be yet another older man. Yet another guy who has been not particularly pleasant, especially towards the staff. I noticed him snap his fingers at Karen last night, which is the ultimate sin in hospitality and will get you sworn about among the staff.

Actually, that is a good point. If the murder victims are all older men, then it's much less likely that Rani or I will be the member of our team who is killed. I glance sideways at Theodore. I don't want to lose him to the VIP area, he's been a lot of fun and he's the best chance I have of figuring out who the murderer really is. But, if it's him or Rani? Well, that isn't really a question.

'Let's go for a closer look,' Theodore says, putting down his napkin. 'Before the rest of the vultures descend.'

We shuffle past the table to take a look at the body. My toe hits something and so I reach down to pick it up. It's a small bottle, like the kind that olde worlde apothecaries use.

'What are you doing?' Rani whispers in my ear.

'It might be evidence,' I tell her as I hold it up to the light. There are traces of liquid in the bottom and I give it a tentative sniff.

'Do you have any idea what you're looking for?'

'Well... no, but it feels like the kind of thing people do in this situation.'

She holds out her hand and I give her the bottle. 'Shall we just leave it with the "body"?'

'Absolutely not.' Theodore snatches it from my hand. 'You don't give the other teams the advantage.' He seems genuinely peeved at the idea. He slips it into his pocket and then looks around quickly to check no one was watching. All eyes are trained on the two white overalled figures heading towards us with their stretcher.

'Ladies and gentlemen,' a voice comes over the speaker system. 'We have yet another murder. Tsk tsk, someone really has been busy. You have just over two hours to gather your thoughts and look for evidence in the rest of the hotel. Please gather at twelve sharp in the ballroom for transport to your next adventure.'

'Right then,' Theodore says, 'let's get sleuthing.'

We head towards the bar area so we can get a good table to act as a base for the next couple of hours. I ask the person behind the bar if they've seen Karen this morning.

'She was covering a breakfast shift,' they tell me.

I shake my head. 'She didn't turn up for it.'

They grimace. 'Ouch.'

'Does that strike you as odd?'

'Holne House has a policy for management to cover shifts in other business areas as required.'

'I don't mean her having a breakfast shift.' Nearly all hotels do that, much to the chagrin of most of us. 'I mean her not showing up for it.'

'I guess. But you know.' They shrug.

I swallow down the urge to tell them that actually I do know. I know Karen and I know she wouldn't flake out like this. Instead I order a round of coffees. I'll have to find someone else to ask about Karen. While I'm out of earshot from Rani, I try Karen's number again but still nothing.

38

SADIE

To avoid suspicion from my fellow guests, I'd sat back down after Diego keeled over, feigning shock and a need for more caffeine. I want to stay and watch Diego's body being removed from the breakfast room, but Sebastian comes over and interrupts me sipping the last of my coffee.

'Red Library,' he says without preamble.

'Yes, sir,' I mutter under my breath as I put down the cup and gather my things.

I meet Aly on the stairs as she comes down to join the festivities for the day. 'Apparently we're meeting in the Red Library,' I tell her and motion to the lift. She looks kind of tired. 'Are you sure you're OK? There's time for you to grab a pastry or something from the breakfast room. You should eat, you know.'

'You sound just like Mum,' she says with a sad smile. 'She always insisted I eat breakfast when I was at home.'

'She was a wise woman, your mother.' Aly's mum had also been a model in the mid-nineties and had seen the glorification of disordered eating first hand and she didn't want that for Aly.

'She was. But, honestly, I'm fine. I never eat breakfast, but I promise I will eat a huge lunch when we go to Dartmoor later.'

'Deal,' I say as we get into the lift.

'She can't be here,' Sebastian says when he sees Aly following me into the Red Library.

'Why not?' I ask.

Sebastian just looks at me. 'Are you serious?' he asks eventually.

'I know everything,' Aly says.

'Ha. Believe me when I say that you really don't,' he replies.

I hold my breath and wait for her response. She won't necessarily take offence at his words, but she will at the way they were said. He spoke to her like she's a child and it will vex her royally.

'Well, I know you've been interviewed as part of at least four murder investigations.' She cocks her head to one side and appraises him as the shock freezes his expression in place. 'You might get away with things for a while, but it will catch up to you one day if you aren't more careful.'

'Aly, will you be picking up a knife? Or a gun? Or a vial of poison?' El asks from the small sofa in front of the fire. It isn't lit – well, it is only the beginning of September – but this room is toasty in the winter.

'I... err—' Aly starts.

'No. She won't be,' I interject. However much she might think what I do is 'badass' and that the people I've killed deserved what was coming to them, I am drawing the line.

'Well, in that case,' El stands and walks over to us, 'I'm afraid I do need to ask you to leave. I think you can appreciate that this isn't exactly a usual situation. People like us,' she motions between herself, Sebastian and me, 'tend to work alone because it minimises the risk. Believe me when I say that we don't trust easily.'

'And yet here you are,' Aly replies, looking her directly in the eye.

'Here we are. But this room is for killers only. Perhaps you should go and find Samuel. Play the game that the hotel is putting on for you.'

'Samuel doesn't know, does he?' she asks Sebastian. There's a hint of a gotcha in her tone.

'You think I've managed to hide this side of myself from my twin for all these years?' He shakes his head as if she's stupid. 'He knows everything. He helps. Provides alibis. You have no idea how useful a twin can be. But he does not partake. And therefore he is not here in the room.' He pauses for a moment. 'And yet *you're* still here.' His left eyebrow rises a half inch.

Aly turns and walks out of the room. Then she looks back over her shoulder. 'There's a saying about keeping your friends close, you know, especially if they know all your intimate secrets.'

'All you know are rumours.' He sounds confident.

'Banbury, June 2019. They found DNA. All they need is for your sample to make its way into the system...'

He closes the door and leans back against it, glaring at me. 'I suggest that, after this meeting, you find your goddaughter and tell her to back the fuck off.' He hisses the words between his teeth. 'Tell her that we are all implicated in this scenario. El has information on all of us. And I'm sure Aly wouldn't want her favourite godmother to spend her twilight years in prison.' He gives me a pointed look. I don't much appreciate the twilight years comment, if I'm honest.

'Right.' El cuts the tension. 'Let's get to work. Shall we?' She motions to the chairs around the table. 'We have lots to discuss.'

39

CASSIE

I'm returning from a mission to find notebooks for Bea and Rani, when someone literally bumps into me, causing them to fly from my hands and onto the floor.

'Oh shit, sorry,' I say, instantly bending down to pick them up.

'No. It was my fault. I'm sorry.'

I straighten up. It's the young woman who's here with the lady Theodore has a thing for. I have no idea what her name is. All my brain can come up with is the Niece Bowerman. Why am I so bad with names?

'I'm Cassie,' I say in the end, thrusting my hand towards her.

'Aly,' she replies. 'We met yesterday, but I didn't get a chance to introduce myself.'

'Oh.' I want to punch myself in the face. 'Sorry... I'm just...' I peter out.

'Are you OK?' she asks, peering at me from behind her fringe.

'I'm looking for someone. She's an old friend who works here. Her name's Karen.'

'The bar manager?'

'Yes.'

'I met her yesterday. Is everything all right?'

'She didn't turn up for work today and I'm starting to get a bit worried.'

'Hangover?' she asks, but the rising inflection suggests she doesn't really think that's the reason.

'She is the most conscientious person I've ever worked with. There's no way it would be that.'

'Umm... I hate to say it but perhaps she met someone?' Aly twerks her eyebrows, but grimaces at the same time.

'Definitely not,' I reply. 'Well, certainly not one of the guests, anyway.' I pull a face.

'You mean she doesn't have a thing for crusty old men with inflated egos and wandering hands?' she asks with faux surprise.

We both laugh. 'I mean, there could have been someone on the staff. But I think she would have told me. Besides, it's still not her style to skip work. Anyway, sorry. I should let you get on.'

'Need some help?' she asks.

'Aren't you hunting murderers and villains?' I ask, putting on a stupid voice that I instantly regret.

She rolls her eyes. 'My godmother and I had a disagreement.'

'Oh?'

'It's nothing,' she says quickly, but I can see it's something that has properly pissed her off. I guess she doesn't want to talk about her personal life with a complete stranger though. It's funny, when I'm behind the bar people are often very fast at offloading their problems – trauma dumping might be a more accurate description – but in the real world they hold them close to their chests. 'But, I'm serious,' she says. 'I'm more than happy to help, if there's anything I can do.'

'I just don't really know where to look,' I tell her. I try not to sound too pathetic but I think I fail miserably.

'Come on.' Aly takes my elbow. She's younger than me by probably a decade, but she seems so in control that I let her take the lead. It's nice not to feel like I have to take charge for once. 'Let's see if they've cleared away the mimosa station in the breakfast hall and then find a quiet spot to make a plan.'

I follow her gratefully and we find the breakfast room empty of people but the ice bucket still full of Champagne and orange juice.

'Will your team not wonder where you are?' Aly asks as she pours the drinks.

'Probably.' I know that last night it was all I was focused on, trying to find the killer and win the competition, but now I don't even care. What was so important yesterday feels like nothing if something has actually happened to Karen.

'Have you looked at her socials?' Aly asks as we take a seat overlooking the lawns at the rear of the hotel.

I pause with my glass halfway to my lips. Why didn't I think of that? It's the most obvious thing in the world and it totally passed me by.

'I'll take your silence as a "no",' Aly says, pulling out her phone. 'Yes, I know we're not meant to have them but...' She shrugs.

I pull mine out too and she laughs. 'Karen and I are mutuals on Instagram so I'll look at that,' I say.

'Great. What's her surname? I'll look at TikTok.'

'She's Karen Peterson but I doubt she's on TikTok.'

'You might be surprised,' Aly says and less than ten seconds later she turns her screen to face me. 'This her?'

I squint at the screen. 'Yes.' Apparently Karen has ten thousand followers to whom she shows off her skills as a flair bartender. I knew she used to work in a club in Ibiza dazzling guests by juggling glasses and flipping bottles but I had no idea she was demonstrating on TikTok.

'Great. So...' She starts scrolling through the account. 'She posts twice a day, once about 6 p.m. and then again at around ten. She posted last night, but it could have been automated, I can't tell just from looking at the front-end. Hmm...' She taps the screen a few times. 'She tends to respond to comments from midnight to around 1 or 2 a.m.'

'That's when the bar would slow down and she'd finish. I guess she replies before bed. What about last night?'

'She commented on a handful, but the last one was just after midnight.'

'I was still with her then. But she didn't reply to the others before she went to bed?'

Aly shakes her head.

'Weird.'

We're interrupted by Rani. 'Oh, so this is where you are?' she says, leaning over me to pick up my drink. She blows me a kiss and then takes a swig.

'This is Aly. Aly, this is Rani,' I say, grabbing my drink back.

'Lovely to meet you,' Rani says.

'And you,' Aly replies. 'I'm just helping Cassie look for her friend.'

'Karen? Did you find anything?'

I shake my head. 'Nothing concrete.'

'Maybe you'll finally believe me that there's nothing to worry about,' Rani says.

'Maybe.' But we all know I'm lying.

* * *

Half an hour later – and another mimosa down – Theodore comes to tell us that there is someone at the door and we need to come quickly. We follow him into the main hallway with the fabulous staircase where the slight hint of barbeque still hangs in the air. They really did do a good job of staging all the murders, the attention to detail is phenomenal.

Just as we did last night, we arrange ourselves on the stairs looking down to where a man stands awkwardly, his hat held in his hands as if he doesn't know what to do with himself. He's wearing an old-fashioned tweed suit but it looks slightly ragged around the edges and his boots are caked in mud. I think it's the same actor who played the Astronomer Royal last night.

One of the other actors, a tall woman with slightly stern features, comes to join him. She's wearing an austere black dress with a white apron so I assume she's meant to be a housekeeper. 'Welcome to Holne House. And what is your business here?'

'I'm here to speak with the Marchioness of Devonshire,' he replies.

'Alas, the Marchioness is rather indisposed at the moment. What was it you wanted to speak with her about?'

'It's a personal matter.'

I can feel my attention dissipating. This is kind of boring. And I'm feeling a little light headed from drinking too many mimosas before it's even eleven o'clock. I open my notebook and flick through the pages as the conversation between the two actors continues.

But then a sentence makes me look up. Did he just say he was a waiter at the Criterion restaurant? That name keeps coming up. It must be important. Unless it's a clever red herring, something to keep my focus in one direction when I should be looking elsewhere.

'Are you sure they were talking about the Marchioness?' the housekeeper asks.

'For sure, ma'am. They mentioned her by name.'

'And do you know who any of them were?'

'I recognised one of them, ma'am. He used to dine with the Marquess before he passed. They were business partners I believe, used to conduct meetings at the Criterion. A Mr Jameson.'

'One of our victims,' Theodore whispers, bumping my shoulder with his own.

'Anything else you remember?' the housekeeper asks.

'One of them said he had a seafood allergy. He was very insistent about it.'

'How many people joined Mr Jameson and his allergic guest?'

'I don't know exactly. My shift finished before they all arrived. But the table they took was large. It could seat a dozen.'

Interesting. So a group of people met to talk about the Marchioness and at least two of them are now dead.

'We need to figure out who else was at that meeting,' I tell Theodore.

I feel him bristle with excitement next to me. 'Hopefully there'll be some clues on our Dartmoor scavenger hunt.'

We all head back to our rooms to prepare for our trip into the great outdoors. On the way I hear a commotion in one of the hallways.

'Just leave me alone.' It's a man's voice, but there's a slight tremor there, as if he's entering serious panic mode. 'I can't help you.'

'Oh come on. You're in charge here,' another man says.

I peer around the corner to see one of the guests – he's old and a little crusty but I don't know his name – and the compere. Lloyd, I'm sure his name is.

'I have no idea what is going on!' Lloyd sounds almost frantic as he twists away from the other man and hurries away down the corridor.

40

THE HIT LIST

Dossier for Insurance: Lloyd Hawkins

I turn to him. 'I do feel a little bad about this.'

'I know. Me too. But we need to be able to control the game and there is no way he'll let you step in otherwise.'

Name: Lloyd Hawkins
Team: None
Role: Compere
Relationship to the Marchioness: Not applicable
Age: 45 years
Residence: Teignmouth, Devon
Occupation: Founder of Murderous Intentions
Personal Life: Married with one daughter

Most people have something to hide. You just need to dig far enough and you'll find it. Most people will go to extraordinary lengths to bury their secrets, terrified that their whole lives will crumble to nothing if their lies are uncovered.

I don't love preying on that.

But we need Lloyd to become a stuttering fool at Holne House, so he willingly lets me take control of the game.

The threat of his wife finding out what he's been spending their savings on will do nicely. He'll keep his mouth shut and we can put our plan into action.

And don't worry. I wouldn't actually tell his wife!

Additional Notes:

Since 2021, Lloyd has been skimming money from Murderous Intentions to pay for his online gambling habit. To date, he has stolen (and lost) a total of £30,000. But that isn't the worst of it. A few months ago, he started dipping his hand into his daughter's university funds to buy gacha. His wife would probably kill him.

41

SADIE

El has given me a new folder. 'This is the full dossier. Or the "hit list", as I like to call it.'

'How many are on the list?' I ask.

'Nine. Plus there are a few others in the dossier. Yourself. Sebastian.' She nods to him. 'Oh, and Lloyd.'

'Lloyd? As in the compere?'

She grins. 'His crimes are a little less exciting admittedly, but I needed to make sure he was suitably invested in giving me free rein for this week and it's not normally that difficult to find something about a person they'd rather the world didn't know. Check out the last page,' she says.

I open the folder and scan the text. 'Oh,' I say.

'Yeah. He definitely doesn't want his wife to find that out.' She snickers.

Good old Lloyd has been using their daughter's university fund to buy something called gacha. 'You might need to help an old lady out,' I say, pointing to the page. 'I'm assuming it's some kind of porn?'

'Surprisingly no. It's basically gambling.'

'Oh.'

'Yeah. Not technically illegal, but he'd be mortified if his wife knew he was effectively stealing from their fourteen-year-old to do it.' She shrugs.

'Anyway, back to the more important stuff.' She taps the dossier. 'Have a read.'

I flick through: it details each of the men on the hit list, their names and ages and marital status, and also a big description of all their crimes. Whoever has put these together was very thorough.

'I'm impressed,' I say as I continue to turn the pages. Oh, interesting. I take it back. They are not all men.

'At the back of the file are the details of the rest of the weekend and how the game will play out. Obviously this is critical, as we need to make sure the bodies drop at the right time and in the right place.' She smiles at us.

'Hang on,' I say as I flick back to the front. 'So, you always planned for me to poison Diego Perez? This was all established already? What if I'd said no?'

'We had a Plan B,' El replies. 'And a Plan C in case Sebastian didn't want to join in. And a Plan D in case both of you were out. None were ideal obviously, but Plan D especially was seriously risky. It's very difficult to kill nine people in a weekend with only two of you.'

'Two?'

'Oh yes, you haven't actually met yet, have you?' Her smile broadens. If I were a gambling woman, I'd put my money on her being in love. 'He'll be here any second. He's just sorting out the team he's babysitting.'

The door opens and a dirty-blond head pops through. He has a spaniel with him and the dog can barely contain its excitement when it sees El. 'Sorry for being late. Theodore Frillish is a chatterbox.' When he smiles, I can see why El is so smitten with him. 'And apparently a huge dog lover.'

'His father bred springers,' I say.

'Really? Well, that explains it. Are you and Theodore well acquainted?' There's a tiny lift in his voice, just enough that I know exactly what he's asking.

'Not like that. We were friends. Once.'

'But not any more.'

'Things are complicated.' I don't want to go into the detail on why I have pushed Theodore away for so many years, especially not to a stranger.

He nods. 'Oh, how terribly rude of me. I haven't introduced myself. I'm Finn.' He points to the Murderous Intentions lanyard round his neck.

'Darling, I think we can use our real names in here,' El says.

'Right, *Rakkaani*. Sorry. I'm Alvi. It's a pleasure to meet you. And an honour. I'm a big fan of your work.'

'Thanks.' I have to admit he's put me out of sorts a little. 'I don't think anyone has ever said that to me before.'

He laughs. 'Well, probably not. It is rare to be able to be quite so open. But wow.' He takes a long exhale and then plonks himself onto one of the remaining seats. 'Isn't it so wonderfully freeing to be able to be yourself?'

'Are you...?'

He laughs again. 'Of course, darling. That's why Jess— sorry,' he corrects himself. 'I'm still trying to get my head around my brilliant girlfriend going back to her original name. Anyway, that's why *El* and I are such a perfect match.' He smiles at her with so much love I almost want to be sick. But, deep down, I know I'm just jealous. Imagine having someone know your deepest, darkest secrets and still look at you like you're the most amazing person in the world?

'Right then. Let's talk details,' El says, taking charge of the room once more. 'There are two deaths to plan for before this evening's gala, but we'll talk about those at the end as they are probably the trickiest to pull off with guests going off for picnics and whatnot. Then there're two this evening.' She looks up and grins at Alvi. 'Let's discuss those first.'

'Only because you're so desperate to reveal your plan for Viktor Romanoff,' Alvi says.

She grins. 'Yep. You got me. I'm going to kill him with the lowliest of tools. Something so banal it will haunt his ancestors for generations.' She pauses for effect. 'I'm going to stab him through the eye with a pencil.'

'Nice,' Sebastian agrees. 'Am I taking Monty Braithwaite?'

El nods.

'I think I might take a pointy leaf out of your books,' Sebastian says. 'A nice little accidental impaling on one of the stag antlers.'

'Ooh, very avant garde,' El says, before turning her attention to me. 'Sadie, you have Roger Carruthers, but in the morning. Literally the last person to die before the game is up. Obviously, once he's dead then there can't be any more questions as to who the killer is. In the game I mean,' she adds quickly. 'And then there's the denouement, before we head outside for photos and the grand reunion, or at least when the guests expect to be reunited with their murdered team mates.'

'Then... Boom,' says Sebastian.

'Exactly.' El turns to me. 'That's how we cover this all up. A huge explosion in the West Wing. Such a terrible tragedy for all those important men and women to die for real just before the weekend draws to a close.'

I have to admit it doesn't sound like the worst plan in the world. 'What about this afternoon?' I ask, flicking through the dossier to the two people who haven't yet been discussed.

'Sebastian will take Felicity Atkinson.'

'Oh.' I fail to hide the disappointment in my voice. She was the irritating woman who wanted to 'pick my brains' yesterday. She's also the CEO of a company which sells snake oil to desperate cancer sufferers. Utterly deplorable.

'Don't be sad,' El says. 'The other is yours.' She smiles like she's giving me a prize.

And I suppose she is. As a senior member of a South Korean organised crime syndicate, my victim has been recruiting drug mules. Nice British students desperate to earn some money to help pay off their student loans.

Not all of them make it back for the start of the next semester.

Oh yes, I'm going to enjoy killing Rani Kohl very much.

PART V

DARTMOOR SCAVENGER HUNT WITH PICNIC LUNCH

42

SADIE

Every year, they load us onto minibuses and off we go to Haytor. Normally I try to get out of it. But this year is much more exciting. This year, I have a murder to plan and prey to stalk.

But first I have to make amends with Aly, who is looking like a puppy who ate a wasp.

'I'm sorry,' I tell her. 'He shouldn't have been rude to you.'

'I'm not mad at him. He doesn't know me,' she replies, her voice devoid of tone. I remember her mother used to pull the same sullen face and body language when I'd tell her she couldn't join me at my Mayfair members' club for vodka screwdrivers when she was still only fourteen. 'You should have stuck up for me,' she adds.

I take a breath. Aly is kind of right. But, also, she's not thinking things through properly. 'Perhaps,' I start, putting up my index finger so she doesn't try to interrupt me. 'Perhaps I should have done. But this is a delicate situation. I know you are discreet and intelligent and could actually be an asset to this whole endeavour. But they don't know that. You're an unknown entity to them and they're nervous.'

'Fine,' she concedes eventually. 'But you're going to tell me what's going on, right?'

'No.'

'What? Why not?'

'Aly.' I turn to face her full on. 'I am not hiding things from you because I'm being mean.'

She huffs.

'Aly.' This time I use my stern voice. The one I use when other people's children – strangers or otherwise – are acting like little heathens and I want them to stop before I lose my temper. 'I am doing this to protect you. There's risk here. You understand that, don't you?'

'Yeah, I guess. But—'

'No buts. This is dangerous and if things go wrong there could be huge prices to pay.'

'You could go to prison.'

'Yes. Or attract the attention of someone who thinks I've wronged them and who would like to settle the score.'

I watch her expression as she tries that thought on for size. 'I'd not thought of that,' she says softly.

'No. But I have. I've been doing this a long time. I know what I'm doing. But even so...' I trail off.

'I would still like to know,' she says after a few moments' pause.

'I don't think you would. And besides. I want you to have plausible deniability. If we get caught, or there are suspicions from the police, I want you to be able to tell them the truth when you say you don't know what happened.'

'But I'd still be lying. I do know some of it.'

'You know more than I ever wanted you to. You were never meant to know any of it. And I'm sorry that I've put you in this position, in a place where you might have to lie for me. But I won't have you lie any more than you need to.'

She picks at the skin around her nailbed and I squash my instinct to slap her hand gently to get her to stop.

'So. Are we OK?' I ask.

'Yeah. Fine.' However mature I think she is, she still has moments when she sounds like a moody teenager, and this is the perfect example. But I'm not going to dwell on it. I've made my decision and it's final. 'Just remember that I'm an adult and I can make my own decisions,' she says quietly.

'I will remember. As long as your decision is to not get involved.'

She opens her mouth to argue but then closes it again. 'Fine.'

'Excellent. Now then, let's go and join the party.'

She rolls her eyes but follows me as I lead the way towards the minibuses.

* * *

We get to Haytor to find a team of staff from the hotel have already been to set up an area for us, with picnic blankets laid out, scattered cushions and baskets of goodies for our enjoyment.

'Ooh,' Aly says as she begins to unpack. 'There's Champagne. And a whole charcuterie board. And artisan cheeses.' She's deliberately pretending nothing happened earlier in the Red Library and I watch as Sebastian and El start to relax.

I raise my eyebrows to Sebastian. *See, I told you she wouldn't be a problem*, my look says.

We'll see.

I turn my attention to the rest of the guests as they take up spots on their own picnic blankets. I find Rani sitting shoulder to shoulder with her wife. I wonder what she thinks her spouse is up to? When she leaves her to travel to Korea?

'Who are you looking at?' Aly asks.

'No one,' I say quickly and turn my attention back to my goddaughter.

'No one? You keep looking at him, you know,' Aly says as she pops a piece of cheddar in her mouth.

'Who?'

'Theodore Frillish.' She adds a little flourish to his name.

'I am not looking at Theodore,' I reply sharply.

'Oh no no. Of course not.' She nudges my shoulder with her own.

I open my mouth for further protestations, then I close it again. This could be useful. I'm really watching Rani, of course, trying to figure out her height and weight and body composition so I can calculate the perfect ratios. But if Aly thinks I'm watching Theodore, it will keep her off the scent. 'He is rather attractive,' I say, keeping my voice casual.

'Ha! I knew it.' She beams. 'We should go over there.' She makes a move to stand up but I pull her back down to the picnic blanket.

'What are you doing?' I hiss.

'We should go over there,' she repeats. 'I met the ladies he's on a team with earlier and they are such sweethearts. They're married and they just rescued some adorable huskies. Isn't that just the cutest? Anyway, you should meet them. And then you can chat to Mr Dreamy at the same time.'

'Firstly. We are not calling him Mr Dreamy. And secondly. We are not going over there.'

'Spoilsport. Promise me you will at least try to make conversation with Mr Dreamy later?'

'What did I say?'

'Don't call him Mr Dreamy. But I'm ignoring you.'

Sebastian lets out a snort laugh.

'This isn't funny,' I tell him.

'I know,' he says. 'I just think that Aly here is more observant than most people. Which is both funny and also incredibly dangerous at the same time.'

I open my mouth to ask who exactly it is dangerous for, but the words die on my lips.

The look on his face says everything. People who watch too intently need to be careful. Surely he wouldn't actually do anything to keep her quiet?

Isn't that the whole idea of slaying together?

That we look after each other?

43

CASSIE

I've always been a big fan of the great outdoors. Or at least the idea of it. Trekking up mountains and across wide open plains and sleeping under the stars and all that jazz. It just sounds so... well, simple. Easy. Void of any expectation except getting from A to B and then maybe heating up some beans.

There was this guy I used to work with who was a carp fisherman. He'd go off to the lake for days at a time with his little tent and boxes of kit. He invited me to go with him once. There were a few moments of awkwardness when he made it clear he thought it was a date and I had to tell him that I just wasn't interested in him that way. You know, on behalf of the whole being a lesbian thing. He was totally chill though and it turned out to be a fabulous few days. There was no phone signal down by the lake, so no emails to write or phone calls to make. No laundry or cleaning or meal prep. Just total blissful nothingness.

Anyway, unfortunately my wife is into the finer things in life. A proper bed with sheets and a hot shower and a flushing toilet. So that has put paid to any idea of wilderness camping trips and the like.

But now I'm standing on top of Haytor, looking at Dartmoor spreading in front of me. You can see some of the towns and villages nestled in the valleys leading down to the sea, but they are small. Inconsequential.

I pull out my phone and try to call Karen again. I must have tried a hundred times already, but it just rings and rings.

'Can you please put your phone away?' Rani says.

'I'm trying to get in touch with Karen,' I tell her.

'Still?'

'I'm going to keep trying until I get through.'

'We're meant to be here together,' Rani says. 'As in you and me. Together. Spending quality time. Not you running around talking to everyone you bump into.'

'I promise you'll have my full attention when I find her,' I assure her.

'Ha. I seriously doubt that.' She says it quietly, almost under her breath.

I open my mouth to apologise but then I close it again. After all, Rani's the one who's always telling me I don't need to say sorry all the time. And I don't actually think I'm in the wrong for being concerned about Karen.

* * *

We're meant to be on a scavenger hunt, looking for small boxes hidden in the nooks and crannies of the rocks. I know they will contain clues and are probably the key to figuring out the murder mystery, but the longer Karen is missing, the less my heart is in it.

'I have an idea,' Bea says. 'Let's just wait for the others to find them and then follow in their wake.'

'That, my dear sister, may just be the cleverest thing you have ever said.'

We break into two teams, Bea with Rani and me with Theodore.

'You'll find her,' he tells me as we stalk the excited yelps of some fellow guests.

'I hope so. I just wish Rani wasn't being so weird about it all.'

'Permission to speak freely?'

'I've literally known you for twenty-four hours but I don't think you can speak in any other way,' I tell him.

'I think your wife may be feeling a little insecure. Perhaps a little on the jealous side. You and Karen did seem kind of close...'

'We're friends. We've known each other a long time. That's what happens when you work with someone, you spend a lot of time together.'

'Oh, I'm sure it's all perfectly innocent,' he says.

'It really is.' I would never cheat on my wife. Mainly because I love her. But also because a tiny piece of me thinks, if I did, she might just kill me. Or them.

'Make sure Rani knows that, OK?'

44

SADIE

It's just me and Aly sitting on the picnic blanket. Sebastian has left with Samuel, I'm assuming one to find silly little boxes and the other to prepare for Felicity Atkinson's imminent decline.

'Is he setting up for the next one?' Aly asks me, moving closer to me so she can drop her voice.

'Plausible deniability,' I remind her.

'Who is it?'

'What did I just say?'

She rolls her eyes. 'Fine. How about we play a game? If I guess correctly you have to tell me.'

'No.'

She blows out a stream of air. It's the same thing her mother used to do when she was mightily irritated but trying not to show it.

'Just spit it out,' I tell her. 'Whatever it is that's bothering you.'

'I would think it was obvious.'

'I thought we'd been through this,' I say, trying not to sound exasperated.

Aly nibbles the skin around her nails again and it takes all my resolve not to tick her off. Eventually she takes her fingers out of her mouth for long enough to speak. 'I don't like being treated like a child. Like a little kid who has no idea how the real world works and who has to be shielded from the truth.'

'I'm not trying to shield you from the truth because I think you're a child who can't deal with the facts. I'm trying to avoid you becoming an accessory to multiple murders,' I hiss under my breath.

'But I'm an adult who can make my own decisions.'

She does have a point there. 'Fine,' I say, clipping the word through clenched teeth.

She gets straight down to the details. 'Who is your next target?'

'It's Sebastian who is taking this one.'

'I don't care about Sebastian,' she says. 'I care about you. Who is *your* next target?'

I mull for a moment over whether I should lie to her. Tell her it's someone else. Let her think she knows the truth but could never actually be implicated by the false nature of the things she thinks she knows. Could that work? Perhaps. Until the bodies drop and she realises I was lying. 'Her name is Rani Kohl.'

'Rani?' She shakes her head. 'No fucking way. She's a travel agent.'

'She's part of a serious crime syndicate and she recruits young people to act as drug mules.'

'Absolutely not. Just look at her.' I watch as Rani makes Cassie laugh, the two women sharing a moment of cosy intimacy.

'She's playing a role,' I tell her.

'I don't think she is.' Aly is insistent. 'I've talked to her. Quite a bit actually. She showed me pictures of the puppies they adopted a few months ago. She's sweet.'

'She's a conwoman. She's taking you for a ride. You need to be more cynical.'

'I'm plenty cynical.'

I resist the urge to reach out and stroke her cheek; she would probably find the motion overly patronising. 'You're really not. You're taking this woman at face value because... why? Because she's nice. She's kind? She seems to genuinely love her wife and dogs?'

I can see her thinking through what I'm saying, the questions she knows she should ask about the woman she literally met for the first time yesterday.

'I still don't buy it,' she says eventually. But she doesn't sound quite convinced.

'Look.' I give her a long hard stare. 'Intuition can be valuable. But I didn't raise you to rely on that alone, did I?'

She shakes her head. 'No.'

'So, you know what to do. When we get back to the hotel, do some research. You have some time, I still have plans to finalise.'

'You're really going to do it?' She sounds shocked. Aggrieved, almost.

'I think perhaps we should go back to the whole plausible deniability plan. You don't seem to have the stomach for this as soon as it feels a bit closer to home.'

Aly's face drops, then even more as she realises that, yes, I am in fact being serious. This is serious. This isn't a game. El and Alvi brought me to here to help them with a problem.

Now, on the one hand I applaud their cause and every person on that hit list deserves to die. I know we're meant to debate the morality of murder and 'only God should judge' and all that stuff. But we're kidding ourselves. Men like Hugo and Jerome and Mitchell and Diego don't deserve to walk on this Earth, don't deserve to squander our species' limited resources. Especially as they take far more than their fair share of them in the first place.

But there is also one other undeniable fact.

I didn't have a choice.

They might have dressed it up with dossier teasers and cryptic letters and invitations and demonstrations of proof.

But there was only ever one choice I was making.

Kill or be killed.

But obviously I don't say that to Aly.

45

THE HIT LIST

Dossier Five: Felicity Atkinson

I know it looks like every single person on the hit list is male, but, honestly, that is only because men are just worse than women. Actually, there are statistics to back that up. In 2023, the British government released a whole report: eighty-four percent of people arrested are men and seventy-eight percent of convictions. As of 30 June 2024, ninety-six percent of the UK prison population were men. That's actually pretty staggering when you think about it, and yes there are some socio-political reasons for the disparity, but even so.

However, what those statistics don't show you are all the people who never get caught.

Ninety-two percent of murders are committed by men. Except they aren't. We just don't know many of the ones committed by women have even happened.

Apparently, the data shows that nine out of ten serial killers are men. You've watched true crime and the TV series and movies about serial killers. The clever men with their motifs and souvenirs. The ones who stage the body. The ones who scream to the world 'this is me. Look how clever I am'. But most women – or at least the ones I know – don't do that. They mix up their methods, even if they have a preference to kill in a certain way. One poison. One push down the stairs. One quick dispatch with a knife in a dark alley. Different is impossible to track. Men who go missing aren't always even factored in.

Men showcase their kills. Women quietly clean up the mess and get on with their lives.

Sexist? Probably.

True? Absolutely.

* * *

Anyway, back to dear old Felicity Atkinson. Now, she is not your typical killer. And she has never been so much as questioned for her direct involvement in the deaths of at least ten individuals.

Name: Felicity Atkinson
Team: Belstone
Role: Principle investor in MoorWell, a holistic retreat just ten minutes from Holne House

'Do you think it's a bit on the nose?' I ask Alvi. 'That in the game she runs this big wellness thing that we make very clear is a pyramid scheme?'

'You've watched her online. Do you think she is self-aware enough to even notice?'

He has a point there.

Relationship to the Marchioness: The Marchioness is an investor in the wellness retreat
Age: 40 years
Residence: Forest Row, East Sussex

'Is it bad if I put scam-artist down as her occupation?' I wonder out loud.

'Given the teams are getting all this information but without the additional notes, I'd say "yes".'

'Spoilsport.'

Occupation: Entrepreneur, owner of The Green Cure
Personal Life: Single

Additional Notes:

To kill without motive is the sign of the true psychopath. To kill innocent people who are already marked for death is even worse. You might not know Felicity Atkinson, but you will have seen her army of green smoothie-swigging acolytes who claim the expensive powders – at a cost of over £400 per month – have cured their cancer and kept them in perfect health for years since.

It is all a lie. A scam designed to get desperate people to part with their cash.

It is also incredibly dangerous.

People are dying because they eschew traditional treatments to use this so-called miracle cure.

Felicity Atkinson is killing them in the pursuit of profit.

46

CASSIE

Theodore practically jumps out of his skin as a gunshot cracks through the air.

'What the actual f—' Rani says, cutting herself off as she dives to the floor, pulling me down with her.

I just manage to stop my head hitting the ground but, for a moment, the wind is knocked from me. 'What was that?' I try to ask as I press my face into the ground.

'It sounded like a gunshot. Just stay low,' my wife hisses with an air of authority. 'All of you, stay low.' That last sentence comes out as more of a growl, laced with warning. I turn my head to look at her. She's wild-eyed, scanning the horizon like we're in some kind of action movie, every muscle tensed. As I start to sit up, she pushes me back down. 'Stay the fuck on the ground.'

'I think it's just part of the game,' I tell her, pointing to the picnic blanket on my right where a team is sitting calmly eating their charcuterie and quaffing Champagne as if nothing had happened.

She slowly turns her head to look at them. 'Oh.'

'It must be another murder,' Theodore says with glee. I look up and follow the line of the finger he's pointing. At the edge of the tor, I can see a man in a full-on hunting outfit, every single item of which is the same brown-hued tweed, staring down into the abyss below him. He turns slowly. 'It's Felicity,' he says.

A bloodcurdling scream pierces the air.

'Come quickly. She's been shot,' one of the actors announces, running towards the edge of the tor.

We all lumber up from our picnic blankets and crowd round, looking down at the pool below. A woman lies in the water, her hair framing her face, her white summer dress stained red and floating around her.

'She looks like that Ophelia painting,' Rani whispers next to me. Sometimes she sounds so much more cultured than I am and I have to pinch myself that she finds me even vaguely interesting.

'Did anyone see the shooter?' the actor asks the assembled crowd. 'Felicity was just standing here and then she was gone.' The acting is extremely bad.

'Do you think we could get some chips to go with all that ham?' Rani asks darkly. 'He's making such a meal of this.'

I swallow down my laugh as I look around. The group has gone from almost listless in the midday sun to suddenly animated, chattering to each other.

'Hmm,' Theodore says, 'I suppose we can't all be RADA trained.'

'Did you go to RADA?' I ask.

'Maybe I'll tell you about it later. Over dinner.' He gives me a wink.

'There's never been a murder outside the hotel before,' I hear someone say behind me.

A pair of people in white overalls and face masks, one of whom is carrying an old-fashioned stretcher, jog over to the pool. They wade in and then start to pull Felicity back to the shallow end. She manages to stay in character. At least she knows how to act. The pair carefully pull her out of the water and onto the flat bed. Without saying a word to each other, they carry her slowly away.

47

SADIE

Well, well, well. That was interesting. Not Felicity Atkinson, of course, that was really rather dull, even if the Ophelia framing of the body was a nice touch.

No, the interesting thing was Rani.

The way she instantly flung herself to the ground, pulling her wife with her to cover them both.

Very interesting indeed. That was the move of a woman who knows what to do in that kind of situation, who's had some training. I tuck that knowledge away into my arsenal. I might need it later, to make sure she doesn't try to do anything stupid if she figures out her time is up.

I head back to the picnic blanket and make myself comfortable again. There's no point in standing around waiting for the stretcher. Especially as this is a much better vantage point from which to watch the others. El comes to join me. 'You saw the dive?' she asks, leaning over as if she's getting another strawberry so she can say it under her breath. 'Rani, I mean.'

'Yeah. I'll bear it in mind.' Does El think I'm not watching my prey, adjusting my techniques as I learn more and more about her? Does she think I'm an amateur? Or a batty old woman going round dripping poison into cups willy nilly?

* * *

Half an hour later, the body has been removed and loaded into a small van. I don't envy whoever is driving that back across Dartmoor to the hotel. Can you imagine getting into an accident and having that discovered in the boot? You can't? Well, I can.

It was a long time ago, maybe forty years, and I had plotted the absolute perfect murder. An old pal was out for revenge against the man who had killed her daughter when he drove home from the pub high on cocaine. He was convicted of death by dangerous driving but the judge was lenient and all he got was a six-month sentence and a two-year driving ban. She might have left it there, sanguinely accepted that the justice system is a pile of rubbish and got on with the job of mourning her eldest baby girl. But then she saw him in a bar one evening and watched from a distance as he laughed and joked with his friends as if nothing had happened. He wasn't even subtle as he took a bump of coke. And then she followed him to the car park and watched him drive away.

She could have gone to the police and reported that he was not just flouting his driving ban but also still driving under the influence of illicit drugs. Instead she came to me.

'I watched him and it became clear that killing my daughter meant nothing to him. It didn't even mean enough to stop him putting someone else's daughter at risk by doing it all over again.'

'So what do you want?' I'd asked gently.

'I want it to matter. I want him to understand the gravity of what he did.'

'And then…'

'Then I want him to die.'

And so we lured him into the woods and she force-fed him a drink of crushed daphne laureola berries. It took him an hour to die and she spent that time lecturing him. It was extremely therapeutic for her.

Or at least it was until another car slammed into us as we drove home, his dead body in the boot of the car.

'Aunt Sadie.' Aly interrupts my thoughts. 'Time to head back to the hotel.'

'Right,' I say, standing up slowly. My right foot is slightly numb from where I've been sitting on it. Samuel throws me a pitying glance as I limp a few paces before the feeling comes back.

Once again we're loaded into minibuses and off we go back to the hotel, where we're instructed to gather in the main ballroom for another guess in an hour. Apparently that will give the teams ample time to analyse the little caches of clues they found. I really don't care about the mechanics of the mystery at this point. It doesn't matter if people think Team Bowerman are the murderers in the game. It'll all be revealed tomorrow anyway, and then... boom. The evidence will be destroyed and no one will ever know what really happened here this weekend. Just a tragic accident. Boo hoo. No one will put the pieces together.

'Let's go and change shoes, Aunt Sadie,' Aly says, taking my elbow and ushering me towards the lift.

'I'm fine actually,' I reply. I'm wearing trainers – well, we were out on Dartmoor – but they are the Prada ones I treated myself to from Harrods and they fit like a glove.

'Well, come with me anyway.'

'Fine.' I suppose I should pick up the vial of opium while I'm up there. Save raising any eyebrows if people see me slip out later.

'I'm still nervous about Rani,' Aly says as soon as we're inside the sanctity of our hotel room.

'It's all there, in the dossier,' I reply, picking up the folder and handing it to her.

'But what if—'

'It's all there,' I interrupt her.

'But—'

'We're five for five. Five people who you have confirmed committed the terrible things they were accused of. Why would this one be different?' I ask. Then I look pointedly at the safe where she's been keeping her laptop. 'Do your due diligence and then come and tell me I'm right.'

48

THE HIT LIST

Dossier Six: Rani Kohl

Rani Kohl looks like the kind of woman you would want to be friends with. She looks like she enjoys a nice meal and a cocktail and she will regale you with funny stories about her wife and their new puppies. It's all a front.

'Where did they get the puppies?' Alvi asks. He can't help himself if there are dogs involved; he's been running an animal rescue centre for years.

'Rescue. RSPCA, I think.'

'Hmm...'

'It doesn't mean she should be pardoned,' I remind him. 'Not after everything else.'

'I know. You think the wife will keep the puppies after she's widowed?'

I pick up my phone and tap the screen a few times to bring up Cassie's Instagram. It is wall-to-wall pictures of the dogs and she always captions the photos with monikers like 'the fur babies' and 'my son and daughter'. 'I think she'll do the right thing.'

Name: Rani Kohl
Team: Cox

Role: Head of Fundraising, Stop Animal Cruelty (SAC)
Relationship to the Marchioness: The Marchioness has been an avid supporter of SAC for many years and has donated large sums to a variety of their causes
Age: 35 years
Residence: Clapham, South London
Occupation: Travel agent
Personal Life: Married to Cassie (her partner for the weekend)

Additional Notes:

Rani speaks a number of languages, including Korean. Which she finds very helpful for her real job. Not the cover job she tells people about, in which she's apparently a slightly ditzy travel agent, but the actual job that pays the bills on the cute flat she shares with her wife and dogs.

Rani has been working for a major organised crime syndicate for over a decade, since before she even graduated. Now she shares her time between London and Seoul, recruiting mules on the syndicate's behalf. Mainly for drugs, but occasionally jewellery, proprietary technology or even information on data sticks. The mules are generally desperate students.

If the mules are detained by the authorities, she abandons them without remorse.

If the mules are discovered by rival groups... well, let's just say that there is no rescue mission.

49

CASSIE

As the guests start to gather in the ballroom, I take the opportunity to ask the staff members dotted about if they've seen Karen. I get a few blank stares and some polite shakes of the head.

'Can you please just stop?' Rani says, moving to block my way as I start to beeline towards the two men behind the bar pouring drinks.

'Why are you being so weird about this?' I ask.

'I just think you're overreacting,' Rani replies. 'She'll turn up. You don't need to meddle.'

'I'm not meddling.'

'No?'

'I don't meddle.'

'Ha.' There's a hard edge to her tone. 'You meddle constantly, Cassie. You're always sticking your nose into things that don't concern you.'

'Ladies and gentlemen.' Our argument is cut short by the arrival of El and her microphone. 'It is time for another guess. There have been two more murders since last night. Those bodies are really piling up. Someone has definitely been busy.' She pauses for the titter of laughter to ripple through the crowd.

'But is it only one killer? It feels like a lot for one person.' She pulls a face. 'Oopsie, perhaps I said too much. Maybe I shouldn't give the game away. Anyway, the task at hand remains the same. Solve the Marchioness's murder. There are points for whoever is starting to get closer to the truth. So, grab your teams and get guessing.'

We've already been through some of the little boxes we found on the scavenger hunt and analysed them. A ticket stub for a train journey from Reigate into London. A receipt for a union flag ordered from a shop in London on 27 June and signed with the initials MB.

'I remember an MB from the folders,' Theodore had said.

'Monty Braithwaite,' I confirmed. My heart wasn't in it, but I was still part of the team and had a responsibility to help if I could. You can't escape your own conditioning.

There was a copy of the *Racing Post* with an article about a Viktor Romanoff circled. Scribbled in the margin was *The Criterion, 27 June, 2pm.*

A document of minutes from some investor meeting for MoorWell. It listed Felicity as absent and was dated 27 June.

But, as I look around the other teams in the hall, some seem to have bigger stacks of clues, things that we obviously just didn't find.

'What do you think we're missing?' Theodore asks.

'A large gin and tonic,' Bea replies loudly. 'And I'm not joking.'

He throws her a withering look but then his face cracks into a smile. 'That does actually sound good. But, first, we need to solve a murder.'

'I have an idea,' I say. 'I think someone from every team went to London that day and met up at the Criterion.'

'You think it was a group effort?' Theodore drops his voice so none of the other teams can listen in.

'El did say it was more than one person.'

'It's not a bad idea,' Bea says. 'But it still doesn't explain who is killing everyone else.' She does have a point.

'Who would have the means?' Theodore asks.

'What about Team Birch?' I ask. 'They're the equestrian team. Felicity was killed with a rifle. Vets have guns, right?'

'I think they have handguns for humane reasons,' Bea interjects. 'I dated a vet once. She was extremely highly-strung, but also very adventurous if you cat—'

'Enough,' Theodore cuts her off. 'You're my baby sister and there are things I do not need to be party to.'

Bea leans in to me. 'Oh, trust me, it was definitely a party.' Then she cackles.

* * *

As soon as we've given our guess – that a group plotted against the Marchioness but Team Birch are the killers – I start looking for an opportunity to escape from the group for a bit. I'm going to try to get access to Karen's room but I don't want Rani to know. She'll only get even more irritated about me looking for her.

Karen said some of the staff live in a collection of cabins in the woods and she has a little room in one of them. So, if she did just oversleep, or she's sick, then I'll find her there. If she left – although, why the hell she would have done that, I have no idea – then it'll be obvious because all her stuff will be gone. But if something *has* happened to her? Then maybe there are clues. I have to try at least.

I get my moment to slip out when we're told that the lawn games will begin in half an hour at 4 p.m. and we're instructed to 'mingle for a while'.

I pass the old rundown keeper's cottage I overheard someone talking about last night. Not going to lie, it looks haunted, the kind of place that's full of scary stories of witches and ghosts. Not the kind of place you'd want to go on your own. A shiver runs up my spine and I carry on until I find the cabins.

Actually, calling the staff accommodation 'cabins' feels like it's doing some heavy lifting. They're static caravans, ancient things that have probably been here since the seventies, with gaps around some of the windows and rust marring the outside. I bet they're fucking freezing in the winter. Karen did say they have their own bathrooms inside, with running hot water from the main house, so I guess I've seen worse. Staff digs are often pretty horrendous, the hospitality industry can look glamorous as you clack around a stately home in a nice pair of heels and a well-cut suit, but the reality is normally much less salubrious. In my first job, I shared a one-bed flat with four others: we would work opposite shifts so two were working while the other two got to use the twin beds. It was chaos but also kind of fun, at least for the summer; I couldn't hack it for any longer than that.

A tall man with a thin face sticks his head out of the door of one of the cabins. 'Sorry love, this area is out of bounds for guests.' His words are friendly enough, but there's an undercurrent in his tone, like he's pissed off and only half trying to cover it.

'Sorry. I'm looking for someone,' I say.

'This area is out of bounds for guests,' he repeats, a little more of that pissed-off tone leaching in.

'I understand. And I'm really sorry to disturb you. It's just that I'm looking for someone. Karen?'

'This area is out of—'

'Yes, I get it. Do you know her? Karen? She's assistant manager of the bar.'

He does this thing that is like a nod and a shrug at the same time.

'What does that mean?' I copy his action but exaggerate it to make it almost farcical. The look on his face suggests he didn't appreciate the caricature.

He takes a breath in. 'I know Karen.'

'She didn't show up for work this morning and she's not answering her phone. I just want to make sure she's OK.'

'I'm sure she's fine. Probably flaked out. Not everyone can hack it.'

'Karen can. She hasn't flaked out. I think something has happened to her.'

He laughs. 'You her girlfriend or something?' He narrows his eyes. 'Or has she been shacking up with your boyfriend? I bet that's it.' He looks smug.

'She's an old friend. We used to work together. I think something has happened to her.'

Why does no one seem to give a shit? I feel like a detective in a small-town murder mystery where all the other residents are closing ranks. But, in those shows, it's normally because one of the townspeople is the killer. Is that what this is? Did something happen to her last night and the hotel is covering it up? Are the staff part of it? Suddenly the darkness of the forest feels like it's pressing in around me. The tall, thin-faced man with the smirk takes on a more threatening presence.

'I'm sure she's fine,' the man says, making a motion to close his door.

'Wait! Could you just take a look for me? See if her room is empty? If she took any of her stuff with her?' But, even as I'm saying it, I realise that, if the hotel was trying to cover it up, all they'd have to do was clear out her stuff and say she quit. No one would bother looking any further. It would be so easy to conceal something in a place like this.

'Just go back to your party,' the man almost growls. 'I was on the night shift. I need to sleep.'

I wait for him to close the door and then I hurry around the back of his cabin. He kept looking to the cabin to his left. I'm pretty sure that is where Karen lives.

The door isn't locked.

But she isn't there. All her stuff is though. Including her uniform, folded neatly on her bed.

I reach into the pocket of her apron and pull out the tiny notebook she always carried. Inside is her scrawl, barely legible. The first pages are observations about customers, little things they've said, funny anecdotes. The last few pages are things she wants to implement in the bar to improve service and efficiency.

I flick through the rest of the pages and find some where her handwriting is even worse.

I think the murders might be real…

But then who is killing them?

And why?

The word 'why' is underlined three times.

It looks like the ramblings of a nutter. Someone unhinged, unstable. But Karen is none of those things. She's one of the most logical people I've ever met. That's one of the reasons we always got on so well.

If Karen thinks there is something odd going on here, then there is in fact something odd going on.

I scan the rest of the pages.

Why is there a separate roster for the VIP area?

The names on the VIP roster are all agency staff.

Why are we using agency staff for this?

Why would a hotel of this size use agency staff for this weekend? It doesn't make sense to staff an entire area that way. You always mix the agency people in with the permanent staff, that's the kind of thing you learn on day one of the job.

And didn't she say something about a new member of staff being in charge of the VIP area? The concierge who checked me and Rani in. That's weird too, it's the kind of task you'd give to someone more senior and more established.

'What the hell are you doing?' I whirl round to come face to face with the tall man. 'I told you to fuck off back to your party.'

'But—'

'Get the fuck out of here.' His voice booms through the small space. He might be wiry but I notice there's a quiet strength to him, forged by hours on his feet, carrying stuff for guests. He could hurt me if he wanted to.

I run.

50

SADIE

Aly didn't make it down at all for the guessing, not that it matters seeing as we know who the killers are, but we should probably keep up appearances. I want to check on her and so, when we break again, this time to mingle before we head to the lawn for the afternoon of games and even more food, I go back up to the suite. I find her hunched over her laptop, shoulders slumped in a way that will come back to bite her in twenty years. I clear my throat so she knows I'm there.

'Oh, hey Aunt Sadie,' she says without looking up from the screen.

'You OK?'

'I...' she starts but trails off.

'You found something?' I ask gently. 'About Rani?'

She nods, chewing the skin around her nail on her little finger. Such a horrible habit.

'And?'

Aly sighs. 'It's all here. The links to organised crime. The recruitment of mules. I found evidence that two of the people she recruited were students at Surrey University, they were like nineteen years old.' She makes it sound like that is decades younger than she is. 'They got caught. Ten years in prison. Their entire twenties just gone. Poof. And then there was a guy she recruited who went missing in Seoul and a rival gang claimed they had killed him. Another life destroyed.'

'So, basically, exactly like it says in the dossier?' I say gently.

'Yeah.'

'OK. So that's that then.'

'I still don't buy it.' She finally drags her eyes from the screen to turn to face me. 'Rani isn't this person.'

I take a breath. 'Except she is. Look, Aly, I know it isn't what you wanted to find, but people lie to us all the time, they pretend to be one thing and then they turn out to be something entirely different. That's just life.'

'Yeah, but—'

'Haven't you met people who aren't who they seem at the beginning? What about that boy you were dating?'

She shivers involuntarily. They dated for two years when she was in college and he tried to tear her down at every available opportunity. Until he got caught in possession of methamphetamine and was kicked out. She hasn't heard from him since. Or at least that's the part of the story she knows about. He wasn't a drug dealer, never even touched the stuff for his own consumption. Aly thinks he lied to her about that, covered it up as he knew she'd dump him if she found out. All I'm going to say is that it was surprisingly easy to source 'ice' and even easier to slip it into his pocket.

Do I feel a little guilty for lying to her about the boy? Not really. Sometimes you have to break the rules to get an acceptable outcome. And I could have just killed him. I still keep an eye on him, waiting for him to find a new victim, a new girl to control. If he does, then I might have to pay him another visit.

'But what if—'

'Aly,' I cut her off. 'Seriously? The information is right there in front of you. You said it yourself. She did those things.'

'I'm just saying, what if you're wrong?'

But we're not wrong. Rani did those things. She's guilty. I'm doing this and I'm going to feel extremely good about ridding the world of yet another psychopath who ruins other people's lives in the pursuit of their own profit.

And then I'm not going to think about her again.

PART VI

AFTERNOON TEA AND GAMES ON THE LAWN

51

CASSIE

Everyone is still floating around the communal areas waiting for the afternoon's entertainment to start, so I go to find the others, desperately trying to slow my breathing down to something more normal.

'Why do you have leaves in your hair?' Rani reaches out and plucks something from my braid.

'I went for a walk. I needed some fresh air.' I try to sound nonchalant. I fail miserably.

'What did you do?' Her eyes narrow as she looks at me. It's the same expression she uses when accusing one of the puppies of doing something naughty, like chewing her socks.

'Nothing.'

She pulls me away from the others. 'Don't lie to me, I'm not in the mood.'

'I just went for a walk.'

'Fine.' She huffs. 'We're playing this game, are we? So, where did you go?'

'Just on the grounds. There are some woods. It was pretty.' I offer her a beaming smile as if that will help to strengthen my argument of innocence.

She pulls her phone from her back pocket and taps the screen a few times. She turns it to show me the screen. An aerial view of the hotel and the grounds in Google Maps. 'Show me where you went.'

'No phones.' Finn comes striding over, his focus entirely on the contraband technology.

'But—' Rani starts but he cuts her off.

'No exceptions. It's in the rules.'

Rani stares at him for a few moments. 'Fine. We'll take it back to the room.'

'We?' I ask.

'I don't think we've finished our conversation, have we.' It isn't a question. She turns and heads towards the main stairs. I follow her. I'm seething that she's talking to me like I'm a five-year-old but I'm also desperate to apologise, to smooth things over. I hate feeling like this.

We don't speak until the door closes on our room and we're alone.

'You went to the staff accommodation, didn't you?'

'I... I...'

'What did I say? You need to leave this alone. It's none of your business.'

'But maybe it is my business. She's my friend.'

'She was a colleague. Someone you worked with for a couple of years and who you've not even mentioned since she left.'

'You're jealous.' As soon as the words are out of my mouth, I realise how true they sound. Theodore was right. 'You never liked Karen, did you?'

'It's not like that.'

'Did you think there was something between us?'

'Of course not. I know you and I know you wouldn't do that. I just thought she was a bit... well... she'd say things that were a little off and the few times I went for drinks with you and your team, she'd just stand there and give me these looks. Like she didn't understand why you were with someone like me.'

'Is that why you wanted to come this weekend? To find out why she invited me?'

'No.' But she says it so quickly, and she won't meet my eyes.

'Well. The joke's on you. She didn't send the invite.'

'She didn't?'

'No. So you can stop being so fucking weird about her. I think something has happened to her. Something bad. And I think the hotel is trying to cover it up. Haven't you noticed that no one cares? No one seems to be worried. What if they're part of it?' I don't add a 'hmm' to my final sentence, but I want to.

Rani stares at me for a full twenty seconds. 'Jesus fucking Christ, Cassie.' She says it softly, shaking her head at the end. What is that? Pity?

'What?' My defences spring up.

'You sound like a conspiracy nutjob. Like the hotel is covering up an industrial manslaughter or something.'

'What if they are?'

'They aren't.' The words explode from her mouth. She rarely gets angry, but when she does, the entire world knows about it. 'Can't you just leave it alone. Can't you be fucking normal for once. This weekend was meant to be for us. A chance to spend time together. We hardly see each other as it is.'

'And whose fault is that?' I ask, barely keeping my own rage in check. 'You're always away with work, skipping around the world and leaving me in London on my own.'

'You knew what my job was like before we got married,' she says defensively.

'I didn't know what it would be like when it's day after day, month after month. You know I'm not good on my own for longer periods of time.'

'I'm so sorry my job isn't more accommodating to your many needs,' she spits.

'There's no need to be mean,' I reply.

'I'm not being mean. You're fucking exhausting. Sometimes it's like being married to a child who is desperate for everyone to love them, but who won't take ownership for their own actions.'

'I'm sorry.'

'For fuck's sake.' Her voice rises by a full octave. 'You don't have to apologise every fucking time. Stand up for yourself. If you think you were in the right, tell me.'

I don't say anything for a few moments as I try to find the right words to convey how I feel. I don't want us to argue. I hate it when we fight. But I don't know what to say to make it better, and I certainly don't know how to make it better without apologising again. And I don't want to apologise. I *know* it isn't all my fault. I *know* our arguments are because we both have flaws.

'You're not going to say anything?' she asks, that old edge of exasperation back. Once again, she shakes her head a few times. 'I just can't even...' she trails off. 'Fuck this shit,' she says as she turns and walks towards the door.

'Where are you going?'

'Back to the party. We're meant to be playing a murder mystery game, remember?'

I stare at the door as it closes behind her. She's right, we are meant to be playing a murder mystery game.

But what if it isn't a game any more?

52

SADIE

I head to the Red Library to meet Sebastian and El. They want to know exactly what my plan is for Rani. To be honest, I'm not really sure how I feel about having someone mark my homework. This whole 'slaying together' thing does feel like it comes with an unnecessary level of scrutiny. I've been doing this for longer than the rest of them put together. Doesn't experience count for anything these days?

We only have about five minutes before we're due on the lawn for afternoon tea and more games. There's a sign-up sheet in the entrance hall for people who want to play giant chess and shuffleboard and boules.

Sebastian joins me after a few minutes and sprawls into one of the chairs. He seems a little on edge.

'Everything OK?' I ask.

'Hmm?' He acts like he barely realised I was in the room before I spoke. 'Sorry. Just...' he trails off. 'It's nothing.'

'You look like you have something on your mind.' I press the issue. After the way he spoke to Aly earlier, I'm still wary of him and what he might do if he thought things weren't going his way.

'I'm fine. Where's El?'

I'm about to say I'm not sure when she throws the door open and comes into the room, all smiles and bouncy energy. She makes me tired just looking at her. 'Right then,' she says with a grin. 'What's the plan, Ms Rose?'

I clear my throat. 'Well, I've decided to do this one a little differently,' I start.

Sebastian says something under his breath, but it's so quiet I can't hear what he says.

I carry on. 'We've had a lot of murders now and everyone will have figured out there are more to come.' El nods as if I just made a particularly profound observation. 'Which means there are many potential eyes out there, watching, waiting.' I pause for a moment. 'There are too many people ready to spot a sleight of hand if I slip poison into a cup in front of them all.'

'So, you're not going to take her out?' Sebastian asks, finally sitting up a little straighter.

'That isn't what I said, no. What I said is I want to do this one a little differently. I'm going to get Rani out of the crowd and then do it. Use something slow-moving enough that she'll make it back out to the other guests but then...' I clap my hands together.

'I don't get it,' Sebastian says.

'It's really not that complicated,' I tell him. 'The other guests have seen enough to know that one of them from each team is going to "die". They will be expecting it by now.'

Sebastian looks at El. She shrugs. 'I guess Sadie does kind of have a point.'

How very generous of her. 'Anyway, Rani's card last night will have told her she had to lie about not being at the Criterion on 27 June. So, she knows she's part of the game. She just has no idea that it's real. So, I'll get Alvi to take her to one side and he will tell her she's the next victim. She'll simply follow him into the main building as she assumes she's about to be briefed on the how and when and what she needs to do to make it look all nice and realistic.'

'And then?'

'Then I'll get her to drink the poison herself.'

'Right then,' El says, standing up and brushing down her skirt. 'Let's get back to the weekend festivities. I'm assuming you both put your names down for something?' She looks from Sebastian to me expectantly.

'Samuel and I have signed up for Jenga,' Sebastian says.

'Good. And you, Sadie?'

'I shall observe from behind a glass of Champagne. I'm seventy-two, no one is expecting me to play Twister.' El laughs. 'It's just a shame there isn't any poker,' I add, almost under my breath.

'Amen to that,' she replies.

'You play?'

'A bit.' But a smile licks the corner of her mouth, she's being coy. 'You?'

'A bit,' I mimic her response.

'Maybe we should play one day?'

'Maybe we should.'

53

CASSIE

The lawn has been set up similarly to yesterday, with tables for each team, white tablecloths fluttering in the breeze. Dotted around the edges of the lawn are game stations; giant Jenga, shuffleboard, chess. Down some stone steps, the lower lawn has been divided into sections; boules, croquet, mini-golf. It's like the wedding of someone who was utterly unable to say no to the salesman from the hire company.

I'm not quite sure what the link is to the murder mystery weekend though.

'Shall we play mini-golf?' Theodore comes up behind me to ask. 'It might take your mind off things.'

'What's the point?' I ask.

'Err... well...' Theodore tugs at the silk cravat he's wearing, it's the same brilliant blue as his eyes and looks surprisingly dapper.

'This isn't me having an existential crisis,' I tell him. 'I meant in terms of the games.'

'Oh, right.' He visibly relaxes. 'I actually don't think there is one.' He frowns for a moment and then shrugs. 'Oh well. Shall we play pointless mini-golf anyway?'

'Sure.'

'I'll sign us up for a little later.'

He skips off and I head over to our table. I need a drink and I can see bottles of Champagne in ice buckets. I sit down but Rani refuses to meet my eye. That's how I know she's still mad at me. But I'm not actually sure why. Is it for looking for Karen? For daring to have friends that aren't her? She must have thought something was going on between me and Karen – which is so utterly ridiculous, you have no idea – and I think she thought that was why she invited me here. Even if we now know Karen didn't send the invite.

I just don't understand why she isn't concerned. Intuition is telling me Karen is at risk, that we need to find her. Karen thought there was something strange going on too.

And then it hits me.

No.

She wouldn't.

I sneak my wife a look. She's been acting a little off all weekend. But, surely, she wouldn't have done something? I think back to last night and the feeling that someone was watching me in the bar. I'd know if it was my wife stalking me, though, wouldn't I?

And when I got into bed and she obviously hadn't had a bath.

What if she was waiting for me to come back and fall asleep? What if she slipped out afterwards?

No.

This is far too much of a reach.

Isn't it?

54

SADIE

It's showtime. Everything is ready. The scene is set. So to speak, at least.

One of the smaller parlour rooms next to the main ballroom is the perfect setting for this murder. The room is exquisitely ornamental, with so much gilt it's almost blinding. Everything that isn't gold coloured is a pale, almost baby blue. Brocade wallpaper, matching upholstery for the small sofas in a square around a low coffee table. Around the edge of the room are dark mahogany sideboards.

I potter around, touching my finger to a few of the decorative items. Pictures of long-dead relatives of the Holne family, candelabra, a carriage clock on the mantelpiece. There is so much history in this room, so much that it has witnessed.

I'm interrupted by a knock on the door. It opens slowly to reveal Alvi, with Rani just behind him.

'Oh my God,' Rani says, her eyes wide and a huge smile on her face. 'This room is insane. It's like the set of *Bridgerton*.'

I cough quietly to get her attention.

'Argh. It's you! Ha! I never even guessed.' It doesn't feel like it should be possible but her smile grows even wider. 'Theodore and Cassie are convinced it's Team Birch, the horse-trainer lot.'

Somehow it doesn't surprise me that Theodore is barking up the wrong tree. He's always been so competitive at these weekends but he's always wrong. Every single time. And I think he's been almost twenty times. You'd think he'd at least have grasped the basic principles by now.

'How are you going to kill me?' she asks, looking around the room as though searching for a weapon.

'All very boring, I'm afraid,' I tell her.

'Poison?'

I nod.

'I was kind of hoping for a dramatic fall over the balcony,' she says. 'But hey-ho.' I have to admit she is a very good actress. She's so convincing as the sweet woman with the loving wife and cute dogs that I can understand why Aly is so taken in. But a wolf in sheep's clothing is still a wolf.

Can I picture her recruiting innocent students and getting them to mule for her? Convincing them that there is no real risk and it's easy money?

Of course.

But she won't do it again.

55

CASSIE

I come back from the bathroom to find Rani has gone. I take the opportunity to neck another glass of Champagne without her judging me. I've had a little time to calm down and think about things. Of course my wife hasn't done something nefarious to Karen, that's just silly. She might be jealous and occasionally her anger takes over... but she isn't violent. She isn't the kind of person who could hurt someone.

Besides, Karen thought there was something fishy going on in the hotel. It was there in the notebook, but not enough information to actually be helpful. I top up my glass again. I probably should be careful not to get shit-faced this afternoon, but another glass won't hurt. Theodore and Bea are playing chess and I head over to join them.

'Oh, there you are,' Theodore booms, stepping forward to give me a hug. 'Do I detect a little tension still?' he asks kindly, his hands on my shoulders as he looks me directly in the eye. He's like a kindly uncle.

'I'm fine,' I tell him, even though I think he can see straight through the lie.

'Would stronger alcohol help?' He waggles his eyebrows.

I glance at my watch. It's only four-thirty and over two hours till dinner.

'Oh, come on, we can have sandwiches to mop it up again,' he says with a conspiratorial wink.

'Well in that case...'

'Excellent.' He claps his hand on my back. 'Let's go and find that bar manager friend of yours and see if she can wangle us a cocktail.'

'Karen? She...' I trail off.

'She's still missing?' Concern skitters across his face.

'You haven't been able to call her?' Bea asks, joining the conversation.

'I tried. So many times. And then I went to her staff accommodation but she wasn't there and then some dickhead got mad at me and then Rani and I had an argument and—' I cut myself off just as the tears prick my eyes. I feel wrung out. Overwhelmed. I don't know what I'm meant to be doing. Or what I'm meant to think. Rani can't have had anything to do with Karen going missing. She just can't.

Not even if she saw you with her last night?

But that still wouldn't explain the notebook.

This is making zero sense and I can feel a headache building behind my left eye.

'I had a friend who went missing once,' Theodore says, his tone imbued with a level of joviality that I feel is entirely for my benefit.

'Boring,' Bea whispers under her breath. She goes back to the chess game.

'Ignore my sister. Anyway, my friend was meant to meet us at the airport. We were going skiing for the weekend and everyone was extremely excited about a fresh dump of powder and the promise of some really rather good après ski. But he never made it to the airport. We went without him, but it slightly ruined the trip.'

'Did you ever find him?'

'Oh yes. A few months later, he bowled up at the Athenaeum on Pall Mall – we were all members – and he just walked in as if nothing had happened.'

'What had happened?'

'He never told us. Said it was nothing. That it didn't matter. Then he ordered a round of drinks for everyone and never mentioned it again. To this day, I have no idea. Maybe he shacked up with a girl. Or got himself arrested.'

'I always assumed he was abducted by aliens,' Bea says. 'It would certainly explain a few things,' she adds drily.

'My point is that she'll turn up.'

'I hope so.'

'Let's make a deal,' he says, leaning in closer. 'If she hasn't reappeared by first thing in the morning, then I'll come with you to tell the police and file a missing person's report.'

'Thank you.'

'You're welcome. Now then, let's go and find someone to get us a drink. I'm parched. And no doubt we're about to get treated to another dead body.'

We weave through the guests on the lawn and head inside to the bar. 'Shall we have negronis?' he asks as we approach the slab of polished oak.

'Sounds good to me.'

'And for your wife?'

I look around, trying to catch a glimpse of her. 'I don't know where she is.'

'I'll get her one anyway.'

He orders and we wait for our drinks to be made.

'Were you and Karen ever a couple?' he asks, once our negronis have been acquired. He makes it sound oh so innocent. Far too innocent. He's fishing for gossip, it's clear as day.

'No. Never.'

Just as I'm about to take a sip of my cocktail, Aly comes running up to me. 'Where's Rani?' she asks, breathlessly.

'No idea. Why?'

'I think she's next...'

'What do you mean "next"?'

She looks into my eyes and my blood runs cold.

56

SADIE

Rani has a lot of questions about the poison and so I answer her honestly. I have no reason to lie about what a massive dose of pure opium will do. All she doesn't know is that all this is real. I can't risk her trying to run and ruining the whole plan in the process.

I even show her the vial.

'The main thing you'll need to fake is breathlessness, that's the primary symptom with an opium overdose. And then just collapse. Nice and easy.'

'This is going to be fun,' she says with a smile.

'It really is,' I confirm. It's taking all my self-control to retain my composure and not break into a manic grin that might tip her off. It's very rare that I get to talk through my methods with a victim. Most of my kills have necessitated a level of distance between me and them. And the few times I've had more intimacy in my kills, they've been frozen in fear at the realisation of their impending doom. This is completely different to that. A detailed dissection of what is to come, but with no realisation and therefore no fear.

'Just promise there're good drinks and decent food in the VIP area,' she says.

El steps forward. 'On behalf of Murderous Intentions, I can promise you will be treated with all the consideration you deserve.'

I stifle my laugh. El and I both know Rani deserves everything coming to her, including a place on a metal gurney in the hidden cold store within Holne House's secret passageways.

Sebastian comes to join us and gives me the nod to say that everything is ready.

'How about we share a glass of brandy to set the mood?' I ask, motioning towards the decanter on the coffee table.

'Well, it only seems fair I get to have one before I stumble into the throng and fake my death.'

'Everyone else?' I ask the others.

Sebastian and El nod so I pour them a healthy measure and hand it to them.

'Alvi?'

He nods.

A look of confusion crosses Rani's face. 'Finn? Did she just call you—'

'Just a nickname,' he interrupts her. The lie is smooth. 'Apparently I look like an old flame, don't I, Sadie?' He raises his eyebrows.

'Yes.' I lean in to Rani, as if we're sharing girlie secrets. 'Cute but a little too self-absorbed in the end, it didn't last.'

She giggles and Alvi shoots me daggers.

I pour the contents of the vial labelled 'Opium' into the penultimate glass and then top it up with brandy. 'Don't worry, you won't taste it, it's just part of the game.'

Once my own glass is poured, I raise it in front of me. 'Here's to the fiftieth anniversary of Murder on the Moors, and to our sixth victim, Rani Kohl.'

'Shouldn't that be Rani Cox?' she quips.

I watch as she raises the glass to her lips.

But then there's an almighty commotion as the door slams open.

'Don't drink that!' Aly cries as she launches herself across the room. She slaps the glass from Rani's hand. 'The poison is real.'

Rani's wife is right behind Aly. 'What the actual fuck is going on?' she demands.

57

CASSIE

Rani is sitting on a small sofa, her hand raised as if she were still holding the glass.

The contents are splashed over the carpet and the glass itself rolls to a stop, making a tinkling sound against the wooden leg of the coffee table.

Aly's godmother Sadie is standing close to her, her mouth forming a perfect 'O'. El, who has taken over most of the compering, is there, along with Finn and one of the creepy twins from Aly's team.

I take in the scene, time slowing down until it's barely moving.

'What is going on?' I ask. None of this makes sense.

Rani smiles at me. 'I'm the next victim in the game.' There's a waver there, as if she isn't quite sure what's really happening.

I glance at the splash of liquid on the carpet. 'What was in the glass?' I ask Aly, trying to keep my voice level.

Sadie smirks. It doesn't look right on her face, turns her features from cool older aunt to bitter pensioner who thinks she's better than everyone else. 'Don't worry, I can always pour another.'

'Aunt Sadie, you can't do this,' Aly says.

'Aly,' she replies, the warning in her tone clear as day.

'At least give her a chance to tell you the truth about Korea,' Aly pleads.

'What are you talking about?' I ask.

But the others ignore me. Not even Rani acknowledges my existence as she stares at Aly.

'Rani.' Aly steps towards my wife from her position by the door. 'I need you to answer something, OK? This is important.' Her eyes dart from Sadie to me and then back to Rani. 'It might be the only way…' She trails off at the end of the sentence.

'Answer what?' I ask.

'Who are you all?' Rani asks. Her whole demeanour has changed. Where before she was almost giddy, now she's on edge, shifty, nervous.

'I don't think you're the one who should be asking that,' Sadie says, that smug expression mimicked in her tone.

This is going in circles. I want to scream. 'Will someone just tell me what the fuck is going on here?'

Aly throws me a look. One that says be quiet. Sadie throws me one too.

Fuck this! 'If no one tells me what is fucking happening in two minutes, I'll scream bloody murder,' I warn them. I've had it up to here with this. All I want is to have a cocktail, figure out who killed the Marchioness in this silly little murder mystery, and then get a call from Karen telling me she's fine and she just got laid and decided to skive off work. And then I want to have another four cocktails, maybe five, and let the edges get all fuzzy for a little while. Quite frankly, I don't think it's too much to ask.

Aly and Sadie exchange looks. Sadie gives a subtle lift of her shoulders as if to say, 'You created this mess, so sort it out.' Aly turns to me. 'Fine.' She sounds pissed. 'Where was Rani on the 19th August?'

Oh. Well, that wasn't what I was expecting. 'This isn't about Karen going missing?' I ask.

'What?' Aly says. 'Of course not. Why would it?'

'Rani? Did you have anything to do with Karen going missing?' I direct the question to my wife.

'What? No. What are you talking about?' She's looking directly at me and, in that moment, I know she's telling the truth. Shit. I shouldn't have even thought it. How could she have done? Stupid girl.

'Can we please focus here,' Aly says. 'Where did Rani tell you she was on the 19th August?'

If this isn't about Karen, then… Oh. Suddenly my blood runs cold. That's the kind of question someone asks if they think someone has been cheating. But not Rani. She wouldn't do that. She doesn't have it in her. I try to think back to last month.

The answer comes to me. 'Amsterdam.' I sound kind of smug to my own ears, like I'm patting myself on the back for having such a good memory and being able to prove where my wife was. 'You were reviewing some of the hotels at Schiphol Airport. You went for four nights and I remember it specifically because one of the puppies was sick and so I slept on the kitchen floor with them. We FaceTimed from my makeshift nest on the lino.'

'Except you didn't go to Amsterdam. Did you, Rani?'

Rani gives Aly a look that would freeze water in its tracks.

'Where did you go? Tell your wife where you really went that week.'

'Rani?' I ask. 'What is she talking about? You went to Amsterdam. You bought me back that huge bag of Tony's Chocoloney from the airport shop. I remember because I didn't believe the company was Dutch and so I had to google it.'

I wait for Rani to make a comment about how I always have to look things up when a question arises and how irritating it is when it interrupts the flow of conversation or I make her pause the TV for a moment. But she doesn't. Instead she says, 'Cassie... I...' as she twists her hands together and refuses to look at me. 'I did go to Amsterdam. I flew from Gatwick to Amsterdam on the 19th and then came back on the 23rd.'

'I don't understand.'

'I went to Amsterdam. But then I took another flight. From Schiphol to Incheon. Seoul. In South Korea.'

I stare blankly at her. I have no idea what I'm expected to say. I have too many questions. But, I guess in the end, there is only one that matters. 'Why did you lie to me?'

'Look,' Aly says. 'It isn't that I don't want to witness you two having an argument. But we really need to focus right now.'

I spin round to face her. 'Sorry. But why the fuck is this any of your business?'

She looks at me for a moment before visibly sighing and turning back to Rani. 'Are you working for a Jopok syndicate?'

'Who are you?' Rani asks, all the emotion drained from her voice. I've only heard her sound like that once before. When she thought there was an intruder in our house and she made me hide under the bed while she went to investigate. It turned out to be nothing but, at the time, I remember her being so calm, it was uncanny. Something is very wrong here. I glance around, instinct telling me to find a weapon. Any weapon. There's a folder on the sideboard next to me. I edge my hand towards it, my finger curling around the edge. It's stupid really, but, if push came to shove, I could lamp someone round the head with it.

'Are you working for a Jopok syndicate?' Aly asks Rani again. 'Just answer the question.'

But Rani doesn't answer. Instead, she turns to me. 'You have to trust me, Cassie. Do you trust me?'

I nod. Our relationship isn't perfect and we argue a lot more than I'd like, but I would go to hell and back for this woman. Even though I have no idea what is going on, what a Jopok is or what was about to happen to Rani when we burst in.

'OK.' She gives me an intense look, as if she's weighing up the options. But what options? I have no idea what she's thinking. Then, suddenly, she leaps to her feet and rushes towards me. 'Run!'

I do what she says and together we burst out of the room.

We keep running without looking back.

58

SADIE

Merde.

59

CASSIE

I can hear Rani behind me as I run. But from what? Or from whom? None of this makes any sense. Rani asked me if I trust her, and I do, or at least I think I do. Is it possible to both trust someone and still question everything they do? Perhaps if you're like me and have to constantly overthink everything to the nth degree.

I'm still carrying the folder I picked up and it's digging into the flesh under my arms. But I can't drop it and so I just hold on for dear life. If they catch us, I'll be glad to have it.

'Head towards the woods,' Rani says. She's so much fitter than me and she doesn't sound out of breath at all. On the other hand, I can feel my heart thumping in my chest, my breathing becoming faster and faster.

'There's a cottage,' I try to say, but it comes out like a garbled squeak. I really need to start exercising a little more. We've only been running for a minute or two and I can barely squeeze out a few words.

'Cottage?' Rani asks.

'In the... woods. Old. Grounds... grounds... groundskeeper.' I manage to get the words out eventually. I debate telling her that I overheard some crusty old dude talking about it last night, but I decide it's not worth the energy. I don't have enough of it to waste.

I keep trying to look back to see if anyone is chasing us. 'Just run. Don't look,' Rani tells me in a strict voice she rarely uses. 'We need to get out of sight as quickly as possible.'

'Then. Will you... tell. Me... what—'

'Just stop fucking talking and run. Jesus Christ. We need to get you in the gym.'

'Just... promise you—'

'I promise I'll tell you what's going on,' she says. 'That is if they haven't caught us first. When did you get so slow?'

I don't tell her that I've always been this slow. That she's barely ever around for us to do nice couple's things like Saturday morning jogs in the park. Actually, scratch that. Running is not a nice activity, even if it was with her and there was the promise of a fancy coffee and possibly a joint shower afterwards.

We reach the trees and take the left-hand path. I can just see the tiles of a roof through the green of the leaves. And then there it is in front of us.

It looks like something out of a fairytale. But not one of the nice modern ones. It looks like the kind of place where children's nightmares come true, where witches boil the bones of the naughty kids who cross their paths.

Rani speeds up to get in front of me and leads me towards the rear of the cottage. With a leap she rams her shoulder against the back door, causing it to fly open.

'Where did you learn—'

'Just get inside.'

She slams the door behind us and then pulls me to the floor. She starts to crawl her way towards the corner of the room. We're in the kitchen but it looks utterly deserted, as if no one has been inside for years.

'We need to get to the pantry,' she tells me. 'Somewhere without windows at least.'

I start to stand up.

'For fuck's sake, Cassie. Get down. Do you have no survival instincts at all? Stay low, so, if someone was following, they can't see you. Jesus Christ.'

'Sorry,' I whisper.

'And why are you carrying a folder?' she asks.

'Sorry.'

She makes a guttural noise in the back of her throat like a growl. 'Please stop saying sorry.'

'Sorry. I thought it might be useful.'

We reach the pantry and crawl inside. She pulls the door closed behind us, plunging us into darkness. 'Fuck,' she says. 'Hang on.' She cracks open the door again and looks around the tiny pantry. There's no food, but there are some boxes on the bottom shelf. 'Aha!' she exclaims and pulls out a handful of candles and a box of matches. She lights one and then waves it towards me. 'Close that door and sit back against it.'

I do as I'm told and then she hands me the candle. 'When are you going to tell me what's going on?' I ask.

'I actually have no idea,' she replies. But it sounds like a lie.

'No idea? Really?'

'I don't know who they are or what they want. I need to think.'

'What were you doing in Korea?' My voice is small, even in the tiny space.

'It was work.'

'You need to talk to me, Rani.' I don't like my pleading tone.

'Just give me a few moments.'

'But—'

'Cassie. Please. Just give me a few minutes to figure this all out.'

'Fine.'

She starts to pace and I want to scream. The white of the folder gleams in the candlelight. I flick it open and idly leaf through the pages, trying not to lose my shit as my wife tries to concoct a lie for my benefit.

'Oh.' I can't help the word from slipping out when I get towards the back of the folder.

'Cassie. Please.'

'You might want to look at—'

'For fu—' But she cuts off the expletive as I turn the page to face her. 'That's...' she says, staring at the photo in the flickering candlelight.

'I think they're up to something,' I say, still trying to process what I've just read.

'But...'

'And they think that's you,' I add. 'They think you're a member of a Korean crime syndicate.'

60

SADIE

Alvi slams the door closed and stands in front of it, creating a human barricade against any of the rest of us from leaving.

'We need to go after them,' Sebastian says.

'No,' Alvi replies. 'We need to figure out what the actual fuck just happened and then make a mitigation plan.'

Sebastian squares up to him. It's like watching two lions size each other up. Ridiculous. Unnecessary. Likely to end in violence.

We don't have time for boys to play at being men. Rani might already be on her way to find a phone. Given the kind of people she mixes with, I highly doubt she would call the police. But – given the kind of people she mixes with – calling her colleagues could be *very* bad for us.

'Aly,' I say to get her attention. 'Tell me what the wife thinks she knows.'

Aly looks down at the ground. 'I don't know. I think just that Rani was at risk, that something was going to happen. For real, not just in the game. She told me as we ran here that her friend, that bartender, had some suspicions that the deaths were re—'

'One of the staff knew what was happening?' El interrupts, stepping forward.

'Apparently, she made a few notes of things she thought were odd for a hotel like this during an event. I don't think it was anything more than speculation. But she didn't show up for work this morning. The other staff think she flaked.'

'We don't have time to discuss some ditsy barmaid,' Sebastian says. 'A fucking *Kkangpae* just ran out of the fucking door.' He makes a move as if he's going to rush Alvi, but then thinks better of it and steps back again.

'I believe *Kkangpae* is used for street thugs, she would likely be considered a *geondal*,' Alvi says.

'Not the time, *Kultaseni*,' El tells him.

I give them both a withering look and turn my attention back to Aly. 'What else did the wife know?'

'Just that something might be about to happen to Rani. And it was linked to information you had on her. Information that I think is fake.'

'*Pour l'amour de Dieu*, Aly,' I say softly. 'I thought we talked about this. Just because she seemed nice doesn't mean she's innocent.'

I throw an exasperated look at El and Alvi. They stare back at me. Their expressions are clear: they want more information and they want it now.

'I found something,' Aly tells me.

'You might want to be a little more specific,' I reply.

'I found something about Rani.' She sounds... well, she sounds excited. Like she's found the keys to a secret room and it's full of sweeties.

I pause and wait for her to continue.

'So, I found the same information online as in the doss—'

'Yes, we already established she was guilty,' I interject.

'Well kind of... except—'

'Isn't it fairly binary? She did those things and so therefore she *is* guilty.' Yes, I understand the importance of nuance, but I also understand how to compartmentalise my emotions. Someone seeming nice or sympathetic or suave cannot erase the crimes you know they have committed. That part is black and white. If you did it, you are guilty. A tiny voice in the back of my brain pipes up with 'but guilt doesn't mean punishment, that depends on motive'. I shush it, now is not the time for moralising.

'But she's not.' It's no longer a question from Aly, this time she's adamant.

'All right, you've lost me.'

'What if the information isn't real? What if it's faked? What if someone put it up online to try to trap her?'

I look at her and wait for her to really think about what she's saying.

'I know I sound like a conspiracy theorist,' she says. 'But what if I'm right?'

'And who exactly would be trying to trap her by planting false information?'

'I... I... don't know.' Aly deflates in front of me, her bravado and excitement dissipating into the air and leaving her to crumple onto the pale blue sofa.

Alvi opens a cupboard by the door and pulls out a tray of fresh glasses. There's also another bottle of brandy in there that he opens without saying a word. A measure is poured for everyone and handed out. Aly tries to refuse, but Alvi just stares at her until she takes it.

'Now then,' he says eventually, before pausing to take a sip. 'The current situation is a clusterfuck. But nothing is insurmountable. We just need to find Rani and Cassie. Explain that it's all a misunderstanding and part of the games. Obviously we still kill her, but only in a way that stops Cassie getting suspicious. When it all goes up in a bang tomorrow, there'll be no evidence to corroborate Cassie's story anyway.'

'Tori and Grace?' El says to a random plant in the corner. 'Can we cut cell comms?'

I nudge Sebastian. 'Who is she talking to?' She looks like she's totally lost the plot.

He shrugs.

'Who are you talking to?' I say more loudly, directing the question at El.

'Tori and Grace. They're keeping an eye on things.'

The women I saw in the room in the VIP area. Of course.

61

CASSIE

Rani says nothing as she reads the dossier another three times. I track the movement of her eyes on the page.

'Are you going to say something?' I ask, unable to bear it any longer.

She remains silent but I can see she's stopped reading.

'Rani? Why do they have all this information about you working for this organised crime group?'

Still she says nothing.

Eventually I can take it no longer and the question explodes from me. 'Is it true?'

Her silence speaks volumes.

'Jesus Christ, Rani! You're actually working for this group? Recruiting mules for them?'

'It isn't what you think,' she says quietly.

'Well, why don't you fucking tell me what I should think.' My words are almost a whisper, but only because they are filtered through the red-hot rage I can feel building in my chest.

'Cassie. Please. It's complicated.'

'So, explain it to me in words of one syllable.' I finally look up and meet her eye. She looks like she's about to burst into tears and her pain hits me like a stab to the heart. How can I be angry and sympathetic at the same time? The dichotomy threatens to tear me apart.

'I'm not a travel agent,' she starts, before dragging in a ragged breath. 'It's a cover. A front.'

'So you do work for these Koreans?'

'No. No. I… I…'

'Just spit it out.'

'I'm a…' She laughs softly to herself. 'You're not going to believe this anyway.' She spreads her hands in front of her as if to say she may as well give up now. 'I'm a spy.'

It takes me a few moments to process what she says. 'Are you serious? That's the best you can come up with? I'm not a five-year-old, Rani. Who are you really?'

She clears her throat and straightens her shoulders. 'I work for the British Government,' she says, her whole accent, posture and mannerisms changing in front of me. 'I'm part of a small team of specialists who are infiltrating major criminal networks to gather evidence in the name of national security.'

I laugh. 'Fuck off, Rani.'

'It's the truth,' she says in her new voice. 'I was recruited just after I graduated from Cambridge and I've been working for them ever since.'

'You went to Oxford.'

She shakes her head. 'No. I went to Cambridge and did Linguistics.'

Is there any chance she's telling me the truth? Or am I just being a total idiot in even contemplating she might actually be a spy? I feel like we've stumbled into the pages of a book with a plot that is so far-fetched it's almost laughable. But I can't deny that I'm desperate to believe her. 'So…' I motion to the folder. 'What is this then?'

'This is my cover story. My in with the people we're investigating. Some of these reports have been fabricated, and the story about the students who got caught? They were junior operatives. It was all fake.'

'So, you aren't one of these… whatever the Korean is for gangster?' I can't hide how desperately I want it to be true.

She kneels down so we're face to face. 'Of course I'm not, you bloody idiot.'

'I have no idea who you are.' My voice breaks as my heart shatters. Whoever she is, she isn't the woman I married, the woman I fell in love with. But then the sadness dissipates and once again my anger boils to the surface. She's been lying to me. For years. 'Oh my God. All that stuff about you wanting to leave the agency and become a travel journalist? That was all bullshit too, wasn't it?'

She at least has the humility to look embarrassed. 'It's what I wanted to do when I was a kid.'

'That doesn't answer the question.'

She sucks in a deep breath. 'Fine. It was a lie. But it would look completely suss if I like my job in corporate travel booking. It's normal for people to have career wobbles. Especially at our age. And I just got married. Who would believe that wouldn't change my professional outlook?'

'And has it? Has *our* marriage...' I put extra emphasis on the 'our', 'changed your opinion on your work? Your *real* work.'

She breaks eye contact with me. 'Of course it has. Of course you've changed me.' She sounds hurt. Good.

'But you're still working?' Suddenly something else clicks into place. 'Oh my God. How could I have been so stupid?' I resist the urge to slap myself across the face. 'How didn't I see it before? That's why you didn't want me to leave the Raven and get a desk job. You wanted me to still be out in the evenings and on weekends so you'd never have to tell me where you were when you were off doing your spy stuff. And then, when we got the puppies and you'd tell me you were taking them to the park, or for a puppy playdate, or to agility classes. Were you doing any of those things?'

She shakes her head.

'When you got stuck on that broken-down train and I offered to take them to agility and you told me not to bother? That was because there was no agility.'

I need to pace but the space is too small. I start jumping up and down on the spot instead; I need to move, to help me to process this information, to get my thoughts in order. I fear that, if I stop, I will do something I regret as the anger boils over. 'Is Rani even your real name?'

She turns away.

'Shiiiit.' I feel the fight leave me. Even her name is a lie. Which means that *our* name is a lie too. 'We chose Kohl because it was a mashup of both our names. Kumar and Ohlson. Kohl.' I can hear my voice breaking again as I say the words.

'I'm sorry, Cassie.'

'Please stop saying you're sorry.' It feels odd to be the one saying those words to her for once. 'Sorry isn't good enough.'

'It's the truth though.'

'You wouldn't know the truth if it jumped up and bit you in the face. You know I was named after the Cassandra of Greek myth? Cursed to see the future but be helpless to stop it? How fucking ironic that I'd fail so unequivocally to see the truth right in front of my own fucking face.' Oh good. The anger's back. It hurts less when the fire rages.

'Please, Cassie,' she says softly, but I'm not listening to her. My brain has fired off on a tangent. I suppose looking at the ashes of my marriage was too much for my subconscious, so it's had a new idea instead.

I tap the folder. 'So, this information was planted. Distributed online so, if someone from one of these organisations you're cosying up to went looking, they'd find it.'

'It's called a pedigree. But, yes, that's the crux of it.'

'So it's real? Or at least people would think it is,' I add.

'It's what could be found online, yes.'

'So, at least on the face of it, the dossier about you is real. So, what if all these other ones are real too?'

'Others?'

'They all have information about terrible things they've done. Hugo and Jerome and Mitchell and—'

She cuts me off. 'So?'

'Read the pages about Sadie and Sebastian,' I tell her, handing over the folder.

I sit in silence as she reads. 'Their dossiers are different,' she says. 'And they say they are "for insurance".'

'Exactly. Their dossiers read like they have some kind of code. Like they're…' I try to think of the right word.

'Like they're vigilantes?'

'Exactly. What if…'

'What if they're vigilantes and this is basically their hit list?' Rani asks.

'Exactly. You always were far cleverer than me.'

'So, you think they're vigilantes and they're picking off the people on this list? And I was on the list because they found all the planted information and therefore I was another target.'

'Does that sound utterly bonkers?' I ask. I already know the answer, of course it sounds utterly bonkers. But that doesn't necessarily mean it isn't true. 'So, we could explain to them that you're not really a drug mule recruiter person,' I pause for a moment, I might need to think of a snappier title for what Rani pretends to do, 'and you don't work for this organisation because you're some kind of evil mastermind, but in fact you're doing good service in the name of your country.'

'And you think they'll let us walk away? You think they'll just let an employee of the government walk away when she knows they've been on a killing spree?'

'But they're good people.'

She doesn't say anything, just stares at me as I listen to my own words ringing in my ears.

Good people don't play judge, jury and executioner.

Good people don't kill other people.

62

THE HIT LIST

Dossier for Insurance: Sebastian Radley

Alvi brings me a cup of tea and looks over my shoulder at my screen as he places it on the coaster. 'Sebastian Radley,' he reads.

'You sound a little weird.'

'It's just... I'm not sure about him, you know. Like, I think there's something not quite right going on "upstairs".' He points to his own head as he says it and screws his face up a little.

'Ha! You're kidding? Of course there's something not quite right. He's a serial killer.'

'Fair. But that isn't what I mean. I think he might be trouble.'

'Well, then we will deal with him,' I say with a shrug. I take a sip of tea and get back to work.

'But, if we have to get rid of him *and* Sadie? How are we going to cover up multiple people from the same team? It kind of goes against the whole idea of the game.'

'Have faith, dear boy,' I tell him. 'It isn't going to happen. But, if it does, well that's why we have help on the ground.' I give him a wink. Our clean-up crew is exceptional, a pair of women with a new venture who are desperate to prove themselves. Smart, hungry and reasonably priced. What's not to like?

Name: Sebastian Radley
Team: Bowerman
Role: The Twin
Relationship to the Marchioness: Distant relative
Age: 41 years
Residence: Newcastle
Occupation: Trader
Personal Life: Single. Sebastian has an identical twin brother, Samuel, who is attending the weekend with him.

Additional Notes:

The people in Sebastian's life have proven to be rather accident prone. But he always has an alibi, someone who saw him elsewhere, away from the scene of the crime. I suppose it is rather useful to have an identical twin.

63

SADIE

The Marchioness of Devonshire slips into the room via a secret passageway even I didn't know existed. She's no longer dressed in that gorgeous 1920s dress, she's now in jeans and a plain white t-shirt, face scrubbed free of makeup and her blonde hair in a messy ponytail. I can see why she had a moderately successful modelling career, she's beautiful in that gloriously relaxed way so many try to emulate but few achieve.

'Is Grace still watching the cameras?' Alvi asks.

'Yeah. We thought it was better if I was the one people potentially saw. Not great for immersion in the weekend's story to find the Marchioness walking about, but might help to cement the idea that this is all surface level theatrics.'

'Clever,' Alvi replies. 'Did you cut the comms?'

'Of course. We've used a jammer so all mobile phones are now useless. And we blocked the WiFi too. Grace started a call to BT so she'll be on hold for the next three hours which means no one can use the landline.'

'Do you know where Rani and her wife ran to?'

'They're in the old groundskeeper's cott—'

'And you have eyes in there?' Sebastian interrupts.

'No. It's derelict. We have cameras going into the woods and then around the perimeter of the hotel grounds, but we can't see every square inch.' She pauses and cocks her head slightly. 'Didn't we talk you through the camera system yesterday?'

'So, they're hiding in the one place we can't see them?' Sebastian says. I can see the anger coiling beneath the surface of his features. 'Jesus fucking Christ. I knew I shouldn't have got involved with you amateurs.'

It feels a bit rich given how keen he seemed yesterday. Didn't he kill Hugo within three hours of being here?

'Anyway,' Tori says, turning her attention back to Alvi. 'They're inside the cottage and, although we can't see them in there, we will know if they leave.' She unclips a small walkie-talkie from her belt and waggles it. 'Grace and I are in constant contact with each other via this.'

'Great, thanks Tori,' Alvi says.

'Umm...' El says. 'Who has my folder?' she asks, her voice quiet, the same tone you'd use if you were trying not to frighten a distressed cat.

'What folder?'

'The one with all the dossiers in it. The one that lists everyone's real crimes.'

'Define "everyone's",' Sebastian demands, his teeth gritted.

'There are twelve. One for each of the people we will kill—'

'Which is nine,' Sebastian says.

'One for Lloyd, the compere, to persuade him to hand over the reins of the story to me and Alvi so we could twist it as needed...'

'You stupid fucking bitch,' Sebastian says, rounding on her. 'Why the fuck would you carry that around with you?'

'Don't talk to her like that.' Alvi steps between them.

'Do not get in my way,' Sebastian hisses.

Right. I've had enough. 'Will you all just sit down and shut up!' I bellow.

All the attention in the room turns to me.

'You're all acting like little children. We have a problem here and we need to decide, as a collective, what we do.' No one moves. 'Sit down.'

They all do as they're told.

'Right then,' I say. 'Let's be clear on the facts. The wife was already suspicious about what was going on, and now she has a folder with the dossiers that detail everyone's real crimes. Rani may not be guilty of hers, but that is as yet uncorroborated. They have run to the groundskeeper's cottage on the hotel grounds, where we know they remain, even if we can't see them. So, we need to assume they are reading the dossiers and starting to build a picture of what may or may not have been happening this weekend. Are we all in agreement that is the situation as it stands?'

The others all nod.

'We need to kill them both,' Sebastian says. 'We need to go right now and sort out this... what was it Alvi called it? Clusterfuck.'

'Cassie is innocent,' I tell him.

'And Rani,' Aly pipes up.

'So?' Sebastian replies.

'I'm not killing an innocent person to protect my secrets.'

'It's self-defence,' Sebastian says with an air of nonchalance, like he doesn't care about the morality of it. Like he would do anything to save himself and never think of it again.

A chill runs up the back of my neck.

I thought we were all alike.

I was wrong.

64

CASSIE

'What are we going to do, Rani?' I ask her. 'We can't just stay here in this pantry forever. Can't you call it in?'

'Call it in? This isn't a TV show, Cassie.'

'But you must have a number to call if you get into trouble. A team to come and extract you when the shit hits the fan.'

She shakes her head and a wry smile curls the corner of her mouth. 'It doesn't work like that. I'm a small cog in a big machine, a complex network of other agents who are scattered across the globe.'

'So what are you saying?'

'I can "call it in". In theory. But then what do you think happens? Some analyst somewhere runs the numbers, looks at the possible outcomes of my extraction, sees the house of cards we've built so carefully collapse.'

'You're saying they'd just leave you here?' I'm shocked and appalled.

'It's what I signed up for. It's a special mission.'

'A fucking suicide mission, you mean.'

'It was a risk I was prepared to take. Look, Cassie, you wouldn't understand.'

'So, help me to understand,' I demand.

She shakes her head.

'There's something more, isn't there? Something else you aren't telling me?'

'The mission is beyond top secret. No civilian can know.' She says the words carefully, enunciating each syllable.

'Oh. You mean, *I* can't know?'

She arches an eyebrow. 'Exactly.'

'What… what would happen?' I trip over my words a little.

She breaks eye contact, staring at the floor as she shifts her weight from foot to foot. 'I don't know. But you understand now why I can't call it in. We're on our own. We need to find a way out of this, and without anyone else finding out who I really work for.'

'Any ideas?' I ask. 'Because this might be a life-or-death situation, but I am also very close to wetting myself.'

She looks at me, her eyes crinkling at the edges. 'You and your bladder.' She laughs. 'Fine, let's get out of this pantry and see what else is here in the cottage. Perhaps it will give me some inspiration.'

We blow out the almost guttering candles and then I go to open the door. But she pulls me back inside, her arms around my waist. The kiss is deep, urgent, tinged with fear and an even greater sense of desperation.

'I love you,' Rani says as we break apart. 'I just hope…' she trails off.

'You've lied to me, Rani. I don't know who you are. I don't know if I can get past that.'

She rests her forehead against mine in the dark.

'Let's just try to survive the next twenty-four hours and then we can talk,' I whisper.

* * *

Rani shoves a chest against the back door and then checks that all the other windows and doors are locked. 'That should at least give us a warning if someone finds us. Stay low and out of sight of the windows and I think we might be all right.'

We go through the cottage room by room, but there isn't much to see. Dust covers every surface and the corners are full of cobwebs.

I can't stop running the last twenty-four hours through my brain, like a movie on a high-speed fast-forward setting. Occasionally I'll snag on a memory, turning it over and over in my mind. The first death, what was his name? Hugo. I thought at the time that his acting of anaphylaxis was particularly good. The smell of pennies in the air after Jerome had been stabbed. Karen telling me she thought something odd was going on. Finding her notebook.

How did I not think of it before?

'Do you think they killed Karen?' I ask.

'I don't know,' Rani replies, but it's clear from her tone that she thinks that's exactly what happened. She goes back to the cupboard under the stairs she was looking through.

A few moments of silence pass. 'Feeling inspired yet?' I ask her as I rummage through the crooked Welsh dresser in the hallway. It's empty except for some old tablecloths and what looks suspiciously like mouse droppings.

Rani stops what she was doing and turns to face me. 'Look, I know you're still pissed off with me, but can we cut the attitude?'

'Are you actually shitting me?' I ask.

'Is this about Karen?' She sounds almost bored, like she isn't at least partially to blame for the situation we're in. Or like she thinks I'm overreacting again.

It lights a touchpaper under me. 'You told me not to worry about Karen. You said, and I quote here, that *not everything is my problem to fix*.' Rani at least has the grace to look slightly guilty. 'You made me think I was blowing things out of proportion, doing that thing where I make myself responsible for things I don't need to.' I take a ragged breath. 'You know I've been trying to work out some things, Rani. You know I've been trying to stop myself from being that person. And then the one fucking time when actually I *wasn't* overreacting, when I *needed* to push for answers, when someone was in trouble and I *could* actually help them, you used that against me.'

'It wasn't like that.'

'Wasn't it?' I raise my voice but I don't like the way it makes me sound. Like I'm out of control. Maybe I am?

'I was trying to keep you safe.' She says it softly, her eyes meeting mine. Her gaze is strong and steady. *Trust me*, she's saying. But I have no way to know if she's lying. I thought I knew my wife, but now I know nothing about her, who she really is.

'Well look how that worked out.' I walk back into the kitchen, I don't want to even look at her right now. This whole situation is a nightmare and I know I'm not overreacting. In fact, I'm starting to seriously consider if I'm *under*reacting, if maybe I've been doing so for far too long, letting my wife run rings around me as she trapped me in a web of lies.

Eughh, I don't know. Maybe I'm just being melodramatic.

'Have you gone to the basement yet?' she asks when she comes to find me a few minutes later.

'No.' I move closer to her and follow her gaze to the floor.

'Then why isn't there any dust here?'

She's right, there's an area in the middle of the corridor where there's no dust, but everything around it is covered. It looks like something has been dragged across the floor towards the basement stairs.

'This feels like a bad idea,' I say over my shoulder as I put my foot on the first step. 'I'm fairly sure this is how people die in horror films.'

'This isn't a horror film.'

'Isn't it?' I reply quietly. I'm in an abandoned house with a woman I thought I knew, who turned out to be a complete stranger, being chased by a group of serial killers and I'm about to head into the fucking cellar.

There's a scratch of a match being lit and then a flicker of orange-hued light. Rani passes me a candle. 'Better?' she asks.

Great. So now I'm heading into a cellar with a tiny flame for protection against the monsters in the dark.

I'm basically the full cliché now.

65

SADIE

There's a knock on the door before it opens a crack.

'Uh... El?' the man says. He looks vaguely familiar and he's wearing the same black outfit and lanyard as El and Alvi.

'Yes, Matty, what is it?'

'It's just... umm...' He taps his watch. 'We're kind of on a bit of a deadline. It's not too long before dinner and we're expecting another murder.' He sounds nervous, like he's genuinely in awe of El. But then he catches sight of Tori and his entire face flushes bright red. 'Oh. Umm... hi... uh... Tori.'

'Hey sweetie,' she says and gives him a wink. I didn't think it was possible but his blush deepens. He looks like an overripe tomato. 'We're just trying to figure a few things out. We hit a teeny snag but I'm sure we'll be back on track in a little while. Do you think you can find a way to keep our guests entertained?'

'Err. Sure. No worries.'

'Thanks.'

He leaves and closes the door behind him.

But then it opens again. 'Oh, and the phones don't seem to be working. I tried to message you but nothing...'

'I'll get one of the hotel staff to look into it,' El assures him, the dismissal in her tone clear.

'Coolio.' He leaves again and once more the door closes.

'We need a plan,' El says after a pause. 'Matty's right. The guests are expecting another murder imminently.'

Sebastian stands up and wipes his hands on his trousers. 'Enough is enough. I'm not getting fucked over because the rest of you don't have enough of a stomach to do what needs to be done.' He stomps out of the room and the door closes behind him.

66

CASSIE

The basement stairs are steep and it takes all my concentration not to fall down them. The air thickens as I descend, making it more and more difficult to breathe. It feels as if there is something primal hidden down here, something better left alone.

I curse Rani under my breath for bringing us to this point. Is it really less than a day ago when we pulled up in front of Holne House, giggling like teenagers at the thought of the weekend ahead of us? It doesn't feel possible for life to collapse so quickly, for utter chaos to replace the quiet calm. Or at least what I was thought was quiet calm, it seems it might have been hiding a raging storm, an inferno of lies. Jesus. I need to stop overthinking everything, it's making me weird and melancholic.

My toe catches something on the bottom step of the staircase and I crouch down to see what I kicked. It's a torch. I flick it on and am instantly almost blinded by the light.

'Jesus,' Rani says, 'why is that so bright? It's like that one you got your dad last Christmas.'

'The million candle one? Yeah.' I can't help but smile. He was inordinately pleased with it and kept making us go outside to test it as twilight descended.

'It's freezing down here,' Rani observes, rubbing her arms.

I shine the torch around. The basement is fairly large, spanning most of the floorplate of the kitchen above. There isn't much down here, just the usual detritus and boxes of junk. One is even labelled 'STUFF' in uneven capitals. I move towards the corner.

It takes a few moments for my brain to catch up with what I'm seeing. She's lying behind the boxes, and she looks almost peaceful, as if she's sleeping. But I can tell from the colour of her skin that she isn't just having a nap away from the busy hotel.

'What is it?' Rani asks from behind me. 'Oh. Oh shit,' she says when she sees what the torch is illuminating. Or rather, whom.

'It's Karen.' The words are barely out of my mouth before I turn and vomit onto the floor behind me, a stream of Champagne and negroni and finger sandwiches.

Rani carefully takes the torch from my hand and moves closer to the body. 'I'm no expert but I think she was probably killed last night. She's wearing running gear, was she into late-night jogging?'

'She mentioned it, yeah. Said she liked to take a jog around the grounds after her shift, to help her relax before she went to bed.' I force myself to look at her. 'Do you think it was my fault?' I ask softly.

'Why would it be your fault?' Rani asks. Kneeling down to look even more closely at Karen.

'I told Aly she was missing. Do you think someone went looking for her?'

'You're not making any sense,' Rani says.

'Or do you think it's because I didn't look hard enough? I could have helped her.'

'No, you couldn't. None of this is on you. Hang on...' She crouches over the body.

'What is it?'

'It looks like she was strangled. With a necktie. It's plain black though, and there were so many guys wearing ones like this last night, I can't say whose it was.'

It rings a bell. A faint one admittedly but... 'I think I've heard that before. Strangulation with a silk tie.'

'Me too.' Rani sits back on her heels.

'The dossier.' We both say it at the same time.

We head back to the kitchen, leaving Karen where she is. We don't want to disturb the scene. Whatever else happens today, the police need to find her and bring her killer to justice.

Rani grabs the dossier and flicks through it. 'Roger Carruthers,' she says, tapping the page. 'Last year a woman was found dead in his hotel room. He claimed she was a stalker who broke in and he had no choice but to defend himself. And before that...' She trails off as she continues to read. 'Jesus, this guy is a fucking piece of shit.' She looks up.

'So, Roger Carruthers killed her?'

'It certainly fits his MO.'

'So it wasn't that twin and Aly's godmother?' I ask.

'Sadie and Sebastian,' she corrects.

'Whatever, I don't really care what their names are.'

'Fair. But, no, if I had to put my money on it, then I'd say it was this Roger Carruthers guy.'

I narrow my eyes at her. 'Did you really just say, "if I had to put my money on it"?'

'Yes...'

'You realise you are literally about to bet your *life* on it?'

'Touché.' She smiles, just for a moment.

'Don't you fucking dare.' My anger goes from not quite zero to a million in a flash. 'Don't you fucking dare smile like maybe there is any fucking humour in this situation. My friend is dead. Lying down there, strangled. And now, because of you and your stupid fucking web of lies that you've been spinning for fucking years, now I have to decide what we do about that. Because, oh no. We can't just go to the fucking police and tell them that my friend is dead. Oh no. We can't get them to come here with their CSI people and their fancy testing kits and collect all the evidence into nice little bags. Oh no. We can't get the police to arrest this piece of shit Roger Carruthers and bring him to trial so they can find him guilty and he can spend the rest of his shitty life rotting in prison. Oh no.'

'Cassie, please.'

'Cassie, please,' I mimic her. 'What? You don't like me ranting at you?

You don't like me pointing out that you've got us into a hideous shitty mess and you have no fucking plan to get us out of it?'

'I… I'll figure something out,' she says.

'I'm going to deal with this,' I tell her. The edges of a plan are coming into view through the veil of my rage. I have always been rather good in a crisis.

'You have no idea what's going on.'

'And you do?' I counter.

'This isn't your problem to solve.' I make a rather unattractive snort but I don't actually give a fuck any more. 'You don't have to fix everything all the fucking time,' Rani adds.

Oh, that's it. 'Don't I? *Don't I?*' My voice raises to a strangled scream.

'No. You don't.'

Except I do. 'Look at the fucking mess we're in.' I motion around us. 'How the fuck can you look me in the eye right now and tell me you'll figure this out? I don't even know who you really are.'

She remains silent and I take a few deep breaths, desperately trying to get my heartrate back under control before I give myself an embolism. Eventually a strange sense of calm falls over me and a plan begins to reveal itself.

I don't condone what Sadie and Sebastian have done. Being a vigilante isn't cool or clever or edgy. It's a gross overstep. It's putting yourself in a position to determine the future worth of another human. No one has that power.

But. And Jesus, if it isn't a massive 'but'. Some people deserve to be punished. They deserve to feel the same pain they've so readily inflicted on others.

I turn to Rani. 'I think I know what we need to do.'

67

SADIE

No one has said anything for ten minutes, we're all just sitting here, playing things over in our own minds. I can only imagine the others are thinking the same thing as me: that they hope someone else has a brilliant idea. Or possibly that Sebastian takes matters into his own hands, and stops us from having to make a decision.

The walkie-talkie on Tori's belt crackles and another voice comes through. 'Control to Tori. Over.'

'Tori to Control. Go ahead. Over.'

'They're on the move. Heading back to the hotel as if nothing has happened. Over.'

'Any sign of Sebastian? Over.'

'He went to his room. Rani and Cassie appear to be making a beeline towards you. Over.'

Five minutes later there's a knock on the door and it swings open to reveal Cassie and Rani. Cassie is holding a white napkin and she waves it a few times. 'We request a parlay.'

Alvi laughs. 'Oh shit, you're serious.' He motions for them to enter. 'Come on in then. I'll get some drinks.'

'I'm not sure I'll be drinking anything in this room,' Rani says, looking directly at me. She does kind of have a point.

'Suit yourself,' he says. 'But I'm having one.' We all wait as he gets more fresh glasses from the cupboard closest to the door and pours us all a healthy measure.

'We want to know how exactly you're planning on getting away with this?' Rani says, her voice containing the merest hint of a tremble.

'With what?' El asks, her voice dripping with faux innocence.

'We know this isn't a murder mystery weekend.'

El laughs, a short sharp bark, and then she points to the lanyard around her neck. 'It kind of is.'

'This might be the first time I've been to Murder on the Moors, but I'm pretty sure that normally people don't die for real.'

El glances at Alvi, who gives her a tiny nod. She turns back to Rani. 'We have a plan. Let's just say this weekend is going to have a slightly explosive end.' She makes a hand motion like a magician.

'You're going to blow up the hotel?' Cassie appears shocked.

'The West Wing. Just enough to destroy any chance of forensic analysis on the people we've dispatched. We'll obviously make sure everyone else has already vacated. No harm, no foul.'

'No harm, no foul?' Cassie raises her eyebrows. 'Except the hotel will be destroyed. And that feels like a crime in itself.'

'It's just bricks.'

'To you maybe,' Cassie replies. 'Anyway.' She shakes her head, as if reminding herself of the script she's deviating from. 'We have an alternative proposal.'

El looks at her and then at me. 'O... K...' She shrugs.

'We have a way you can walk away risk free.'

I lean forward slightly. 'Ha. You realise you are the biggest risk here.'

'No. Your biggest risk is that the explosion doesn't burn hot enough, that evidence is left behind and it becomes clear that these people were murdered.' Cassie sounds extremely confident. I narrow my eyes. How much is bravado? An act? A lot, that's for sure. But I think she genuinely does believe in what she's saying.

'And you have a better idea?' I ask.

'Roger Carruthers.'

Roger Carruthers is number nine on our hit list. I am currently planning how I will kill him slowly and painfully. He's a weaselly little bastard and I want to find a way to make him suffer.

Aly sucks in air between her teeth. 'Pervy little shithead.'

Rani nods. 'Yes. He is. And a murderous one too.'

'He killed one of the staff. Her name was Karen. Roger Carruthers killed her.'

'Karen's dead?' Aly says, her hand flying to cover her mouth.

'Yeah,' Cassie replies. 'We found her body in the old groundskeeper's lodge. Hidden in the basement.' Did Cassie know this Karen well? She sounds genuinely traumatised by this. I file away that nugget of information, it might be useful down the line. 'We know it was Roger who killed her. And we know he was on your "hit list".'

'I have no idea what you're talking a—' El starts but she cuts herself off as Cassie pulls a folder from the shopping bag at her feet. Did she carry that in with her? I didn't even notice.

'Number nine on the hit list, I believe,' Rani adds. 'You recognise the folder, El? The folder of all the people you've killed this weekend. And the ones you're still planning to kill.'

'But here's the thing...' Cassie takes over before pausing for a few moments, assumedly for dramatic effect. 'He deserves something much worse.'

Oh. Well, that isn't what I was expecting. I lean forward a tiny bit in my seat. She has my attention now.

'And what is the thing that's worse than death?' Cassie looks directly at me as she asks the question.

I shrug. 'Enlighten me.'

'The thing that's worse than death,' she starts again, 'is the loss of everything. Imagine what a man like Roger Carruthers would do if he had to spend the rest of his life in prison. It would destroy him. And be justice for Karen.'

'You want to call the police and have him arrested?' El asks, making it abundantly clear that particular scenario is never going to happen.

'Eventually.' Cassie takes a sip of her brandy before she puts down her glass and then smiles. 'But they won't come to arrest him for just Karen's murder.'

'You want to set him up for the others?' El asks.

'I'm assuming you designed this weekend so any one of the teams could be the killer in the game, depending on who you allocated it to on the first day?'

Cassie nods. 'Yes. That's the way Murderous Intentions always does it, it means the story can be used multiple times across different venues. We knew it would look suspicious otherwise, if anyone ever thought to go digging. But we've obviously deviated slightly from standard by necessity.'

'But not by much? You could still change who the killer was in the story?'

El and Alvi share a look, an entire conversation passing silently between them. They remind me so much of myself and my dear first husband, Tommy. Thick as thieves and so in love it's almost sickly to witness.

'You'll ruin the final twist,' El says.

'Can't we still make it work?' Alvi asks.

'No. It'll be lost in all the excitement.' She sounds disappointed. 'It was going to be such a fun reveal.' She sighs and then does a little shimmy as though she's shaking her feelings off. 'I'll get over it.'

Alvi touches her shoulder gently, then turns back to Cassie. 'It'll be tricky to change the story at this late stage. You think you can help us pull that off?'

Rani and Cassie nod.

'And then what?'

'Then we all go our separate ways,' Cassie says.

'Just like that?'

'Just like that. You forget you ever met me and Rani. And we forget we ever met all the rest of you.'

Another look is exchanged between Alvi and El.

Tori steps forward. 'And why exactly should we trust you?'

'Because you have no choice.'

'There's always a choice,' El says.

'Look. My wife needs this Roger punished for what he did to her friend. I've made a lot of mistakes and this is... well, let's call it a gift. To her. You do this for her and I will let you all walk away.'

'Sebastian thinks we should kill you and remove any threat that way,'

Alvi tells her, putting his hands up in a defensive action. 'I'm not saying that the rest of us think that but…' he trails off.

'Fine. Let's put this another way.' Rani drops her voice. 'If anything happens to me, the people I work for would come for you.' She slowly makes eye contact with each of us. 'All of you.'

'So, if you die, we all die?' Tori asks.

'Exactly.'

'Mutually assured destruction. Well, I suppose it wouldn't be the first time I've made an agreement like that.' Tori offers up a small smile.

'I still think we should stick to the original plan. Blow up the hotel, get rid of any evidence,' I say. 'If I get to have an opinion here…'

'If you blow up the hotel, the deal is off,' Cassie says. 'Roger Carruthers needs to pay for what he has done, but the hotel is innocent in all of this.' She sounds like she has a genuine affection for this place, and I suppose I can see her point. It has been a pretty important part of my life for a long time.

'Well,' says El, 'I guess this is welcome to the team.' She reaches out a hand for Cassie to shake.

This is either a very good, or a very bad, idea.

I'm going to reserve judgement on which one for now.

68

CASSIE

The way they are looking at me makes me think they're not all one hundred percent convinced this is a good idea. Especially Sadie, who looks like she ate a wasp. I'm going to need to do more work to 'capture their hearts and minds', as my wanker boss likes to say in staff meetings to try to gee us up before a shift. Maybe I should channel his energy, wear his persona like a mask I can hide behind. Managing a crisis is always much easier if you pretend to be a middle-aged white man who is blissfully unaware of his own mediocrity.

'OK,' I start. 'The first thing is to figure out how to pin the murders that have already happened on Roger.'

'We're all ears,' Sadie says, with a sly grin.

'Umm... well, I don't...' I put my hands out, palms up. My bravado already starting to collapse. 'I mean, I don't know how you actually...'

'Killed them?'

'Yes.' I don't like the way she says the words so easily. Like it doesn't weigh on her in the slightest.

'So, you don't actually have a plan?'

I feel like a small child being ticked off by an adult who isn't technically in a position of responsibility. Like I should respect their opinion for being my elder, but I'm also resentful because I don't understand why they should have an opinion, but also scared that I have done something so wrong even a stranger feels the need to tick me off. Jeez, I really do have a complicated relationship with authority. But I guess now isn't the time for self-reflection.

'I think what Cassie is trying to say—' Rani starts, but I cut her off. I don't need my wife to speak for me. I try to turn off the tiny voice in my brain asking if she even is my wife any more, given how many lies she told me and the fact our entire marriage is built on bullshit. Now isn't the time for that particular meltdown.

'I do not have access to all the specific details of every one of your... murders.' I force myself to say the word and it actually doesn't feel too bad. Especially if I remember all the things they did. 'That is by your own design. You were hardly advertising your actions to the rest of us. And you all seem very adept at covering your tracks.'

I watch as Sadie softens slightly. I guess, to her, that was a compliment. Perhaps that should be my tack here, a change in direction to bring them on side?

'If circumstances had been different, I would never have guessed what was going on,' I say and Sadie softens even more. 'You had me fooled. And everyone out there too.' I motion to the door. 'So, yes, I'm sorry but you're going to have to help me out with the specifics.'

'Fine,' Sadie says.

'Thank you.' I offer her a tentative smile and she returns it. Or at least it's half a smile. I think it's as good as I'm going to get. 'So, how do we pin these murders on Roger Carruthers?' I ask again.

'Method. Motive. Opportunity,' Tori rattles off.

'You sound like you're reciting something you learned by rote,' El tells her.

'Grace is an excellent teacher. Even if she can be rather exacting.'

The walkie-talkie on her hip crackles. 'I heard that.'

'Umm... who is that?'

'That's Grace, my business partner,' Tori says.

'But you're...' I tail off. Hang on. Why exactly *is* the woman who played the Marchioness here? Shit. Have I missed something?

'You don't play poker, do you?' Sadie asks.

'What? I... No...' What is she talking about?

'Only that we all saw the questions you just asked yourself, they were etched so clearly on your face it's almost laughable. You're going to need to be a lot better at hiding what you're thinking if we're going to get away with this.'

'Sadie has a point,' El says. 'But, also, I'm conscious we haven't introduced you to Tori properly. She's working with us, her and her business partner. They run a very discreet and very efficient service in... what do you put on your business cards, Tori?'

'The removal of unwanted problems,' Tori replies. 'Grace is in our CCTV room keeping an eye on things.' She pats the walkie-talkie.

'OK. So hi, Tori and Grace. I'm Cassie.'

'It's a pleasure,' Tori says and flashes me a stunning smile.

'And this is my wife, Rani.'

The smile on Tori's face drops. Well, I suppose she does think my wife works for a Korean organised crime syndicate. I take a deep breath and go back to what we were talking about before, trying not to stumble over my words in front of her. 'So, we need to go through each murder and work out how we can convince the police that Roger killed them, make sure we have a motive and then ensure there's opportunity,' I say. It sounds impossible. The edges of my plan begin to crumble. Fuck.

'I think between us we can make that work,' Aly says, standing up. 'We do have a rather wide-ranging skillset, after all.' She seems genuinely confident. I just hope it isn't American bravado.

'Great,' I say to her and she grins. 'And then there's the *coup de grace*.'

Everyone's attention turns back to me and for a moment I worry I butchered the pronunciation, languages were never my strong point and Rani has to frequently correct me.

I swallow down my insecurities. 'We need something to arouse the initial suspicions of Roger's guilt. Something that points the finger to him in an instant, so every piece of evidence is viewed through that lens. One thing I've learned in my hospitality career is that people will see what you tell them to. If we tell the... what, sixty people, including staff, here at the hotel, that he's the killer, they will start to come forward with titbits of evidence to corroborate that. Snatched conversations, times when he slipped away to take a call, all that kind of thing.'

'You know,' Sadie says, leaning back in her seat, 'that's actually pretty clever.'

Something tells me that's the highest compliment she'll ever give me. I'll take it. And I need her onside to make this part work.

I take a breath. 'Also. There needs to be another murder. Mine.'

PART VII

GALA DINNER

69

SADIE

Well, that wasn't what I expected.

'Obviously the murder will be fake this time,' Cassie says with a slightly nervous laugh. 'We need to stage my murder and then I'll hide somewhere, ready to burst out at the right moment and say I've found the bodies and Roger was the one who killed them and he tried to kill me.'

'That won't work,' El says.

'Of course it'll work.' Cassie is adamant. I have to admit, I also think it'll work. It's actually almost genius.

'No, it won't,' El says, shaking her head. 'The game is designed so that any team could be the killer, depending on who we pick on the first day. So, Roger Carruthers can be the killer. But you can't be the victim. It has to be Rani. All the clues are designed for the death in your team to be the person playing the Head of Fundraising.'

A look passes between Cassie and her wife. I'm assuming they're weighing up their thoughts on this major change to their grand plan.

Eventually, Rani nods. 'Fine. I'll do it.'

'Great,' El says. 'Well, in that case, I think that sounds like it could work.'

There's one more thing though. 'I'll need to partially dose you,' I tell Rani.

'Sorry?'

'The police will test you for the presence of opium. It's probably the first thing they'll do,' I explain.

'Absolutely not,' Rani says. 'Or are you forgetting that it hasn't been very long since you tried to kill me for real?'

'The circumstances have changed,' I tell her.

I can see the conflicting emotions on her face. She wants to trust me, but she knows that maybe she shouldn't. Her primitive lizard brain is telling her to run for the hills while her neocortex is saying that I actually do have a good point. It's really rather fascinating to watch.

My brandy glass is almost empty, but I take a sip of the final dregs as I wait for her to make a decision. There's definitely something more to her and her situation. Aly thinks she's innocent but Rani's threatened me with 'her people'. None of it really makes any sense. All that information exists online about the things she has done, even if Aly is convinced it's fake. But, if it wasn't true, then why wouldn't Rani just say that? Why wouldn't she tell us that she's innocent and it's all a misunderstanding?

'OK. I'll do it,' Rani says eventually.

'Excellent,' El says, clapping her hands to show that everything is decided. 'Now, we need to get the rest of this murder mystery weekend back on track. I'll go and brief the rest of the team. They were expecting Rani to "die" this afternoon but I'll say we've decided to do it during the pre-dinner drinks.'

No one moves.

'Well, come on people,' El adds. 'Chop chop. Time to dress for dinner. It's the big gala this evening and everyone out there is expecting a show. Let's not disappoint them.'

* * *

Back in the Christie suite, Aly turns to me. 'Are you going to do it?' she asks.

'Do what?'

'Rani.'

'Do you really think she's innocent? You heard her threaten us.'

'She's desperate. Scared.'

I make a non-committal noise in the back of my throat.

'So, you're going to kill her?' Aly presses.

'I'm going to give her the partial dose we agreed to,' I say, but only after a moment of hesitation.

'Really?' She raises an eyebrow then turns back to the closet. She pulls out a gorgeous navy-blue beaded flapper-style dress and lays it on the bed.

I wore something similar the first year I came to Holne Hall. I was so much like Aly back then. Bright and inquisitive and with an unwavering sense that I knew the difference between good and evil.

But now I'm not so sure. Is it really as simple as I thought, so binary? Right and wrong. Black and white. Or is there a grey area in the middle?

70

CASSIE

'Do you think I should wear the teal or the black?' Rani asks, standing in front of the wardrobe. She pulls out one of the dresses and holds it against herself. 'The teal is much brighter, much more of a statement.' She throws it onto the bed and grabs the other. 'But the black feels like it's more fitting.' She turns to admire herself in the mirror. 'You know, given I'm going to die tonight.'

A shiver runs up my spine. 'Fake die,' I correct her.

'So, you think the teal?' She puts the black dress back and picks up the teal again.

'It's a beautiful dress,' I tell her.

'Well, I do want to be a gorgeous corpse.'

I'm not sure she should be this flippant given that she did in fact come to within seconds of actually dying this afternoon. But her humour is keeping our spirits buoyed and going a little way toward stopping me from spiralling about the absolute shitshow our lives have become.

'Do you think this is going to work?' she asks as she bends over to extract her shoes from the bottom of the wardrobe.

I want to ask if she means the plan for tonight, or if our marriage can be salvaged from the wreckage of her lies, but I don't. 'I hope so.'

We carry on getting ready in silence. I'm wearing the same trousers as last night, but I'm adding a pair of black suspenders. I've switched to a fitted white silk blouse, unbuttoned to my navel to show off my lacy black bra, with an undone bowtie around my neck. Instead of the fancy headband I wore last night, tonight it's a simpler affair, just a row of black diamantes that glitter in the light, and a single black feather. One of the girls at work made it for me. Using a real feather from our mascot raven in the entrance hall that gives the hotel its name. I think Karen would have loved that detail, but I'm going to try to put all thoughts of her to one side this evening. There is far too much going on and my brain already feels like it's going to explode. I raise the long black cigarette holder I bought to complete the look.

'Jesus,' Rani says when she sees the full effect. 'You look...'

I turn back to the mirror, raking my eyes over the ensemble... have I missed something? Do I look like a fool?

'You look like the sexiest thing I've ever seen,' Rani finishes, coming up behind me. She runs her hand over my waist. 'You're a fucking smoke show.'

I waggle my cigarette holder at her. Acting goofy has always been my defence mechanism for being told I'm attractive.

Rani gently turns me to face her. 'I love you, Cassie,' she says. 'And I know I've fucked up so fucking badly. And you have every right to hate me. But I promise that, of all the lies I've told, there is one thing I have never lied about. And that's my feelings for you. I love you and I will spend every day for as long as you'll let me trying to make things up to you.'

'Let's just get through this weekend, OK,' I say, pulling away from her. I want to forgive her. I want to tell her that we can get through this, that I understand why she lied and it'll all be all right.

But I'm not sure I'd be telling the truth.

* * *

Theodore is bouncing on the balls of his feet as we head toward him and Bea.

'He looks like a kid who's been at the Christmas chocolates,' Rani says in my ear.

'I think I know who the killer is,' he says, the moment we're within hearing distance.

'Thank goodness you're here. He's been a nightmare for the last half hour without anyone to tell his little theory to,' Bea says, almost cutting him off.

Rani squeezes my hand and I squeeze back. This is it. Showtime.

'Oh wow, really?' I ask.

'It's been staring me in the face since this morning.' He grins. He's suddenly distracted by something behind me. Or some*one*, I suppose, judging by the way he's furiously waving them over. 'I got Champagne.' He sounds so proud of himself and for a moment I forget that Rani and I have a new objective.

He makes a scene of popping the cork and then sloshes the pale liquid into the flutes.

'To us,' he says as he raises his glass aloft. We all follow suit.

'So, are you going to tell us who you think the killer is?' Rani asks, before taking a sip.

'Oh, of course. Now then,' he drops his voice so we have to lean in closer to him. 'You will remember earlier when our lovely Cassie picked up that little bottle, after Diego keeled over?'

We all nod. It was only a matter of hours ago but it feels like a million years have passed since then.

'Well, when I took it back to my room I had another look at it. And I noticed something.' He takes a long drink of Champagne. He's enjoying this, drawing out his big reveal. 'The label said "Belladonna", and there was something a little unusual about the "B". So I sat there and I thought to myself, "I recognise that "B"", I've seen it before.' He pauses for a moment to make sure we're all still under his thrall. 'And then finally I realised where I knew it from.'

He takes a step backwards, a smug smile on his face.

'Aren't you going to tell us?'

'Sadie Rose.' He looks directly at her as he says it. 'The Dowager Bowerman.'

Shit.

Shit.

Shit.

For a split second my brain goes into full meltdown mode, but then it scrambles for a solution. 'And how exactly do you know what Sadie's handwriting looks like?' I ask him. I make it sound like a joke. Like this is still just a murder mystery weekend and we're playing for kudos and clout and not a real-life attempt to pin a string of murders on someone who deserves to burn in hell for what they did to Karen. I try to keep my expression neutral, to keep the mask in place. *You can do this*, I tell myself. You were born to do this. Think of all the times you've solved everyone's problems, picked up the pieces of everyone else's lives.

The smug smile on Theodore's face slips a little. 'Once upon a time, she called me Beau.' The words are so soft they hang in the air like miniature clouds.

'You were a *thing*?' Rani asks, her professionally cool demeanour cracking.

'I thought so. We spent the weekend together. She wrote to me after. Told me she'd had the best time. That she just needed to get her divorce finalised and then we could be together.'

'So, what happened?'

'A few months later, I met a man in Singapore. He told me about his beautiful wife. How they'd been married for five years and they were happy, the rocky patch they'd been going through finally solved, so they could continue with their marriage.'

'Sadie's husband?'

'Of course.' He sounds heartbroken.

'How long ago was this?' I ask.

'Oh, a while.'

'A while?' Bea scoffs. 'It was at least thirty years ago. You can't play the lovesick boy any more, Theodore. You've been married twice since and goodness only knows how many lady friends you've had in that time.'

'She was my one that got away.'

'From what I heard,' Bea says, 'she definitely should have chosen you. That man was her second husband and he was hideous.'

I've always loved to hear other people's love stories and I can't help but wonder if there would still be a chance for Sadie and Theodore. She's clearly single, as is he. He's aged well, surely she'd still find him attractive. A finger pokes into my back. Rani. Bringing me back to reality. Sadie's a killer. And not just in the game. I can't possibly think about Theodore and her.

'Unfortunately, Theodore,' Rani says. 'I think you're wrong about Team Bowerman being the killers.'

'I'm never wrong,' he says with a smug smile.

Bea rolls her eyes and shakes her head at him.

'Well, I guess only time will tell,' I say enigmatically, already wondering how the fuck I'm going to change his mind.

71

SADIE

Aly looks incredible in the navy-blue flapper dress. There is flirty fringing that sways as she walks and an asymmetric neckline. I've opted for a slightly more staid floor-length number in a deep green, with a beaded bodice and high neck.

'You look amazing, Aunt Sadie,' Aly tells me. 'Mr Dreamy is going to fall over himself when he sees you.' She grins.

'Ha ha.' But I can't help but look at my reflection another time. I'm not interested in Theodore. I'm not interested in anyone. And certainly not this weekend, there are far too many moving pieces to even consider it.

'Shall we go?' Aly asks, as she slips her feet into some killer heels.

'Why don't you head down and find the others? I need to double check my dosage calculation.'

'I'll save you a cocktail,' she promises as she slips out of the door.

'You'd better,' I call after her.

I like to do the maths the old-fashioned way, pen and paper, a careful calculation of height and weight and how much they've likely eaten already. If they are on any medications that may contra-indicate. If they've been knocking back brandy like it's going out of fashion.

Now, normally the calculation is fairly easy. All I'm doing is making sure that the dose is high enough, there isn't a ceiling, but there is a floor as it would be a disaster for them to survive. With Rani, however, I need to make sure that there is a high enough dose that there will still be some in her system when the police test her, but nowhere near enough to actually cause her harm. Ideally, I don't even want her to pass out.

There's a knock on the door. It's Sebastian. He's brandishing a bottle of Dalmore, the silver stag head glinting in the light. 'Peace offering,' he says as he takes a step inside the room.

I didn't actually invite him in, but I stuff down my irritation at his lack of etiquette.

'Did El brief you on the new plan?' I ask.

'Yeah,' he says, looking around the suite.

'Are you looking for something?'

'Where's Aly?'

'She already went downstairs to get a cocktail.'

He relaxes a little. 'Good.' He turns to face me. 'We're alone.'

It's very rare that good things happen when a man says that to you.

'What do you want, Sebastian? I'm in the middle of something.' I motion towards the desk and my notebook of calculations.

He walks over to take a closer look. 'A lethal dose?'

'No. That isn't what's been agreed.'

'But it's what you want to do,' he says as he straightens up and smiles at me. 'We both know that this plan is a farce. We don't do fake murders and tricks. It isn't who we are.'

I think back to the speed at which he recommended taking out Cassie as well, to keep our secrets. I'm not sure we're the same at all.

'Or are you worried about upsetting your darling Aly?' There's an edge to his tone, like he's mocking me. 'Poor precious Aly who doesn't think Rani is guilty because she has a hunch she can't back up.'

'What if she's right?'

'Alvi told me she threatened us with "her people".' He cocks his head as he stares at me.

'I'm not sure I buy it.'

'That "her people" would come for us?' He makes it sound like a joke, like she's a silly little girl invoking the old 'my brother will get you' warning. 'What if Aly *is* right and these "people" are made up?'

'For fuck's sake, Sadie.' I blanch slightly at his tone. 'Who cares? These women know far more than they should and we ought to be trying to find a way to silence them instead of getting into bed with them for some stupid games.'

'That isn't—'

But he cuts me off. 'Why the fuck do you care what happens to Rani and Cassie?' His raised voice echoes through the suite and I try not to flinch. I don't want to give him the satisfaction of thinking he can scare me.

'Because I'm not a psychopath.'

'Ha. You keep telling yourself that.'

'I don't kill innocents.'

He drops his voice to little more than a whisper. 'You know you would kill in an instant if it meant saving your darling goddaughter.'

'Is that a threat?'

He smiles and then holds up the bottle. 'How about we have a little conversation?'

72

CASSIE

Alvi comes up to Rani and asks for a word.

'But we're having fun,' Theodore tries to object. 'It isn't every day I get to spend time with the two most beautiful women in the room.'

Bea coughs pointedly.

'Sorry, the two most beautiful women in the room and my slightly grumpy sister who I'll admit has put on a fairly nice frock and doesn't look too hideous this evening.'

She punches him in the arm.

'Ouch.' He rubs the area, acting like it's all a big joke. But you could tell by the sound that she walloped him with quite a lot of force.

Before she peels away, I pull Rani to me. 'Good luck,' I whisper in her ear, taking in the scent of her perfume. She kisses my cheek and then follows Alvi. I can't help but cross my fingers at my side that this all goes to plan.

We mingle with the other teams, everyone making small talk. I try to look relaxed. Like I'm a guest at a murder mystery weekend and everything is fine and fun and games.

'Is everything all right with you and Rani?' Theodore asks. 'We missed you guys this afternoon. We were meant to play mini-golf...' he trails off, as if expecting me to launch into my story.

'We're fine,' I say quickly.

'Ohhh. Lovers' tiff,' he says and taps his nose. 'Say no more. I just hope you have fun making up later.'

'Don't be gross, Theodore.' Bea punches him in the arm again.

* * *

She stumbles as she heads towards us, hair loose down her back, hand at her neck. She's breathing incredibly quickly, her face turning red.

'Rani?' Theodore steps forwards and goes to grab her.

She collapses against him and then slowly slides to the floor, first onto her knees and then to the ground. She doesn't make a sound. I want to tell her to up the theatrics but I don't want to draw attention to the fact I've been waiting for this, that I knew this was going to happen.

Suddenly, Bea snaps to attention. 'Argh,' she lets out a pathetic half scream.

'I think it's obvious my sister didn't join me at RADA,' Theodore says. Then he winks at me before crouching down next to Rani. He slips off his dinner jacket and drapes it over her lower half to ensure her modesty. He's wearing the most ridiculous shirt underneath; the front looks normal, but the sleeves and back are printed with little pictures of gatling guns and porkpie hats. 'What?' he whispers when he catches me looking. 'It's a 1920s theme. Gangsters and all that.'

Then he rocks back onto his heels and looks up at the ceiling. He closes his eyes and takes a deep breath. A wail comes from his lips, like one of those women at funerals who are paid to mourn. He cracks open one eye to make sure people are starting to pay attention to him. I don't think he needs to worry about that. A crowd begins to form.

'Another murder?' a voice with a clipped accent asks. 'Before dinner?' I wait for them to add the word 'preposterous' at the end. They just grumble instead.

'I thought we were eating at eight,' someone else says.

'There's been a murder!' shouts Theodore. But the crowd is already dispersing as quickly as they gathered. I guess that six – well, seven, if you count the Marchioness – murders in about thirty hours is kind of a lot.

'You may as well help me up,' Theodore says, holding out his hand to me.

The two people in overalls come out once more. Now that I've met her, I recognise one is Tori. I suppress my urge to wave. The other must be Grace. I still haven't actually met her in person.

I'm waiting for Rani to break character, just a tiny bit, a wink or a hand motion or something.

But there's nothing.

She doesn't move a muscle as she's carried out.

'Your wife has some quite impressive acting skills,' Theodore whispers.

73

SADIE

Given the whole ugly situation with Sebastian, I approach dinner with a sense of dread. I know I've done the right thing – the only thing I could do given the circumstances – but still. He'd better stay as far from me as possible this evening.

El has changed the seating plan and we're now on a table with Cassie, Theodore, and his sister. I could really do without this, Aly is going to be insufferable about the whole Mr Dreamy thing and I'm going to have to try to find it amusing, even though I'm very far from being in the mood. On a positive note, our actors are joining us and El has put me next to Alvi so I don't need to put up with Aly's constant nudging and whispered comments.

However, I'm also sitting next to Cassie. There are little menu cards on each place setting and I watch as she carefully reads every line. She pulls a face after each item; sometimes a frown and sometimes a tilt of the head like a grudging acceptance.

'Do you approve?' I ask her quietly.

'Personally, I wouldn't serve Jerusalem artichoke at a gala,' she says. 'But wellington is always a good choice. As long as it's cooked well.'

The red-waistcoated waiters bring out tiny plates and place one in front of each of us.

'A smoked salmon macaron,' Cassie tells me.

It's delicious but I wish they served more than one. I'm not a fan of all these single bites of food that have become all the rage in recent years.

The plates are cleared and more wine is poured. Conversation around the table is stilted, as if we're all strangers who barely know each other. Although I suppose that is the case as far as Theodore and Bea are concerned, they have no idea I've spent most of the afternoon either with Cassie and Rani or at least talking about them at length.

'You promise she'll be all right?' Cassie whispers.

'Rani will be fine,' I tell her quickly. I want to shut this particular topic down as fast as possible. Aly looks up at that moment and catches my eye. My goddaughter grins at me and then looks at Theodore. If only Aly had any idea of what happened earlier and the threats Sebastian made.

The soup is served and, as it's placed in front of me, I think I can understand why Cassie said she wouldn't serve it at a gala. It smells earthy and I have a suspicion it will repeat on some of our more flatulent guests later.

I select a bread roll from a waiter and then turn to my left. 'Could you pass me the butter please, Alvi?'

'Alvi?' Bea asks, looking at the actor they've been calling Finn all this time.

'Apparently some former flame of Sadie's,' El says quickly. 'She said Finn reminds her of him.'

'Well, there have been a few,' Theodore mutters into his soup. Fucking cheek. Like he can talk, with all the women he's paraded around over the decades.

I take a bathroom break before the main course and relish the few minutes of solitude in the stall. But, as I leave, I find Cassie standing by the washbasins waiting for me.

'Theodore thinks it's you,' she says without preamble.

'He what?'

'He was very pleased with himself, just before Rani...' she peters out rather than saying the words.

'Why does he think it's me?'

'He has the bottle of belladonna from Diego's murder. He recognised your handwriting. Apparently you sent him a love letter many years ago.' She raises her eyebrows. 'Called him your beau.'

For fuck's sake. Is this all going to end in tears because of fucking Theodore fucking Frillish?

I narrow my eyes at her. 'You look like you have an idea.'

'Just prove to him it couldn't be you,' she says and then turns on her heels and leaves me in the bathroom.

I make a quick detour to the evidence room on my way back to the table. I'm going to need a prop.

The rest of the dinner passes with little note. The wellington is tasty if a little on the dry side and the dauphinoise it's served with is infused with nutmeg for an autumnal twist. Or at least according to Cassie. The food is obviously a safe subject and so it's all we talk about.

'The vegetables are well seasoned,' she tells me.

I'm so bored I want to gouge my own eyes out with a spoon.

Dessert is an espresso nougat tarte with cognac and blood orange salad. 'A really good balance of flavours,' Cassie decrees.

A selection of petit fours is brought out with coffee. I put a generous slug of brandy in mine to take the edge off.

Cheese and port follow. I was trained since childhood to endure bone-dripping boredom and still look like I'm having a thoroughly spiffing time, but this meal is taking all my resolve to get through.

Finally we are done and released from our prison at the table.

'Shall we retire to the ballroom?' El asks. 'There are still games to enjoy.'

Oh goodie. I can't wait.

Cassie leans in so she can whisper in my ear. 'This is your chance to talk to Theodore.' For a moment I think she's talking about him like Aly does, as Mr Dreamy. But she isn't. She means it's time for me to convince him I'm not a killer.

I touch his elbow as we start to head into the ballroom. 'I feel like we haven't had any time to chat this weekend, Theodore,' I say. It feels almost alien to be talking to him like this, trying to entice him into my orbit instead of pushing him away.

'Well,' he says, tucking my arm into his elbow. 'I think you may have been rather busy, Ms Rose.'

'Perhaps a drink now?'

'Before the next round of games? That sounds delightful.'

We find a quiet corner in the bar area and order Espresso Martinis from a passing waiter.

'So, any idea on who the killer is?' I ask, trying to sound as innocent as possible.

'I think you already know.'

'I have my suspicions, yes.' I pull out the small notebook I filched from the evidence room. 'Perhaps we could compare notes?' I flick to the middle of the notebook and write a list of the team names. Luckily there are five who begin with 'B', plenty of opportunities to showcase my handwriting.

I watch his gaze snag on the words on the page and a quick flash of confusion skitters across his brows.

My father believed that a lady should know how to write a proper letter and spent hours drilling me in fancy cursive handwriting. The ability to use a hand other than my own, or even to mimic someone else's, has proved to be extraordinarily useful in my life.

74

THE HIT LIST

Dossier Seven: Viktor Romanoff

I stare at the name. 'This has got to be fake, right?' I ask, turning to face Alvi. 'There is no way we have a bad guy here and his genuine name is Viktor Romanoff. He sounds like a Bond villain.'

'Sometimes the truth is stranger than fiction.' He shrugs.

Name: Viktor Romanoff
Team: Birch
Role: Equestrian Trainer
Relationship to the Marchioness: Trains the Marchioness' prize racehorses
Age: 70 years
Residence: Monte Carlo
Occupation: Businessman
Personal Life: Unknown

Additional Notes:

Viktor Romanoff is the man who bought the three lions from Jerome Fulker. He is also an international arms dealer. And not the legal kind.

No more needs to be said.

75

CASSIE

We gather in the ballroom and once more El takes the stage. She seems different to before, a tension in the way she holds her shoulders. Well, I suppose we have rather ruined her plan for the weekend and forced her to make a new one with very little time to iron out the details. It's hard to feel too much sympathy for her though.

'Ladies and gentlemen,' she says and waits for everyone to quieten down a little. 'I hope by now you are feeling a little closer to uncovering the truth of the Marchioness's murder?'

There's a murmur through the crowd. Perhaps I'm tired or just feeling a little jaded, but no one sounds particularly enthusiastic.

'Well, I've got something that will cheer you all up and galvanise you into action.' Her eyes meet mine across the room. 'Something very special indeed.'

What is she talking about?

'Tonight we are taking it back to the prohibition era. The East Orangery has been converted into our very own speakeasy. A place to drink gin, dance and, of course, to gamble.'

This time the murmur from the crowd is a little more interested.

'You will find a range of games, including roulette and of course some blackjack. But bet wisely. You will be able to convert your winnings at the end of the night into currency. And guess what that currency will buy you? Clues!'

I have no idea if this was always the original plan, although I suppose she wouldn't have been able to procure a speakeasy set-up that quickly so it must have been. But I'm a little irritated she didn't mention it earlier. Just so long as she isn't planning on making any other changes to the agreement.

Theodore and Bea excuse themselves to hunt down some drinks and I turn round and find Sadie right behind me. She has a little grin on her face. I raise an eyebrow. 'Care to explain that look?' I ask.

'Nothing. I've just always been a bit of a gambler.' But then her face drops. 'Not that it's going to make up for everything.'

'What do you mean?'

'Well, you have rather ruined it all. And I was very much looking forward to seeing him removed from Earth.'

'Who?' I ask.

'Viktor Romanoff. I didn't realise who he was before I read his dossier and started to piece together a few things from a very long time ago. A life-time ago – forty years at least – he came to my house to talk to my then husband.' She pauses and takes a breath. 'He has no idea who I am now, of course. I had a different name and different hair and I was quite the stunner at the time.' There's a touch of pride there. 'Do you know what my then husband did for a living?'

I shake my head.

'Let me tell you. He was a jewel thief.' She touches her hand to the chain around her neck and pulls it up to reveal a red stone glittering in the candlelight. 'This was what he gave me for our first anniversary. It once belonged to a member of the German royal family. He stole it from the safe of a Hollywood actor and left a dupe in its place.' A look of reminiscence lights up her entire face. She loved this man.

'What happened to him? To your husband, I mean,' I ask, fascinated by the idea you can still – forty years later – be in love with a criminal. Perhaps, if there was a chance for them, then I can find a way forward with Rani, despite all the lies?

'He died.' She keeps it simple but I can see the pain etched into her features. 'A long time ago. Anyway,' she clears her throat, 'the point being that Viktor Romanoff wanted to do business with my husband.'

'What kind of business?'

'Guns.' She sounds so disapproving. Like this was a step too far in terms of morality. Well, I guess even jewel thieves have lines they won't cross. 'Tommy didn't operate like that. But, anyway. Did you read the dossier? Did you see what happened to those lions? That's not the worst thing this man has ever done, mark my words. Aly gave me a lecture in the arms trade earlier, about how they need a steady stream of conflict to find new markets, literally creating wars for profit.'

'So, you think he should die?'

'You don't think we should make that decision, do you? You think that the justice system should lead the way, find the bad guys and punish them.' She makes me sound like a naive little child.

'I know it isn't perfect. But that's the way it needs to be. If everyone runs around playing vigilante, then there would be chaos. Innocent people would get caught in the crossfire.'

'How many people, innocent people, do you think have been caught in the literal crossfire of the guns this man puts on the streets?'

'That's not the poi—'

But my words are cut off as the crowd turns to face the doorway. Viktor Romanoff comes staggering in, his hand covering his eye, a pencil clearly visible between his fingers. He makes a grunting noise and then collapses.

There's a collective gasp from the other guests.

Theodore is on his way back to us with drinks and almost drops the tray. 'But I thought he was the killer,' he says in total disbelief as he reaches us. 'When I realised it couldn't be Sadie,' he nods at her, 'I figured it must be Team Birch, like our earlier guess.'

'I think we might have to re-evaluate,' I say. But I'm not really replying to Theodore.

I'm talking about the whole situation.

This wasn't what we agreed. There was never a plan for more people to die.

Which means it could still be a lie.

All of it.

Including Rani.

76

SADIE

Cassie grabs my wrist, her nails digging into my flesh. 'What the actual fuck,' she hisses under her breath.

'I'm just thinking that exact same thing myself,' I reply.

'What have you done?' Her nails dig deeper.

'This obviously wasn't me. So, if you could kindly get the hell off my wrist...'

She releases her grip but follows me as I head towards the main door into the lobby of the hotel. I stop at the bottom of the staircase and turn to face her. 'You can't come with me.'

'I'm not letting you out of my sight until you tell me what's going on.'

I take a deep breath. 'I didn't do this, remember. This wasn't me.'

'But you knew it was going to happen? You knew that he would still die tonight?'

I don't reply.

'I trusted you,' she spits the words.

I leave her standing by the main staircase and head towards the ladies' bathroom. Inside the last cubicle, I use my Swiss Army knife to unscrew the panel and slip into the passageways.

Viktor Romanoff had to die, I never really debated that, especially after Aly verified his crimes. But it was meant to be El who killed him, she was so excited about the whole pencil-as-murder-weapon thing. She was on stage when Viktor came staggering in to die, so there is no way she could have done it.

And that only leaves one possible perpetrator. Sebastian.

This may have been the only time I've killed as part of a team, but everyone knows there are rules in any sport, and the first one is that you don't take someone else's turn.

What the hell is Sebastian up to?

* * *

I keep my Swiss Army knife in one hand and take my heels off to carry them in the other as I follow the curve of the passageway. I should have left my shoes in the bathroom cubicle but I was a little distracted by the... what was that word, clusterfuck?... that appears to be unfurling. The stone floor is cold beneath my feet.

There's a sound behind me and I whirl round, knife out, expecting to come face with face with Sebastian.

'Woah, Aunt Sadie!' Aly jumps backward. 'It's only me.'

'And me.' Oh goodie, Cassie is behind her.

'You both shouldn't be back here,' I hiss, turning to look over my shoulder at the direction I was previously heading.

'We need to know what's going on,' Aly says. 'If the plan is changing, I need to be briefed. Viktor wasn't meant to die for another hour.'

Cassie grabs her arm and turns her so they're face to face. 'Hang on. *You* knew he was still going to die?'

'Cassie, I know you don't think it's our place to decide who should die, and that you're only tolerating—'

'You can't—'

'Let me finish.' Cassie closes her mouth slowly. Aly takes a breath and continues talking, 'and that you're only tolerating any of this because you want to punish Roger for what he did to your friend.'

'Karen.'

'Karen. But you need to let Sadie and El finish what they started. And trust me when I say this will help the case against Roger. I've planted some really rather juicy evidence to prove he killed Viktor.'

'Let's just hope Sebastian hasn't messed it all up though,' I add.

Cassie and Aly look at me expectantly.

'Because that wasn't his kill to make. It was meant to be El with the pencil,' I clarify.

'You think...?' Aly asks. She doesn't add 'that he's gone rogue and is about to screw up everything?' But she doesn't need to.

'I don't think we can trust him any more,' I reply.

'Oh, come on, Sadie,' Sebastian says from behind me, causing all of us women to jump. 'That feels a little harsh.'

I turn to find him wiping his hands on a handkerchief. It's streaked with blood.

'You know,' he says, casually leaning against the wall as if he doesn't have a care in the world. 'There's a saying about the best-laid plans. The best-laid plans of mice and men often go awry. Well, you are the mice. And your silly little plan was never going to work.' He smiles.

'What did you do?' I ask, the words sticking in my chest.

His smile widens. 'What was necessary.'

He looks at me, eyes boring into mine. He doesn't say the words but his expression is clear as day. *What you refused to do.* His gaze drifts to Aly.

Earlier, I told him I wouldn't tolerate his threatening behaviour and demanded he keep to the plan. I didn't take him seriously. I think I misjudged him.

Has he killed Rani?

And if he has, what does it mean for all of us?

77

CASSIE

What was necessary? What the hell does that mean? I open my mouth to ask but my eyes snag on a smear of red on Sebastian's collar. Blood. I knew this man was a killer but to see the evidence so casually displayed brings the reality home. He's a psychopath who ignores all of society's rules.

I should never have trusted him. I should never have trusted any of them.

'Take me to her,' I demand, trying to keep my voice level and not give away just how terrified I am. For myself in a dark secret tunnel with two serial killers. For Rani. I believed them when they said they wouldn't hurt her. What if... but I swallow the thought down. I cannot fall apart. Not yet.

'Take me to her,' I demand again.

Sebastian actually has the gall to look puzzled. 'Take you to who?' he asks.

'Take me to my wife. Right fucking now.'

'Woah. What's got into you?' he asks.

'We had a fucking deal. A fucking plan. But you obviously didn't give a shit about that. So take me to her. So help me God.' A few months ago I had to go all kamikaze on some prick at the dog park with an off-leash bully and a serious attitude problem. I didn't know I was capable of that level of anger, but this burns even hotter. I would fight this man with my bare hands to save my wife. I just really hope I don't have to.

'Calm down a little, OK,' Sebastian says in the kind of patronising tone mediocre men so often reserve for women they feel threatened by.

'I will not calm down.' I take a few steps towards him, my face up in his space. 'Take me to her or I will fucking end you.'

'Cassie?' a voice behind me says. 'Did you really just threaten to kill this man?' She laughs, a sound far sweeter than I ever thought possible.

I spin to watch my wife sashay towards me. Her hair is unravelling from her braid and there's a ladder up one of her tights. I don't think she's ever looked more beautiful.

Relief floods my system and I almost stagger under the weight of it.

* * *

The rest of the evening passes in a blur. I try to avoid Sebastian, mainly because I think I might punch him on the nose if I see his stupid smirking face. He actually laughed when he realised I thought he'd killed Rani. Like my distress was funny to him.

I don't know what's been said to him by the others but Aly assured me that he'll fall into line and not deviate any more from the plan.

'Does that plan include the death of Monty Braithwaite?' I'd asked.

'The dossier says he's a paedophile. But it's worse. He's involved in the trafficking of the girls too. There's already been an investigation but it was all swept under the carpet. He will never face traditional justice for his crimes.'

'OK,' I'd said eventually.

The orangery windows have been draped with dark purple curtains, leaving the ceiling to draw the eye upwards to the stars glistening in the night sky. There is a row of casino tables set up down the centre, each one staffed by a waistcoated croupier. The space is lit by wrought iron candelabra and hundreds of tealights that flicker on every surface. It's probably a terrible fire hazard but the effect is incredible.

Theodore tries to teach me how to play blackjack but my brain is so full of everything else that I struggle to pick up all the rules of his magical strategy. When I try to split my tens, he harumphs loudly. I excuse myself to go to the bathroom, trying not to cry in front of him as my emotions start to crescendo.

I spend five minutes in the ladies composing myself. I've never been that good at showing my true feelings in public, something that has earned me the moniker of 'ice queen' on more than one occasion. A number of ex-girlfriends have suggested I think about an autism test. Normally when they broke up with me, of course. I've never been formally diagnosed, although I'm fairly sure I'm neurodivergent in some way, but I do feel things. I just choose to cry in the ladies bathroom instead of in front of other people.

Back in the orangery, which is now buzzing with guests gambling and drinking, I stand at the edge and watch them all. Everyone else is having fun but I just feel washed out. Overwhelmed. All I want to do is go to bed and get some sleep but I still need to convince Theodore and Bea that Team Black – and specifically Roger Carruthers – are the killers. A headache builds behind my left eye. I'm so sick of feeling like I'm on the back foot; I still have no idea how to do it.

Theodore and Bea have moved on to roulette and I force myself to join them. At least I can't get this game wrong if I stick to betting on either red or black.

'I'm sorry if I was short with you,' Theodore says as he puts his arm around my shoulder and pulls me into the game. 'I can get a little too competitive sometimes.'

'It's OK,' I reply. 'Sorry I wasn't better at blackjack.'

'You should really cut yourself some slack. You're a highly intelligent and thoroughly impressive young lady. It took me weeks to learn all the rules when I first started playing and you were picking it up at practically the speed of light.'

I think he's just being kind, but it's sweet of him to say it.

The roulette dealer asks for our bets.

'Shall we go all in on a single number?' Bea asks with a twerk of her eyebrow. 'I'm in a gambling mood.'

'Thirty-two,' I say. 'It's always been my lucky number.' I don't add that I don't feel particularly lucky at the moment. You never know when things might change.

The ball bearing spins around the wheel at lightning speed and I watch it carefully. Eventually it drops and I close my eyes in anticipation as it bounces a few times before settling, fingers crossed on both hands.

'Holy shit,' Theodore whispers. I crack an eyelid. Holy shit indeed.

'We won?'

'Yes, we did. And you know what this means?' He grins.

I breathe a sigh of relief. What it actually means is that I don't have to find a way to convince my team that it's Team Black instead of Willhayes or even Bowerman; we can buy the clues to do it for me.

'Let's go clue shopping,' Bea says as she scoops up the winning chips.

Grace and Tori spent the early part of the evening creating new clues to point everyone towards Roger and Team Black and I'll admit they did a pretty good job.

'Look at this,' Theodore says, thrusting a pamphlet into my hands. 'It's about the dangers of electricity. From the Wiltshire Anti-Pylon League.'

'Wiltshire?' I ask. 'I'm sure one of the remaining teams has a guest from Salisbury.'

'See, I told you you're highly intelligent,' Theodore says.

'There's also a receipt for a dagger,' Bea says. 'A dagger inlaid with a coat of arms. Oh, with the Marquess's coat of arms.'

'But only family could use that.' Theodore's brow crinkles as he thinks.

'What about an illegitimate son who thought he might be about to claim the title he always thought he deserved?'

'Aren't Team Black meant to be relatives?'

I nod.

'Well then, ladies, I think we have our killers.'

PART VIII

BREAKFAST

78

THE HIT LIST

Dossier Eight: Monty Braithwaite

Name: Monty Braithwaite
Team: Willhayes
Role: Bishop Absolute, Order of the Patriots
Relationship to the Marchioness: The late Marquess' grandfather founded the Order
Age: 50 years
Residence: Cayman Islands
Occupation: Investment banker

'What's the collective noun for bankers?'

'A wunch. You already made that joke.'

'Wow, tough crowd.'

He blows me a kiss. 'You're still adorable though, *Rakkaani*.'

Personal Life: Married with two sons. His old schoolfriend Felix is with him at Holne House.

I take a deep breath before I fill out the final section of Monty's dossier. To me, he is the worst of them all.

Additional Notes:

There have been rumours about Monty Braithwaite for years. Whispers that he likes his women on the younger side. I hate that euphemism. Let's just call a spade a spade, shall we? Monty Braithwaite is a paedophile who thinks children aged around fourteen are a delicacy.

This one needs to be painful.

79

SADIE

The morning air is cold against my face. I've always loved this time, just before the dawn breaks and the world stands still in anticipation of the new day.

It's even better when you're preparing for a kill.

Technically this one will belong to El – Sebastian having conceded his claim after the pencil debacle last night – but it's so ambitious, she needs all of us to help. She talks about us 'slaying together' but, until now, we were still doing our own thing, just with the others having knowledge of it. This one will be a genuine collaborative effort.

Monty Braithwaite is a man I have heard rumours about for years. Whispers about how he liked his women 'a little on the younger side' – so, girls then, not women. Nothing concrete, mind; someone describing him as 'noncey' like it was a cutesy term, a grainy picture of him and Epstein, the daughter of a family friend posting an oblique comment on social media. I was lucky to not actually ever meet him in real life. Or was he the lucky one? I would have killed him in an instant and thought nothing of it.

I know Cassie has this simplistic view that you can't play judge and jury, but I'll just say this: you don't get that kind of reputation without being guilty.

Monty is attending the Murder on the Moors with an old school pal of his.

'I'm going to look at the friend,' Aly told me last night.

'You think he's the same?'

She shrugged. 'Why else would you want to spend time with a man like that?'

In the end, though, she'd been pleasantly surprised. The friend was exactly the opposite. A man who donated huge sums to charities protecting women across the world from exploitation.

'Unless it's a cover,' I'd said somewhat cynically. 'A way of rebalancing the scales.'

Aly dug deeper and found repeated mentions of an unnamed source popping up in relation to a number of open investigations into the trafficking of teenage girls. The source was described as a British aristocrat with a decorated military record.

'You think that's the friend?'

Aly nodded and then sat back in her chair. 'At least there are a few good men out there,' she said with the relief of someone who spends far too much time looking at all the awful ones. I felt a stab of guilt at my part in bringing this batch to her door. When this is all over, I'm going to take her on holiday somewhere nice. Somewhere there isn't a whole collection of criminals to be dispatched. A place with cocktails and shirtless waiters and hope mingling with the scent of coconut in the air.

* * *

My role in this morning's fun is to lure Monty to the courtyard where El is waiting for him.

Grace, dressed in her concierge uniform – apparently she's been working at the hotel for a month or so to ensure everything would go to plan – has already woken him, spinning some tale about reports of a potential gas leak in his suite. She has deposited him in the hotel bar with the promise of a coffee.

I step inside the building and spot him immediately. He looks dishevelled, a man who has partied a little too hard and is now regretting it the next morning. The buttons on his shirt are done up incorrectly. I really hope that you go to the afterlife in the clothes you're wearing when you die. Imagine spending eternity with a flappy piece of shirt because you couldn't dress yourself properly.

'Your suite also affected?' I ask as I slide onto the stool next to him.

'It's diabolical. I'll be sending them back the whole bill for this weekend.'

Typical man, getting his knickers in a twist about a minor inconvenience. If there really was a gas leak, you'd think he'd be thankful they discovered it in time. But, anyway. 'I've heard the sun is about to rise over the moors and the view is really rather impressive.'

He mumbles something under his breath.

'I would have thought you were rather a connoisseur of beauty,' I say, smiling sweetly. 'Didn't I see you admiring the F. J. Widgery in the hallway yesterday?' I didn't, but I can absolutely imagine that at some point over the weekend this disgusting man has paused to view the painting of a gorgeous sunrise over the sea at Teignmouth, featuring the very pretty – and very young – wife of some former Holne House resident. The painting would have caused quite the stir when it was commissioned, given she's in the sea in just her shift, the white cotton clinging to her skin.

He's caught in a trap with no choice but to come with me to appreciate the scenery, or admit the human subject of the painting was the true point of interest.

El is waiting in the courtyard.

I leave her to work her magic and head back inside to get a drink.

80

CASSIE

I wake up alone, the sun just rising above the horizon. I have the uneasy feeling that I've been having terrible dreams but I can't remember any details. Rani told me once that I was lucky I don't remember them, she can recite hers beat by beat like a movie. But I disagree, I think it's worse if you can't remember anything but your sleep is still interrupted, as your body pumps you full of adrenaline against a monster you cannot see.

It also invariably means my anxiety is on high alert for the first thirty minutes after I wake up, searching for something – anything – to latch onto.

Oh shit. And there it is. There *is* something we've not thought about.

It's so fucking obvious as well. How the hell did we miss it?

It's all well and good to point the finger at Roger Carruthers and have him deny everything, but still be found guilty when all the evidence is analysed.

But his team will corroborate his story. They have not been the killing team for the weekend. Maybe we could get away with saying his girlfriend is lying to help save him. But the two strangers on his team, people he wouldn't have met until Friday afternoon? Why would they lie? And if Team Black hasn't been the killing team all this time, then there is no way that Roger Carruthers killed all those people in real life either. Unless he snuck into the VIP—

I cut off my own thought process. That's just stupid. Why would he sneak in and then kill them in the exact same way they were fake killed in the game by another team? Idiot.

The only way this works is if the murders were premeditated by Roger. If he was able to disrupt the hotel operations sufficiently so that no one noticed there weren't actually any real-life people in the VIP area. If he was always in control.

His team have to have been the killers the whole time.

Fuck.

Fuck.

Fuck.

I drag myself out of bed and pick up the dossier from the coffee table in the seating area. What are we going to do? Who are the other members of Team Black?

When I see him, I can't help but laugh. It's probably delirium.

* * *

I head down to breakfast to find an absolute ruckus in the entrance hall. I guess they found Monty's body then. I still don't know how I feel about his death, it definitely feels wrong to have taken the law into our own hands. Not that my hands were anywhere near this, of course, but you know what I mean.

'There's been another murder,' Theodore says, running up to me.

I paint a confused look on my face, as if I had no idea Monty Braithwaite was currently impaled on a deer statue. 'Another?'

'It's really rather good, this one,' he tells me. 'They've done such an incredible job in the staging. It's truly chef's kiss.' He kisses the tips of his fingers. 'Just fabulous.'

'I don't think my brother is going to stop talking about this one on our trip back to London,' Bea says, coming to join us.

I think he's going to have plenty more to discuss, but I keep quiet. I feel kind of bad that Theodore's bubble is going to burst so dramatically in just a few short hours. I think it's going to put him off murder mystery weekends for the rest of his life.

'You know what this means, though?' Theodore says. 'We are definitely right about it being Team Black.' He rubs his hands together in glee.

'I think it's probably time we came clean,' Bea tells me. 'There's something we've been hiding from you.' She sounds nervous, like she's truly worried about telling me. 'Umm... well, the thing is... we don't normally do very well at these weekends. We're always so completely wrong it's embarrassing.'

'I'm sorry I lied to you, Cassie,' Theodore says. 'I was just so hoping we'd have a better chance this year, what with being in a team with you and your delightful wife. I didn't want you to cut us out when you discovered we were so bad at it all.'

I want to laugh at how earnest he is. It's adorable. If only he had any idea what was really going on.

'Now then,' Theodore says, 'shall we get some breakfast?' He looks at me expectantly.

I want to sit with him and Bea and drink coffee and eat some pastries. But first I have one last problem to solve. 'I'll join you in ten minutes,' I promise. 'Save me a seat.'

* * *

Theodore and Bea admitting they were bad at murder mysteries has given me an idea. They are smart people, well educated, able to follow clues and make reasonable deductions. If even *they* admit to being rubbish, then how bad would someone be if they weren't very smart and they weren't able to follow basic instructions?

Remember the utter imbecile who didn't understand the game at all during the 'where were you the day the sun went dark' thing? Guess who's a member of Team Black? I assume his girlfriend is also pretty lacking in the brains department – harsh, but probably true.

So, the final question remains.

Can I convince good old Jasper that he's been on the killing team this whole time?

PART IX

DENOUEMENT AND PRIZEGIVING

81

SADIE

For the final showdown, I need a poison that cannot be found in my garden here at Holne House. It must be one that leads the police away from here and towards a man who is an opportunist and not someone who has spent their life studying the art.

Now, there are some misconceptions with poisons. Most people think there is a certainty to them: calculate the perfect dose and the result is guaranteed. But that only applies to a very limited number of poisons. Many people also think poisons are instant, that the person will keel over and die as soon as they ingest one. Again, that only applies to a narrow range.

Poisoning is very hit or miss to the hobbyist.

I'm sitting in the Christie suite, pondering the conundrum, when inspiration strikes. After all, who better to take my cue from than the Queen of Crime herself? In *Lord Edgeware Dies*, she used a barbiturate known as Veronal. It was a fairly common sedative at the time but was also linked to numerous suicides. It is notoriously unreliable. You can take a huge dose and suffer little in the way of ill effect, or find that a small dose is lethal.

Now, I would never use a barbiturate to kill someone. There is far too much of a chance that they would survive. However, I have used them to subdue a victim before administering something more... how shall we say?... reliable. So I have a small amount with me, ground to a powder and hidden in a small makeup compact.

It's perfect.

82

CASSIE

I finally find Jasper and his girlfriend on the patio, admiring the view out across Dartmoor. There are just ten minutes left before the final showdown. I'm only going to get one shot at this.

'Gorgeous morning, isn't it?' I say as I stop beside them.

'Indeed,' Jasper replies.

'I bet you two are excited for the final denouement.' I throw him a wink.

'Indeed. I'm intrigued.'

I take a breath. 'Intrigued. Oh, Jasper, you're such a rogue.' I laugh loudly. Then I drop my voice and lean in to him. 'I know it's Team Black.'

'No. I'm Team Black,' he says, before glancing at his girlfriend for her confirmation that he is indeed on Team Black.

'Of course you are, silly,' I say. 'You have been so discreet too. I'm very impressed.'

Confusion clouds his face and he looks at his girlfriend again for moral support. She just shrugs. I honestly don't think she cares either way. 'But...' He shakes his head. 'I...'

'You really had me convinced it wasn't you that first night, you know,' I tell him. 'Honestly, hats off to you. I would never have guessed.' I lean even closer to deliver my coup de grace. 'I only know because I cheated and managed to sneak a peek at one of the staff's folders.' I make a face. 'Naughty me.'

'No... I...'

'You're far too modest, Jasper. You really did pull a fast one over everyone. Your teammates must have done a sterling job too. Anyway, I think it's time for the final game.' I turn to walk away but then stop and return to face them. 'Bravo,' I say, clapping my hands together in applause. 'Bravo indeed.'

And then I walk away. Is it enough?

I really hope so.

* * *

We are gathered in the ballroom for the final denouement. A raised area has been erected, on which there are two rows of chairs, one on either side of the makeshift stage, a low coffee table in front of each. El stands in the middle. She catches my eye across the crowd and I give her the briefest of nods.

We're ready.

'Ladies and gentlemen,' she booms and silence falls over the guests. 'The moment you have all been waiting for has arrived.' She pauses for the ripple of excitement. 'Now then, you may be wondering what all these chairs are for? Well, I think you've all figured out by now that only two teams could possibly be the killers. No one has been murdering their teammates, after all. So, I would like to invite the members of Team Black and the members of Team Bowerman up onto the stage.'

There's a round of applause as they head up to the front and take their seats as directed by Lloyd. We barely saw him yesterday and today he is looking both extremely peaky and very relieved that El is still holding the reins.

'I think we can all agree that this weekend has been a rollercoaster,' El says. 'And I hope you have all had a fantastic time getting to know your fellow guests and enjoying sleuthing not just one death, like is normally the case at Murder on the Moors, but nine!'

She motions to the two red-waistcoated waiters who are standing by each row of chairs. 'We have prepared a congratulatory drink for the finalists, based on what we know to be their favourites.' All the drinks are different. I have no idea what Team Black are drinking, but Sadie's is a gin gimlet and Aly's is a mimosa.

'No surprise my niece has gone for a buck's fizz,' Sadie says loudly. There's a titter from the crowd, Aly made a bit of a thing at breakfast about her love of orange juice mixed with Champagne. I mutter under my breath that a buck's fizz and a mimosa don't have the same ratios but no one hears.

'Does the Dowager not approve?' El asks.

'I just think you should enjoy a proper drink,' Sadie replies, raising her glass.

'Hear, hear,' El says. 'So, if you will raise your glasses. To the finalists!'

But, just as Aly lifts her mimosa to her lips, there's an almighty crash from behind one of the curtains next to the stage. Out stumbles Rani, her hair even more dishevelled than last night, another ladder in her tights and a wild look in her eyes.

'No!' she screams, running towards Aly and knocking the glass from her hand. The crystal shatters as it hits the floor, spraying the contents across the parquet.

There's a gasp from the crowd.

'There's a murderer on the loose,' Rani says. She turns to point at Roger. 'This man tried to kill me.'

For a moment, silence falls and then there's a few bursts of nervous laughter. No one quite knows how to react.

'Is this part of the game?' someone behind me asks.

Rani falls to her knees, as if exhaustion has taken her. She begins to sob, covering her face with her hands.

'What's happening?' someone else whispers.

Rani takes her hands away to reveal thick tears running in rivulets down her face. Jesus, my wife really is a *very* good actress. Perhaps I should stop beating myself up for not seeing through her lies before. She stands up on shaking legs and turns to face us. 'Someone needs to call the police. It's all real. All the murders. Roger Carruthers has killed them all.'

I push through the crowd to the front and gather my wife into my arms. Her body is racked by her tears.

'Get out of my way.' I hear Theodore coming through the guests behind me. He marches up to the clearly shell-shocked Roger and grabs one of his arms, twisting it behind his back.

'What... what...' Roger splutters, trying to free himself.

'What have you done?' Theodore asks. All trace of the gentle affable man I've been drinking with all weekend is gone. In his place is 6 ft 2 of pure rage. I guess Rani's performance has convinced *him*, at least.

'He tried to kill me, Theodore,' Rani says softly. 'It's all real. And I think he was about to kill Aly.'

'Poison?' Theodore asks.

'I think so,' Rani says. 'Check his pockets.'

Theodore reaches into Roger's jacket and pulls out a small clear bag, the remnants of some white power at the bottom.

Sadie stands up and walks towards Roger. 'What is that?' she demands.

'I... I... have no idea,' Roger stutters. 'What the hell is going on here?' He tries again to twist out of Theodore's grip. 'Ow. You're hurting me.'

Sadie takes the bag from Theodore and opens it carefully, giving it a delicate sniff. 'Odourless.' She holds it up to the light. 'Crystalline.' She turns to Rani. 'This could be recreational?'

Rani shakes her head. 'It's poison. He was going to poison Aly, just like he poisoned me.' Then she faints in my arms.

'We need an ambulance,' I say. 'And the police.'

83

THE HIT LIST

Dossier Nine: Roger Carruthers

Name: Roger Carruthers
Team: Black
Role: Illegitimate son of the Marquess
Relationship to the Marchioness: She only discovered his existence at the Marquess' funeral
Age: 35 years
Residence: Salisbury, Wiltshire
Occupation: Managing Director of Carruthers Enterprises

Roger Carruthers earned over a million pounds last year as the MD of the company established by his father. Who says nepotism is dead?

Personal Life: Divorced, no children. Attending Holne House with his new girlfriend, Tamara

I do not know how many people I've killed in my lifetime. But there is one thing I do know: I have never killed someone who didn't deserve to meet their demise. Same for Alvi.

But not Roger Carruthers.

Additional Notes:

What we have discovered about Roger is likely only the tip of the iceberg. He is clever and cunning and knows how to cover his tracks. At least up to a point. He may have evaded arrest so far, but he does leave a signature with his kills. All of them were strangled. And the weapon in each case was a silk necktie.

The first one he dressed up as a suicide, claimed the woman – his girlfriend at the time – had used his tie to kill herself. Then there were a few Jane Does who turned up in various secluded spots, the neckties all purchased at charity shops and impossible to trace. Last year the police got involved when a woman was found dead in his hotel room. He claimed she was a stalker and he had acted in self-defence, grabbing the closest thing to him to subdue her as she tried to stab him with a knife.

Roger has murdered at least five women.

We do not condone the murder of innocents.

84

SADIE

There's a secret passageway directly behind the parlour room the police have taken over as their HQ. Every single person at the hotel is to be interviewed over the next few hours, and so I've bought a lawn chair to make the spying a little less uncomfortable. I can't see them, but I can listen to every word that's said.

* * *

Jasper Price-Evans proves he is just as stupid as I always assumed.

'I had no idea what was going on,' he tells the police. 'I didn't actually realise we were the killing team until about ten minutes before that lady, Rani, I think her name was, burst onto the stage.'

The police assume he's lying and keep repeating their questions over and over in an attempt to trip him up. But he just gets more and more flustered.

'Ask Matty. He was the person from Murderous Intentions who was helping us. He didn't know either.'

'None of the staff knew. The game was designed that way, so they couldn't be blackmailed by other teams to give away the killer's identity.' The police have already spoken to Alvi who was especially convincing in the way he spun the story. If I ever need another pair of hands to take someone out, I wouldn't hesitate to bring him in.

* * *

Aly acts like she's shell-shocked over how close she got to becoming another victim. They ask her a few general questions about where she lives and what she does for work, but nothing detailed.

They don't ask her if she would be able to plant false evidence on a person's laptop to suggest that they had been organising a murder spree.

They don't ask if she'd managed to fake a time stamp on an email so it seems Roger had access to the 'game bible' the staff at Murderous Intentions had used to plan the event.

They don't ask if she could hack his WhatsApp and create a message chain between him and a hospitality temp company, telling them not to send staff for the weekend. This was especially tricky as the original conversation had been between Alvi and the company, but Aly was able to repoint everything so it looks legit.

They don't ask if she would be able to make it look like Roger had ordered poisons on the dark web, including the opium he apparently administered to Rani and the barbiturates in the bag Theodore found in his jacket pocket.

* * *

Grace is interviewed in her role as the concierge in charge of the VIP area. She does an impressive piece of acting, playing a traumatised staff member held hostage by the evil murderer. The police even buy that she was forced to collect the bodies she knew were really dead while telling Tori they were just pretending. I hold my breath through parts of her interview. This is the weak link in the story. All the guests saw the murder victims being removed so there is no way around it. But, at least it does explain any traces of the two women's DNA found during the autopsies.

* * *

When it's Sebastian's turn, he stays fairly quiet, answering the questions quickly and concisely. Samuel is interviewed directly afterwards. He doesn't mention the magic course he did when he was a student, or how he occasionally delights his friends with his sleight-of-hand tricks.

* * *

Cassie plays the wife of the woman who was almost killed to perfection. She basically just repeats, 'How did I miss that it was real? She was almost dead and I was partying,' over and over again.

* * *

And then it's my turn in the hot seat.

'I've been coming here for fifty years,' I tell the detectives, who are both suspiciously young. They have definitely been through some fast-track scheme for 'bright young things', which is all well and good, but they are completely out of their depths here. Although I suppose that could work to our advantage, as long as they don't mess up the whole thing and let Roger Carruthers walk free.

'Fifty years of Murder on the Moors and there has never been anything so shocking as this. A real murderer on the loose? It just doesn't bear thinking about.' I play into the whole 'batty old woman' thing. It doesn't take long before they bore of me and tell me they have no further questions. I'm told to expect a visit from other detectives in the next few days if further details need to be corroborated.

'Of course,' I say, smiling sweetly. At least I'll have plenty of time to rid the apartment in Mayfair of anything incriminating.

85

CASSIE

Rani has to be taken to the hospital so they can check her over and make sure the opium won't cause any lasting damage. She was flanked by two uniformed officers as they wheeled her stretcher onto an ambulance, for her protection, in case she's still at risk. I promised I'd go to the hospital to find her as soon as the police had finished their interviews here.

But now I'm standing outside Holne House, finally free to leave, and I'm torn. Part of me wants to see her, to talk about everything that's happened this weekend, to find a way through all of this. And part of me wants to get in the car and drive as far away as possible.

'Follow your heart,' Theodore says, coming up behind me. 'But remember that, if you walk away, you will never know if you could have worked things out. Don't be like this old fool who didn't take a chance.'

I turn round and see his attention isn't on me. It's on Sadie, as she waits with Aly for their driver to collect them.

'I thought you said she was married to someone else?'

'She was. But Bea said he was a hideous bully. I could have helped get her away from him.' He sounds sad, almost guilty.

'It wasn't your job to save her.'

'I should have made it my job.' He's adamant. I wonder what he'd think if I told him she didn't need him to save her and that she saved herself perfectly well in the end?

'But, anyway. Things with Rani are too complicated. I can't just forgive her.'

'You can if you try hard enough,' he says, resting his hand on my shoulder. 'But only if you want to.' Obviously, he has no idea what is really going on but I appreciate his kindness anyway.

'We need to go, Theodore,' Bea says as she comes over to us.

'I was saying goodbye to Cassie,' he tells her. 'Who was about to promise that she will come and visit us in Gloucestershire very soon.'

'I wouldn't miss it for the world,' I assure him.

He pulls me into a hug and squeezes me so tightly I can barely breathe.

'It has been a pleasure, Ms Kohl.'

I watch him and Bea drive away. I suppose at least one good thing has come from this weekend.

El comes over just as I'm finally getting into the car. She leans through the driver's window. 'You're good at this,' she tells me quietly. She sounds so genuine and, for a brief moment, I allow myself to bask in the idea of a job well done. But then I remember she's a killer. An actual bona fide serial killer. Yes, she might only kill the bad guys, but even so...

'I couldn't do what you do...'

'No. But maybe something a little less splashy...' She gives me a pointed look. 'I think it would do you good to let go a little more often.'

ALY'S EPILOGUE

The train to Newcastle from London takes three hours and we are packed in like sardines. Luckily, I pre-booked a seat and I find myself with three brothers returning home for the Christmas holidays. They have flasks full of mulled wine and are more than happy to share.

'Why are you off to Newcastle?' the eldest asks me. He's cute, with floppy dark hair and brilliant green eyes like the cliché love interest in a romcom.

I give him the same answer I gave Aunt Sadie when I left her Mayfair flat this morning. 'Just visiting an old friend.'

El and Alvi never bothered to make a dossier for Samuel Radley. I suppose they weren't quite as good at research as I am...

Name: Samuel Radley
Team: Bowerman
Role: The Twin
Relationship to the Marchioness: Distant relative
Age: 41 years
Residence: Newcastle
Occupation: Trader
Personal Life: Single. Samuel has an identical twin brother, Sebastian

Additional Notes:

The people in Samuel's life have proven to be rather accident prone. Sometimes a few questions are asked of his brother's whereabouts, but Samuel is good at helping Sebastian with his alibis.

It goes both ways, of course. Samuel couldn't possibly have killed those girls in Exhibition Park. Or that man who was dumped in South Shore Road Car Park.

Roger Carruthers was a terrible man who deserves to spend the rest of his life in prison. But he didn't kill anyone that weekend at Holne House. Including Karen Jackson.

Samuel Radley did.

And I'm going to make him pay for it.

I reach into the pocket of my coat and touch the vial of cyanide, then I pull out a pen and a crumpled receipt for the Agatha Christie novel I bought at JFK. On the back, I scribble my phone number.

The green-eyed boy winks as he slips it into his pocket.

Maybe I'll let him take me for a drink while I decide if I'm going to deal with Sebastian while I'm here too. Sadie told me about the threats he made, and I remember the way he laughed when Cassie thought he'd killed Rani. He's a liability. But I need to choose my time wisely.

CASSIE'S EPILOGUE

We meet at the water cooler in the hospital corridor. Dad had a heart attack three days ago and I've barely left the building, except to ferry Mum back and forth and pick up one brother from the station, and get everyone snacks, and pick up some toiletries for my other brother who forgot the bare essentials.

The woman smiles at me but I can see the exhaustion etched into her features. We're probably about the same age, but both of us look a decade older under the harsh lights.

'My mum,' she says. She reaches out to take a stack of cups. 'I honestly think the rest of my family would turn into desiccated husks before they actually went to get the water themselves.'

I lift my jug and multiple cups in solidarity. 'My dad,' I tell her. 'And my family are the same.'

'My husband keeps saying I should tell them to bugger off.' She laughs softly.

I glance at the diamond on her left hand, glittering in the harsh overhead lighting, and, for a moment, I touch the place mine once resided. Rani and I are taking a break. I don't know who she is or if I could ever really trust her again. She's said she'll wait for me to change my mind, but I don't think I'm going to. Life is too short to waste it.

* * *

We smoke under the canopy of the bike store down the side of the hospital, not far from the entrance. It provides vague protection from the rain as it lashes down. Both of us studiously avoid looking at the sign that says 'no smoking'. I get it's a hospital, but they must realise that, for a lot of people, this is the most stressful place in the whole world.

'You're the eldest?' she asks.

I shake my head. 'I have two brothers who are older than me.'

'So, you are the eldest.' She grins. 'The eldest daughter, at least.'

'Is it that obvious?'

We both laugh, but it's more of a rueful chuckle.

'Sometimes I wish I could just let it all out,' she says, before taking a long drag on her cigarette. She blows a plume of smoke directly upwards towards the canopy ceiling. 'Blow it all up. Let loose.'

I think back to the way I felt as they led Roger Carruthers away in handcuffs, his face beetroot red in rage. Karma really is a bitch. And letting her out for a few hours was so ridiculously cathartic.

'What if there was a way?' I ask my new friend.

'Ha. Are you planning a crime spree?'

'I think we'd be really rather good at it. We could call it the Eldest Daughters' Crime Collective.'

* * *

MORE FROM SARAH BONNER

Another book from Sarah Bonner, *How to Slay at Work*, is available to order now here:

https://mybook.to/HowtoSlayatWork

ACKNOWLEDGEMENTS

Firstly, a huge thank you to my wonderful agent Hannah Sheppard for being such a champion of my writing.

To the fabulous Francesca Best for your editorial wizardry. To Amanda Ridout, Wendy Neale, Marcela Torres, Isabelle Flynn, Grace Cooper, Hayley Russell, Ben Wilson, Paul Martin, Justinia Baird-Murray, Arbaiah Aird and everyone else at Boldwood for all your hard work in getting my books into the hands of readers.

To my family and friends for everything you do, especially to my amazing husband who (once again) put up with me during the writing process and kept me topped up with tea and biscuits and the occasional gin. To Lily for your constant companionship. A special mention to the Sbooky Bitches; for being the best group of writer friends I could have wished for.

And finally a massive thank you to all the other authors, reviewers, bloggers, and readers. Bookish people really are the best people!

ABOUT THE AUTHOR

Sarah Bonner is the author of bestselling psychological thrillers, including *Her Perfect Twin*. She lives in West Sussex with her husband and very spoiled rescue dog.

Download your exclusive bonus content from Sarah Bonner here:

Follow Sarah on social media here:

x.com/sarahbonner101
facebook.com/sarah.bonner.35574
instagram.com/sarahbonner101
tiktok.com/@sarahbonner101

ALSO BY SARAH BONNER

How to Slay at Work

How to Slay on Holiday

How to Slay at Christmas

A Killer Guest List

THE *Murder* LIST

THE MURDER LIST IS A NEWSLETTER DEDICATED TO SPINE-CHILLING FICTION AND GRIPPING PAGE-TURNERS!

SIGN UP TO MAKE SURE YOU'RE ON OUR HIT LIST FOR EXCLUSIVE DEALS, AUTHOR CONTENT, AND COMPETITIONS.

SIGN UP TO OUR NEWSLETTER

BIT.LY/THEMURDERLISTNEWS

Boldwood

Boldwood Books is an award-winning fiction publishing company seeking out the best stories from around the world.

Find out more at www.boldwoodbooks.com

Join our reader community for brilliant books, competitions and offers!

Follow us
@BoldwoodBooks
@TheBoldBookClub

Sign up to our weekly deals newsletter

https://bit.ly/BoldwoodBNewsletter

www.ingramcontent.com/pod-product-compliance
Ingram Content Group UK Ltd.
Pitfield, Milton Keynes, MK11 3LW, UK
UKHW041906300326
11592UKWH00001B/2

9 781836 335610